Hot Dish Heaven

A Murder Mystery with Recipes

Hot Dish Heaven

A Murder Mystery with Recipes

Jeanne Cooney

North Star Press of St. Cloud, Inc.
St. Cloud, Minnesota

ISBN: 978-0-87839-645-0

This is a work of fiction. Names, characters, places, and incidents are the products of the author's imagination or are used fictitiously. Any resemblance to actual events or persons, living or dead, is entirely coincidental.

First Edition: June 2013

Printed in the United States of America

Published by
North Star Press of St. Cloud, Inc.
P.O. Box 451
St. Cloud, MN 56302

www.northstarpress.com

Facebook - North Star Press

Twitter - North Star Press

Dedication

This book is dedicated to my mother, who showed by example that you are never too old to pursue new interests and ideas. She also instilled in me the work ethic needed to foster the dedication it took to write this book. For all of that, I love her and thank her.

Acknowledgements:

Books are hard to write. First books are almost "killers." I must thank my sister Mary for being with me every step of the way, debating ideas, telling tales, slogging through drafts, and never losing faith; Gary and Myron for taking me seriously enough to answer all my questions about farming; all the relatives who read various versions of this story and cheered me on when I doubted myself; my mentors and peers at The Loft and Sisters in Crime for helping a novice find her way; the people at North Star Press for giving me this chance; and everyone in the Red River Valley. No matter where I live, I'm proud to say I grew up in the Valley. I will always be a "Valley girl."

Hot Dish Heaven

A Murder Mystery with Recipes

Part One

Brown the Meat

Chapter One

IT ALL BEGAN WITH HOT DISH. That's right. Hot dish.

As the most junior writer for the "Food" section of the Minneapolis paper, I, Emerald Malloy, was directed to scour rural Minnesota for popular "church cuisine." Since funerals and other church functions were major social events in rural communities, my editor thought the recipes for the dishes served at those get-togethers would be of interest to our readers, many of whom lived in the country or, at least, had grown up there. "No country funeral is complete until everyone has waded through a buffet of tuna-noodle hot dish, red Jell-O salad, and frosted pumpkin bars," he said, handing me his notes. "Now don't look so glum. Our readers will eat this stuff up." He flashed me a snaggle-toothed grin. "Get it?"

I got it, but I didn't think he did. You see, I considered myself a serious journalist. I'd earned a master's at Northwestern and had interned at the *Chicago Tribune*. I deserved more prestigious assignments than copying down recipes. I wanted to be an investigative reporter. But since my work experience was limited, and no other paper was clamoring for my services, I swallowed my pride and began my research.

I pulled several weekly newspapers from around the state, skipping the front-page articles and turning to "Community News," where weddings and funerals were described in detail. I wasn't sure what I was searching for but hoped I'd know it when I saw it.

Sure enough, while combing through several editions of the *The Enterprise*, I found something. Margie Johnson, the owner of a café called Hot Dish Heaven, seemed to be in charge of most of the church dinners in that area. And at the end of each article about one of those gatherings, she was congratulated for preparing another "pretty good" meal. Even the piece about the untimely passing of her brother, Ole Johnson, age fifty-five, closed with, "Thankfully, funeral guests found solace in the pretty good lunch served by Margie and the church ladies."

Margie sounded like an interesting subject, so I pleaded with my editor to let me write about her while compiling her favorite recipes.

He contemplated my request, the florescent lights in his office reflecting off his long, shiny forehead. Finally, with a shrug, he agreed but warned that the piece might never make it to print. "Emme," he said, "'Food' section readers want recipes, not stories!"

Excited to do some real writing, I dismissed his reservations, lined up the interview, and spent the next day reading about northwestern Minnesota, where Margie Johnson lived. I was raised in the southern part of the state and knew little about the north other than it was "lake country." My destination, however, was well beyond most lakes. In fact, it practically bordered Canada. Nonetheless, the following Friday, I dragged myself out of bed at the ungodly hour of 6:00 a.m., eased behind the wheel of my Ford Focus, and headed out, a Diet Coke and a one-pound bag of M&Ms in hand.

After six hours of Willie Nelson music, one stop for the bathroom, and another for more pop, I'd passed through lake country and had entered the Red River Valley.

While hypnotized by the flat, seemingly endless road, I exchanged one thought for another until settling on my initial phone call with Margie. She had loved the idea of sharing her recipes and being the subject of an article that could appear in Minnesota's leading newspaper. "Uff-da," she had said, "this is pretty darn excitin'." We must have talked for an hour. I learned she was in her early sixties, had never married, and lived in a town of 193 people.

Upon exiting Interstate 29, I crossed the Red River, which seperated North Dakota and Minnesota, and journeyed on. The wind blew hard, the grain in the fields rippling like waves in a chain of green and gold lakes. Gravel roads dissected occasional oak groves and led to the type of farmhouses featured in the books I read in my early teens. They were big, square, and white, and I imagined they, like those in my books, were inhabited by grandmothers who baked bread and cured the ills of visiting grandchildren with hugs and homemade apple pie.

I always wanted to be one of those kids, lucky enough to spend time with loving grandparents on a picturesque farm. I hadn't recalled that fantasy for years. Pleased it still comforted me, I clung to it, letting it go only after I spotted a water tower in the distance. As I got closer, I saw from the name on it that I'd arrived at my destination, Kennedy, Minnesota.

I parked the car and checked my watch. Right on time. Margie had asked that I wait to meet with her until one o'clock, "after the lunch rush." I surveyed my surroundings. A grain elevator sat on one side of the highway, a bank and post office on the other. The VFW, Hot Dish Heaven, and the Senior Citizens Center were lined up alongside the bank. I counted just three parked cars, two men outside the elevator, and a lone boy biking down the train tracks, a golden retriever trotting behind. *Lunch rush? Hard to believe.*

I unfolded myself from my seat, broke the silence by slamming the car door, and crossed the sidewalk, heat shimmering off the concrete. Northern Minnesota was much hotter than I'd expected.

Opening the steel door of the clapboard restaurant, I met the chill of air conditioning and the smell of french-fry grease mixed with the sounds of John Prine on the jukebox. He was singing, "In a Town This Size." No lie. That's what he was singing. "In a town this size, there's no place to hide."

I stepped inside and pulled the door closed behind me. When my eyes adjusted to the dim light, I saw the patrons—all five of them—gaping in my direction. John Prine was right—there was no place to hide.

A shiver ran down my arms, though I couldn't tell if it was from the cool air or my self-consciousness. Whatever the case, a tall, sturdy, middle-aged woman quickly rescued me with a warm smile. "You must be Emerald Malloy," she said. "I'm Margie Johnson."

Scuttling out from behind the counter, Margie extended her red, chapped hands and briefly cupped mine before pointing to the men sipping coffee on the stools beside her. One was the mayor, she said, the other, the local banker. They greeted me and then took off, joking that they had to get back to work before the whole town fell apart.

Margie also introduced her aunts, the Anderson sisters, who shared a nearby booth. The collective age of the three ladies was at least 250, yet they were full of life. Talking over one another, they said their hellos and explained how they'd like to stay but couldn't because bingo was about to begin at the Senior Center. So with promises to return, they too went on their way, stiff and hunched over, like a trio of traveling garden gnomes.

Once we were alone, Margie unplugged the juke box, poured us both some weak-looking coffee, and took hold of what I assumed was a recipe box. It was the size of a shoe box but shaped like a treasure chest, its finish worn. Margie handled it with great care, gently setting it on the table in a booth before retrieving our coffee and inviting me to join her.

Sliding across the cool, black, Naugahyde seat, I inspected the place. No doubt, it had been around for a while. The wood floor was warped, and the Formica counter was chipped and badly stained. Chrome-legged tables cluttered the middle of the room, while booths hugged the outside edges. The walls were plastered and cracked but hidden in large part by dark wainscoting, faded advertisements, and community flyers.

"How long have you owned this place?" I clicked on my tape recorder and placed it on the table between us.

"Oh, gosh," Margie replied, glancing at the tiny machine, "it's been in my family for years."

She hesitated, clearly nervous, so I urged her to take her time. I had all day.

Nodding, she continued, "My sister and I grew up waitin' tables and washin' dishes, and my brother did some of the cleanin'.

Ma ran things and served as cook for over twenty years. When she died, I took over."

Margie came across as a no-nonsense woman. Her long, angular face was absent any makeup, and her fine, shoulder-length hair, obviously blonde at one time, was now heavily streaked with gray. She kept it pulled back with a plastic clip, though a few uncooperative strands hung loose over her forehead.

"Has it always been called Hot Dish Heaven?"

"Ever since Ma had it. Hot dishes were her specialty." Margie cocked her head to one side. "They're mine too, but I've also branched out some." She opened the wooden box.

"Does your sister still work with you?"

"Oh, gosh, no. The day Vivian got married she threw her apron on the counter and walked out. Workin' in here was never good enough for her. No, sir-ree."

Glimpsing at the tape recorder, she hastily added, "Now don't get me wrong, I love my sister, and God knows she's had a tough row to hoe these last few years, with Vern's accident and all."

"Vern?"

"Vern's her husband. I'm sure ya heard about him. He got his arm chopped off in a baler accident a few years back. The story was all over the news. It even made the front page of that big paper of yours."

I didn't recall it. "It must have happened before I moved back from Chicago."

"Oh," Margie replied in a disappointed tone before a pencil-thin smile made its way across her face. "In that case, let me tell ya."

She wiggled around in an apparent attempt to get comfortable. "See here," she began, settling her arms on the table, "Vern was alone in the field. Oh, yah, his daughter and nephews helped him out some, but that day he was all by himself. Anyways, he was balin' when somethin' in the baler up and went ka-put. Now, Vern's a darn good mechanic, so he climbed right on down there to check things out. Well, wouldn't ya know, the knotter was jammed, so he reached in to fix it and . . . WHAM!"

I jumped and spilled my coffee.

Looking pleased with my reaction, Margie wiped up my mess with the hand towel she tugged from her shoulder. “Yah, that’s what happened all right. Vern’s arm got pulled into the knotter, and he couldn’t yank it loose. It got real twisted up. He bled somethin’ fierce and knew he’d die if he didn’t get free soon, so by God, he did what he had to do.” She gulped air. “That’s right. He sawed his arm off with his pocket knife. He hacked right through it, bone and all. For sure it took some doin’, but he did it.”

My stomach churned as I shook my head in disbelief.

“Hard to believe, I know, but it’s true. Like I said, your paper even ran the story.”

Margie now seemed totally at ease and oblivious to the tape recorder. “Anyways, he pried his arm out and carried it on back to the house—about a mile away. There, Vivian put it in the Styrofoam cooler Vern used to store fish bait. Now I don’t know if any bait was in there at the time, but that’s where she put it. Then she drove him and the cooler to the hospital in Hallock, just north of here. The doctor on call took one look at Vern and another inside the cooler and loaded both in the ambulance and rushed them to Fargo.

“By the time they arrived, Vern was in mighty rough shape. So was his arm. Surgery lasted for hours, and for a long time afterwards, we didn’t know if he’d make it.” She paused to allow me to absorb the gravity of the situation. “In the end, the doctors saved him but not his arm.”

Margie sipped some coffee. “Well, wouldn’t ya know, Vern and Vivian’s daughter, Little Val, was to get married the followin’ spring. And believe it or not, Vivian was worried Vern wouldn’t be able to do the father-daughter dance at the weddin’ reception, havin’ only one arm and all.”

She pursed her thin lips so tightly they virtually disappeared. “Isn’t that terrible? Her husband barely survived an awful accident, yet Vivian’s main concern was what folks might say if he couldn’t waltz. But that’s my sister.” Again she paused. “As it turned out, she had nothin’ to worry about. It could of been a whole lot worse.” She gave the table a tap of her finger. "The fact is Vern danced pretty darn well, even if Little Val had to do most of the leadin'."

Being a reporter, I should have had a follow-up question ready, but I didn't. What more did I truly want to know about Vern or his severed arm? Nothing, I decided. Absolutely nothing.

Margie handed me a grease-stained card. "This here's my most popular dish. I now call it One-Arm Hot Dish because it's so easy to make, even Vern can do it." Her pale blue eyes danced. "Vivian had conniptions when she heard I'd changed the name on the menu, but Vern said he liked bein' honored with a hot dish. Yah, that Vern is somethin'."

While only half-way listening, I printed the recipe on a blank index card. Yes, that's right, an index card. I'd left my laptop at home, unsure it would work way up here without a lot of fuss. I wasn't a computer wiz, and fussing with it wasn't something I liked to do or did very well. Instead, I planned to tape my interview, jot down the recipes along with my notes, and type up everything back at the office in Minneapolis. Probably odd-sounding coming from me, someone under thirty and raised during the technology revolution, but as my dad often said, I was an "old soul."

"Followin' his accident," Margie said, "Vern still insisted on helpin' out on the farm, though his daughter, Little Val, had to take over most of the operation. Now we tease that when she needs more than 'one extra hand,' she has to ask her husband or cousins to pitch in." She snorted a chuckle.

Without a doubt, Margie enjoyed making one-arm jokes at Vern's expense, and while she was politically incorrect for doing so, I liked the sound of her laugh when she did. It was genuine. Then again, everything about Margie Johnson seemed genuine, from the Scandinavian accent that led her to drop most every "g," to her tee-shirt, which read, "LET ME SPEND ETERNITY IN HOT DISH HEAVEN."

"Anyways, when Vern's not helpin' out on the farm there, he's workin' on his duck decoys. He carves and paints some of the finest you'll ever see. Sure, people don't use the hand-carved ones for huntin' anymore, but they still like 'em for decoratin'." She snuck a drink of coffee.

"After the accident, folks assumed he'd never carve again, but he proved 'em wrong. Of course, with only one arm, he now has to use clamps or his knees to hold his carvin' wood. I joke that he better be careful with his knife when that wood's between his legs, or by golly, he'll be missin' more than an arm."

Another chuckle accompanied by another snort, and this time, I couldn't help but laugh too, although I tried to downplay it by dropping my head and studying the recipe I'd just copied. It wasn't for anything special. Just your run-of-the-mill hot dish. But I soon learned that in Kennedy, nothing was "run of the mill."

Chapter Two

MY VISIT WITH MARGIE was interrupted by two girls with blonde bobs, freckled faces, and sunburnt noses. They wore bright, one-piece swimsuits, their striped beach towels draped over their shoulders. They came in for waffle cones, and Margie made them with hard ice cream from one-gallon buckets.

Handing a chocolate cone to the taller girl and a strawberry one to the shorter, she asked about swimming lessons, informing me they were offered three days a week at the outdoor pool in Hallock. A bus took the kids there and back again.

The girl with the chocolate cone bragged that she was the best swimmer in her group, while the other complained that the breast stroke was too hard and hurt her neck. The chocolate-cone girl then explained that the two of them would be weeding the community garden much of the afternoon.

Margie frowned. "I know it's your job, and ya have to do it, but take lots of water breaks," she warned. "It's so hot out there I swear I just saw my thermometer run into the shade."

"Don't worry," the chocolate-cone girl replied with a giggle, "the hose is on." And with that, the duo padded barefoot toward the exit, licking their ice cream along the way.

"Hey, Margie," the same girl said, twirling on her heels when she reached the door, "don't forget to charge these to Ma." She saluted with her cone before using her butt to open the solid metal door, allowing a wave of heat to sneak into the room.

"Do a lot of people charge food here?" I asked after the door slammed, shutting out the girls as well as the stifling air.

"A few of the regulars do." Margie returned the ice cream pails to an up-right, stainless-steel freezer. "But their ma's no regular, at least not in this part of the building. She spends most of her free time and darn near every dime she makes on pull tabs down the hall." She motioned toward the hallway that apparently connected the café to the VFW.

"I feel sorry for the girls. I like to treat 'em to ice cream or a meal once in a while, but since they won't accept charity, I tell 'em I'll charge their ma's account. They don't need to know she doesn't have one."

Margie freshened up our coffee and fixed a plate of chocolate-frosted mint bars, placing it on the table between us. "Now," she said, sliding back into the booth, "where were we then?"

"Well, you told me your sister quit working here when she got married." I snatched a bar. The scent of rich chocolate and cool mint made my mouth water. Still, I managed to ask, "How about your brother? Does he ever help you out?"

Margie's eyes turned sad. "My brother, Ole, died a few weeks back."

I recalled the article in *The Enterprise* about the "untimely death of Ole Johnson" and the sister who'd cooked the "pretty good" funeral luncheon. "I'm sorry. I knew and simply forgot."

"Oh, that's okay. It's just hard to believe he's gone. Liver failure, don't ya know." Margie stared out the window until the rumbling of a passing train brought her back from wherever her thoughts had taken her.

After the noise died down, she went on to explain, "Ole never worked here much anyways. And he quit altogether when he joined the army, right out of high school. But when he came back home, his wife, Lena, helped me out a lot."

My eyebrows shot up to my hairline. "Ole married a woman named Lena?"

A smile once more brightened Margie's face. "Lena wasn't her real name. Everyone just called her that 'cause she was Ole's better half. He met her down in Texas, when he was in the service. They got married, and after Pa died and Ole got discharged, they moved back here to take over the farm. Her name was Maria, but no one called her anything but Lena." She bracketed one side of her mouth with her hand and whispered, "She was Mexican and Catholic, don't ya know."

Several moments later, as if I needed to digest that information before she could proceed, Margie added, "We don't have many different races up here, but we're used to Mexicans. Before all this fancy equipment, Mexican migrant workers came up from Texas every year to help with harvest. But they seldom stayed on after the crops were in, and they never married locals. So when Ole came home with a Mexican wife who was Catholic to boot, lots of folks, includin' my sister, Vivian, thought the marriage was doomed. But they were wrong. Ole and Lena were happy for many years. I often told them they were like a pair of old slippers. They just fit right."

Margie fingered the cards behind one of the wooden dividers in her recipe box, while I used the lull in the conversation to bite into another bar. I savored its rich taste and buttery texture. "These are incredible."

"Thanks," Margie replied with just a hint of pride. "They won me a grand champion ribbon at the county fair some years back, so I reckon they're not too bad."

I bit back a smile. My editor, a New York transplant, often contended that Minnesotans had a hard time accepting that they were the best at anything. According to him, you only had to look at the state's major sports' teams. He'd say, "If they're about to win a title, they'll choke. Second or third place is good enough for them. Hell, if you give a Minnesotan a gold medal, he'll have the damn thing bronzed!" Margie Johnson, the maker of the best bars I'd ever tasted could only admit they weren't "too bad." She was a true Minnesotan.

"Yah, Lena was somethin'." Margie examined one recipe card after another. "Once she got settled out on the farm, she started waitin' tables and workin' in the kitchen here. Before long, she was a pretty fair cook. I taught her how to make *lutefisk*, even if I couldn't get her to eat it." She tilted her head. "But she liked *lefse*. Sometimes she'd use *lefse* instead of tortillas to make tacos. We'd call 'em Norwegian taco nights."

"I bet you've heard every Ole and Lena joke in the world."

"And some a hundred times." A wistful expression overtook Margie's face. "Followin' Ole's funeral, the 'V' was packed, the beer was flowin', and every toast began with a Ole and Lena joke." Her voice was weighted down with sadness.

Out of respect, I wanted to offer her my undivided attention but couldn't because of the battle waging in my head. It was over whether or not to eat a third bar. Convincing myself I needed to surrender to focus fully on my host, I plucked another from the plate. I was determined to eat this one more slowly, but didn't, and wound up posing my next question amid bites. "Where's Lena now?"

Margie closed her eyes. "She died four years ago this past spring. The doctor said it was due to a broken heart. Did ya know that could really happen?"

Smacking my lips, I shook my head.

"Well, it can, and it did. Lena loved Ole so much she never got over him leavin' her."

Again she stared out the window, her expression remote. "Uff-da, I miss her."

I was confused. "I thought you said Ole and Lena had a good marriage?"

She refocused on me. "Yah, they did, for a long time."

"Then what went wrong? Why'd he leave her?"

Margie heaved a heavy sigh. "Oh, about five years ago, 'round Ole's fiftieth birthday, he started drinkin' and actin' wild. He began neglectin' the farm, spendin' most of his time down the hall in the 'V' with Samantha Berg, the day-time bartender." She tore at the edge of her paper napkin. "Well, one thing led to another, and soon they were havin' an affair. No one could believe it. Ole had always been faithful to Lena, and Samantha had always been . . . um . . . a tramp."

She dropped the napkin and pointed at me with her kitchen-scarred index finger. "Ole's mistake was bein' too nice to her. Most men 'round here only liked Samantha on her back in the bed of a pickup. But not Ole. He wasn't that way. So when she finally got her chance, she was all over him like a bad case of poison ivy." Margie raised her cup to her mouth only to set it back down again. "To make a long story short, he moved in with her and goaded Lena into a divorce."

Ole's affair clearly upset Margie, causing me to wonder why she'd brought it up in the first place. But since she had, I was determined to pursue it. Gathering recipes and material for a short profile piece wouldn't take long. I had time. And Ole's affair was bound to be more interesting than Jell-O recipes or learning what it was about hot dish that excited Margie so.

"What happened next? Did Ole and Samantha get married?"

Margie selected another recipe card. "I guess they planned to. At least that's what that floozy blabbed to anyone who'd listen. But it never happened."

"Oh, really? Why not?"

"Well, first, Ole left her, and then Samantha Berg got herself murdered."

Handing me the card, she uttered in a voice absent any emotion, "This here's the recipe for the bars ya seem to like so much. Ya better write it down."

Chapter Three

BEFORE I COULD INQUIRE about Samantha Berg's murder, two old-timers came in, and Margie excused herself to wait on them. Despite the August heat, both men wore long-sleeve shirts and bib-overalls. Each also sported a baseball cap, one advertising John Deere tractors, the other, chemical fertilizer.

Sitting down at the counter, the chemical-fertilizer guy asked Margie if it was hot enough for her, while the other tipped his head in my direction. Ignoring the weather-related question, she told them who I was and what I was doing there. They seemed impressed.

Margie served them carrot bars and coffee, all the while chatting about the upcoming beet harvest. Even though sugar beets, used to create the alternative to cane sugar, were sometimes grown in the southern part of the state, they were king of all crops in the Red River Valley. According to my research, they'd made wealthy people out of many of the Norwegian and Swedish farmers who called this sparsely populated area home.

The two guys and Margie talked, but I paid little attention. I wanted the men to leave so Margie and I could return to murder. Or, at least, our discussion of it.

I finished copying the mint-bar recipe about the same time Margie began regaling them with a story about an apparatus Ole had rigged up years before to "rotate the filler wheels on his beet lifter."

The men chuckled. "Oh, that Ole," the guy with the John Deere cap said in a Scandinavian accent so strong it put Margie's to shame, "he was a thinker." Although it sounded more like, "he was a tinker."

He swiveled on his stool to face me. "Ya know, he also was the first guy in these parts to try modern organic farmin', and—"

His friend cut him off. "That there's nothin' to brag about."

John Deere twirled his seat back around. "For cryin' out loud, now why would ya go and say somethin' like that?"

"'Cause I don't think much of organic farmin', that's why."

Without making any eye contact whatsoever, John Deere argued, "For your information, Ole got prit near 'tirdy' a bushel for his soybeans one year."

"Ya ain't tellin' me nothin' I don't already know. But he had to work a lot harder."

"There's nothin' wrong with hard work."

"He was always pullin' weeds."

"So?"

"So sprayin' weeds is easier."

"Well, easier ain't always better." That last remark was spoken brusquely and was obviously meant to end any further debate.

"Say, Margie," John Deere then said, shifting both his focus and his tone, "I remembered that Ole and Lena joke I wanted to tell ya after Ole's funeral there. Care to hear it now?"

"Do I have a choice?"

A grin inched across his face. "No, not really."

She slouched against the stainless-steel prep table and crossed her legs at her ankles, "In that case, go ahead and get it over with."

John Deere shoved his cap back from his sunburnt face and scratched his pale forehead. "Well, ya see," he began, looking quite pleased with himself, "like most Norwegians, Ole, a professional fisherman, was pretty dang frugal. But when his wife, Lena, passed away, he reckoned he better put an obituary in the paper. So after fishin' one day, he went on down there to the newspaper office and told the editor to write that Lena had died. Well, the editor said, 'For land sake, Ole, ya gotta say more than that. You were married to the woman for dang near fifty years, and she was your partner in the fishin' business.' Still, Ole kept quiet, so the editor told 'em, 'Now, if it's the money you're worried about, Ole, don't forget the first five words of any obituary are free.' Of course, that got old, tightwad Ole tinkin', and soon he said, 'Well, in that case, write, "Lena died; walleye on sale."'"

John Deere's friend belly-laughed, while Margie groaned, and I couldn't help but smile. These guys weren't the sharpest knives in the drawer, but I found them charming in a "Beverly Hillbillies" sort of way.

"Heard that one before?" John Deere asked.

"No, don't think so." Margie ambled back to our booth. She winked at me, picked up her recipe box, and returned to the prep table.

"Now I better get cookin'," she said to no one in particular before calling out, "Hey, Emerald, why don't ya come on over here and keep me company. Or better yet, give me a hand. You can cook, can't ya?"

"Nothing you'd want to charge money for."

Margie snorted. "How on earth did ya get to be a food writer if ya can't cook?"

I slid from my booth and strolled to the kitchen, a pen and several blank note cards in hand. "My aunt has connections, and I'm a pretty good eater."

"Ya don't look it." Margie's gaze traveled from my head to my toes. "You're kind of skinny."

"High metabolism," I muttered self-consciously.

"Just like me." John Deere rose from his stool and patted his Santa-like paunch. "I have a high metabolism too. I just don't know where I put it." His sidekick laughed some more as John Deere wiped crumbs from the bib of his overalls.

When the laughter died, John Deere added in the direction of his friend, "Say, now, we better be goin'." He shoved the last of his carrot bar into his mouth and washed it down with coffee.

Returning his cup to the counter, he tossed a few dollars alongside it. "Tanks, Margie." He then tipped the bill of his cap in my direction. "And Miss Malloy, it was a pleasure to meet ya."

He lumbered toward the door on the heels of his companion, Margie calling out after him. "Ya comin' back later?"

He answered across his shoulder, "That all depends. Ya servin' Wild Rice Hot Dish?"

Margie huffed, "Of course I am." Her tone implied she could hardly believe he'd ask such a question.

"Then, ya betcha, we'll be back."

The two men stepped outside, though John Deere peeked right back in again, his red face backlit by the afternoon sun. "Eh, Margie, that there was a humdinger of a joke, wasn't it?"

"Oh, get out of here!" she teasingly ordered, causing the sidekick to snicker as the door banged shut.

With a shake of her head, Margie returned to her recipes. "Those two old coots stop in every afternoon. They went to high school with Ole. The three of them were best of friends."

"They seem nice enough."

"Oh, yah, and they're as common as snow in January. You'd never guess that once upon a time, the guy with the John Deere cap was a big-time engineer at Boeing."

"Really? An engineer at Boeing?"

"Yah, but when his pa got sick, he had to come home and take over the farm."

I must have been in shock about the whole engineering thing because all I could utter was, "Well, that's too bad."

Margie handed me the recipe for carrot bars. "Oh, don't go and feel too sorry for him. He may be the valley's worst joke teller, but he's one of its biggest farmers. He works more'n fifteen hundred acres of beets, and I don't know how much wheat and soybeans. On top of that, he's president of the beet growers' association. The growers own the beet plants, which means they decide how many tons get processed each year. In other words, they regulate the price of sugar." She shook her head. "Yep, like a lot of farmers up here, he's worth millions."

I jerked my head so fast I almost broke my neck. "Millions?"

Margie looked embarrassed. "Oh, yah, but I suppose I shouldn't of said that. It wasn't my place."

Chapter Four

I PLOPPED DOWN ON THE STOOL next to the prep table and took stock of everything Margie had shared with me. Her sister, Vivian, was married to a one-arm man named Vern, and together they had a daughter known as Little Val. Her recently deceased brother, Ole, was married to an Hispanic woman named Lena, who died of a broken heart after he dumped her for a tramp who wound up murdered. And the goofy-sounding farmer who frequented the café was really a brainy millionaire. "Hmm." I could hardly wait to meet the fire eater and the bearded lady. But in the meantime, I'd have to settle for watching Margie chop onions with the speed and accuracy of the guy who did the Ginsu commercials.

Awestruck, I asked without thinking, "What are you making?"

She smiled, as if I were oddly amusing. "Hot dish. What else? I've got the ground beef and turkey brownin' and the noodles and rice boilin'. I made the buns and bars yesterday and the salads this mornin'."

Margie had informed me on the phone that she was co-hosting a fund-raiser with the VFW on the night of my visit. It was to benefit a local woman who had breast cancer. The woman needed help paying her bills because her treatment made her too sick to work.

According to Margie, medical fund-raisers were fairly common in the valley. "If ya ask me," she'd said, "the cancer's from all the chemicals sprayed on the fields. But don't quote me on that, or I'll get tarred and feathered and run out of town on a rail."

With a dangerous-looking knife, Margie sliced and diced onions right next to me, my eyes watering as my thoughts returned to Samantha Berg. I assured myself that as a reporter, it was only natural to be interested in her. Only natural to ask more questions.

"Margie," I said, wiping away my tears, "tell me more about Samantha Berg."

She set the knife down. "There's not much to tell, and she sure wasn't worth cryin' over!" She chuckled at the remark.

"Seriously, how was she killed?"

As if doing a dance she'd done a million times before, Margie stepped from the prep table to the stove and on to the sink. There, she dumped a frying pan full of cooked ground turkey into a colander and rinsed it with water. "She disappeared three years ago this past March, exactly one year to the day from Lena's death. It was the spring the Red River flooded so bad that folks got stranded on their roofs and had to be rescued by helicopter." She squeezed her eyes closed in an apparent attempt to shut out the images. "Anyways, when the flood waters receded, Samantha's body was found washed up on shore. She'd been stabbed in the heart . . . or in the place her heart would have been if she had one."

I shuddered. "That must have been a gruesome discovery."

Margie dumped the ground turkey back in the pan, carried it to the prep table, and spooned the meat into an industrial-size baking dish. "Little Val's husband, Wally, found her." She emptied the pan. "Of course he wasn't her husband back then. He was just some guy travelin' from Fargo to Winnipeg on business. He got sick and stopped in Drayton. That's the town ya went through just before crossin' the Red. It's where the beet plant's located."

She aimed her wooden spoon at the cutting board full of chopped onions. "Would ya mind addin' those in here?"

I commandeered her knife and scraped the onion pieces into the casserole dish. At the same time, she retrieved a metal bowl of whole-kernel corn and another of sliced green beans from a massive, stainless-steel refrigerator that stood alongside the upright freezer.

"Fresh from my garden," she reported, tossing the vegetables into the ground-meat mixture.

She handed me one of the bowls. A few uncooked beans remained at the bottom, and I popped them in my mouth. "Oh, these are good," I said as I crunched.

Margie's cheeks flushed slightly before she hurried back to the subject of murder, evidently something far easier for a humble Scandinavian to deal with than a compliment. "Anyways, Wally's aunt lives just north of the beet plant. He wanted to rest at her house until he felt better, but she wasn't home. So he went for a walk along the river there. And lo and behold, he came upon Samantha Berg. She was dead and nearly naked." She pivoted toward the stove before wheeling back around. "Naturally, he didn't know it was Samantha at the time." She arched her pale eyebrows. "Had he been from 'round here, he probably would of. Like I told ya, most men in the county could of identified that big, bare ass." She shuffled to the stove.

"What did he do?"

"He called the police, who called the FBI. They told him to stick around while they investigated, so he ended up stayin' with his aunt for darn near a month, if you can imagine that."

She removed a kettle of rice from a burner and poured its contents into the baking dish. "While he was there, his cousin had a barbecue. That's where he met Little Val." She trudged to the sink and dropped the empty pot into one of the deep basins. The thud made me jump, and she chuckled again.

Once back at the table, she stirred the hot dish a final time before nodding at the double wall oven. "Grab the top oven door, will ya?"

I did, and she slid the dish onto the upper rack. "They hit it off right away," she said. "They're musicians, don't ya know. Little Val plays the piano, and Wally, the guitar, and both sing."

She wiped her hands on the soiled towel that draped her shoulder and headed back to the steel work station. "When they got engaged, he quit his job in Fargo and got another at the crop insurance office in Hallock. Now they're married and expectin' a baby. They're nice folks."

"Did the FBI ever solve the murder?"

"No," Margie replied, handing me the recipe for Uncle Ben's Hot Dish. "They never did, which is just fine by me."

Chapter Five

"UFF-DA, IT'S HARD TO BELIEVE Little Val and Wally have been married goin' on two years. Time sure does fly."

Margie wagged her finger at me. "Now that weddin' was really somethin'." She shook her head. "Little Val's dad, Vern, was still recuperatin' from the baler accident, but that didn't slow her ma down one iota. No, not one iota.

"The weddin' took place in the spring, just before plantin'. The reception and dance were held down the hall, in the 'V.' The band was Mid-life Crisis, out of Grand Forks. Ever hear of 'em?"

"No, can't say I have."

"Oh, they're good. Or, I should say, they *were* good. They just broke up." She'd lowered her voice as if sharing information no one else should hear. Not a problem, I suspected, since we were all alone. "From what I gather, the female drummer ran off with the keyboard player, who happened to be the wife of the bass guitarist. Quite a scandal." She arched her brows and waited, apparently wanting me to think long and hard about what she'd just said. "Anyways, they were supposed to play at the benefit tonight, so now, Jim, the banker you met when you first got here, is tryin' to find a replacement band. Not an easy task on such short notice."

"Why's the banker . . . ?"

"He's also the commander of the VFW and manages things there too."

Stooping over, Margie claimed two more over-sized casserole dishes from where they were stowed under the prep table. "Yah, for

Little Val's weddin' reception, Vivian decorated the 'V' like there was no tomorrow. The streamers and twinkle lights most people use weren't good enough for my sister. No, sir-ree. She had to draw, cut out, and paint a bunch of life-size, plywood, Precious Moments characters and prop them all around the bar. There was a Precious Moments bride, a bunch of bridesmaids, a groom, a flower girl, even a minister."

She brushed by me on her way to the stove. "No doubt Vivian's a good woodworker and a fine artist. That's what brought her and Vern together in the first place. They grew up in the same 4-H club, and one of 'em was always winnin' the blue ribbons in the art competitions, even at the state fair. Just like Vern, Vivian's a wiz with a carvin' knife."

She pulled on a pair of oven mitts, reached for two cast-iron skillets of cooked ground beef, and plodded over to the sink. There, she transferred the meat to her colander. "But what she did for that weddin' was a bit over the top, if ya ask me. With all those big-headed, wooden people standin' about, Little Val's real guests had trouble gettin' around."

I couldn't imagine anyone populating a wedding reception with fake people. "Didn't they look out of place?"

The hot-dish waltz continued. Margie rinsed the ground beef, returned it to the skillets, crossed to the prep table, and spooned the meat into the casserole dishes. "Well, they ended up bein' a bigger part of the festivities than Vivian ever intended, that's for darn sure." Out of the corner of her mouth, she muttered, "Buford kept pretendin' to make out with one of the fake bridesmaids. That boy will do anythin' for a laugh. And Ole got so drunk he couldn't tell the real bridesmaids from the pretend ones. A half dozen times he dragged a wooden one onto the dance floor, only to yell at it for not bein' light on its feet. And by midnight, he was ready to fight the fake groom just because he 'didn't like the look in his eyes.'"

I briefly bit my lip to keep from laughing. "I take it that once Ole started drinking, he didn't stop?"

Margie stirred various Italian seasonings into the meat, the resulting aroma reminding me how hungry I was for honest-to-goodness food. My sustenance for the day had been limited to a half pound of M&Ms, three bars, and four green beans.

"Ole lived with Samantha Berg for five months, and during that entire time, I never saw him sober. Then he just up and left her. I like to believe he woke up one mornin' clear-headed for some reason, saw he was in bed with a pig, and ran like hell. He moved into an old trailer out on Vivian and Vern's farm, quit drinkin', and tried to make amends with Lena." She punctuated the air with her spoon. "But before he succeeded, Lena died, sendin' him right back to the bottle 'til the county judge gave him thirty days in jail."

"For drinking?"

"Not exactly." She laid her spoon on the counter. "At the county fair, some months after Lena's death, Ole got real drunk in the beer garden and ran butt naked through the Future Farmers' cow judgin'." She closed her eyes. "Uff-da, what a sight. I couldn't eat rump roast for a month!"

Again I tried not to laugh, but this time I failed. "Sorry, it's just that . . ."

"It's okay. It was sorta funny. See, there we were, sittin' in the bleachers in the cow barn, waitin' for Buford and Buddy to bring in their heifers, when all of a sudden, Ole ran in wearin' nothin' but his boots and a smile. He couldn't have been drunker if he were twins. He galloped around the ring, swattin' his bare ass like he was whippin' a horse. I thought Vivian was goin' to keel right over."

I laughed even harder.

Margie bent down and gathered up several glass canning jars filled with tomato sauce. "When I make food to sell, I have to use store-bought ingredients." The abrupt change of subject led me to stifle myself, hoping I hadn't offended her with all my guffawing. "But whenever I do private events, I can use vegetables straight from my garden and homemade sauces. They're far tastier." She wrestled the jars and ultimately won, laying the lids on the metal table with a series of clangs.

"Anyways, the police couldn't get Ole under control at first." She scrunched up her face. "I guess it's hard to wrestle a naked man.

Ya just don't know where to grab. Plus, he kept kickin' everyone with his pointy-toed boots. But they got him 'in the end,' so to speak." She snickered, and I lost it. "The judge gave him thirty days and ordered him to quit drinkin', which he did for over six months. But when Samantha disappeared, he went right on back to the bottle."

Margie divided a kettle of boiled egg noodles between the two casserole dishes and gently folded the pasta into the meat mixtures. "Will ya grab the shredded cheese from the fridge there?"

I caught my breath, wiped my eyes, and opened the refrigerator to an array of glass bowls filled with Jell-O in various colors, all covered in plastic wrap. "Where's the cheese?"

"On the top shelf, in front, in the Tupperware."

I peeked under the lid to make sure I had the right container. Grated mozzarella mixed with Parmesan. Even that smelled good.

I handed the tub to Margie, and she liberally sprinkled its contents over the hot-dish mixture in each pan. "As soon as I'm done here, I've gotta start my Tater-Tot Hot Dish."

A smile tugged at my lips. "My mom made Tater-Tot Hot Dish almost every Saturday when I was young. I love it. I made it myself a few times, but it didn't turn out."

Margie appeared bemused. "It's sorta strange ya do what ya do for a livin', bein' you're such a bad cook and all." She brushed cheese crumbs from her hands with a couple of claps. "I suppose it just goes to show that God has a sense of humor."

"Or simply enjoys messing with me." And, man, was I right about that, as my trip to Kennedy proved.

Chapter Six

MARGIE, WHY DID OLE start drinking again after Samantha disappeared?" I posed the question while watching her place tater tots lengthwise across two casserole dishes filled with a mixture of hamburger and cream soup. I'd tried to convince myself that I'd write a better profile if I knew more about her family, but the truth was I just wanted to hear more about the murder and this town. The people here were different, to put it mildly. But I found them and the murder fascinating. Much more so than hot dish. After all, crime was what real reporters wrote about. "You said Ole left Samantha. That means he must not have loved her anymore, right?"

Margie sniffed. "I don't believe he ever did."

"If that's true, what caused him to fall off the wagon when she went missing? Did he feel—"

She didn't let me finish. "Ole was a good person. Sometimes, too good. After Samantha vanished, he told me he felt bad that no one in town cared if she was ever found or not."

With the back of her hand, she wiped a few strands of hair from her cheek. "That tramp used him, yet he never said an unkind word about her. She wrecked his marriage, but he shouldered all the blame."

"Well, he should have shouldered some."

"Not necessarily." Picking up one of the casserole dishes, she again nodded at the wall oven. "When a guy's in a bad state, like he was, those around him need to be more thoughtful. But Samantha never gave a hoot about anyone 'cept herself."

This time I opened the bottom oven door. "Well, Ole shouldn't have let himself get into a 'bad state.'"

Margie slid the dish onto the upper rack. "Yah, he should of asked for help. But that's not easy to do, especially for a man. That's why other folks have to be more responsible durin' those tough times. Like the Lord said, 'You are your brother's keeper.'" She placed the second casserole dish on the lower rack. "But it's also during those tough times that the devil goes to work, and . . ." I didn't hear the rest because the casserole dish banged against the oven wall, but I was certain I'd gotten the gist of it anyhow.

"And Samantha Berg was the devil?"

She bumped the oven door shut. "Well, she wasn't an angel, that's for darn sure. Maybe she was after his money, or maybe she was just plain bored. Whatever her angle, it wasn't love."

"How do you know that?" I returned to the prep table, while she made her way to the sink.

"Less than a month after Ole left her, a new guy moved in. Samantha always liked havin' a man livin' with her, especially durin' the winter. That way she didn't need to pay the heatin' bills all by herself."

Margie went on to rattle off the names of some of Samantha Berg's live-in boyfriends. It was a long list that sounded like a Scandinavian phone book: Alex Anderson, Thor Carlson, Sven Hanson . . .

While only partially listening, I doodled on a blank index card and thought about Ole and Samantha. I routinely doodled when sorting things out in my head. One of my professors suggested it helped "put order to my musings."

I sketched a female stick figure lying dead on a river bank, blood flowing from her chest. "Margie, is it possible Ole came to resent Samantha Berg?" Concerned my picture might be in bad taste or—worse—make me queasy and unable to eat dinner, I scribbled it out and flipped the card over.

"He should of, but like I told ya, he never said anything negative about her."

More doodling on the back of the card. This time mere geometric shapes. "Let me get this straight. Ole's family fell apart because of his affair with Samantha. And his attempt at reconciling with Lena failed because of her death, which was due, at least in part, to that same affair. That means Ole lost everything because of Samantha Berg. Yet she moved on without any trouble whatsoever." I raised my head, then my eyebrows. "That had to make him resent her, don't you think?"

She nodded. "It made *me* resent her, that's for darn sure."

"And exactly one year to the day after Lena passed away, Samantha disappeared, and Ole started drinking again."

Margie remained silent, and later I came to wish that I had too. "Margie, you said Ole fell off the wagon because he felt bad that no one cared if Samantha was ever found, but that doesn't make sense, especially if he never had any real feelings for her in the first place."

My instincts warned me that I was coming on too strong. Yet I couldn't stop. I'd developed a theory about Samantha Berg's death and was hard pressed to keep it to myself. But as I soon realized, Margie wasn't the ideal confidant. You see, I'd concluded that her brother was the murderer.

I had no evidence to support my theory, but that didn't bother me. I thought of myself as fairly knowledgeable about crime solving because of a few investigative journalism classes I'd taken in graduate school. None of my assignments actually dealt with homicide. I always chose non-violent crimes. No blood. No gore. No getting sick in front of classmates. Still, I'd come to believe that most murders were easily solved. Students who worked those cases reported that the killers almost always were found among the people with the strongest ties to the victims. And in this instance, Ole and Samantha's ties were pretty damn strong.

"Margie, I can't help but suspect your brother hit the bottle again to hide from something—something he did—something terrible."

Margie braced herself against the sink. Clearly she was having trouble admitting to a killer in the family. Although as far as I was concerned, Ole wasn't your typical homicidal maniac. His was a crime of passion. And that, I thought, should have provided his sister with at least a modicum of comfort. But I thought wrong.

As soon as Margie turned my way, I could tell from her expression, I'd gone too far. I'd said too much. She wasn't comforted at all. Rather, she looked really ticked off. "Ole didn't kill her, if that's what you're drivin' at. I wouldn't of blamed him if he had. But he didn't."

Ignoring my better judgment, I re-engaged my mouth. "How do you know? How can you be so sure?"

"I just know, that's all. My brother wasn't some kind of crazed killer."

"I didn't say he was. But it's possible he—"

"If he'd killed her, don't you think the FBI would of arrested him?"

Unable to reign myself in, I sarcastically replied, "They didn't arrest anybody, but that doesn't make her any less dead."

Margie again mumbled something, but this time I didn't catch much other than "effin'" this and "effin'" that. And when she was done "effin'," she signaled an end to our conversation by twisting on the squeaky faucets and noisily rearranging the dirty pots and pans.

Once she began scrubbing them, I volunteered to towel them dry, but she insisted they be left alone. Noting silently that the dishes weren't all that needed to be left alone, I sat back down and chided myself for being too impatient.

It's my biggest character flaw. Not my only one, mind you, just my biggest. I'm too pushy. I move too fast. I'm afraid if I take my time, I'll be left behind, all alone. That's what my therapist says anyway.

Yeah, my therapist. And before you get too judgmental, let me just say that I think most people would benefit from a little one-on-one counseling. But I digress.

I shuffled through the recipe cards Margie had given me. In an attempt to ease my discomfort by otherwise occupying my mind, I picked a recipe I hadn't yet copied and began doing just that. It was Lena's Chili Hot Dish. Margie had mentioned it was Ole's favorite.

While jotting down the list of ingredients, I lectured myself on why I should stick to gathering Margie's recipes and profile notes and avoid all further talk of murder. It wasn't as if I'd ever write about the incident anyway, so why work so hard to uncover the details? Besides, if I continued to badger Margie, she might refuse to give me what I needed to complete my real assignment. Then where would I be?

The cooking instructions, like the listed ingredients, were straight forward, allowing my mind to wander some more. And no matter how hard I tried to steer my thoughts away from the murder, they veered in that direction.

I wondered why the police never arrested Ole Johnson. Sure, the best in law enforcement probably didn't get assigned to cases in the middle of nowhere. But how could cops of any caliber overlook a killer who was standing—or staggering—right in front of them?

Chapter Seven

FOLLOWING A GOOD TEN MINUTES of awkward silence, Margie spoke, raising her voice to be heard above the running water and the clanging of cookware. "Men are fools for helpless women, and Samantha Berg knew how to act helpless. She was always complainin' about bein' broke or misunderstood or somehow mistreated. Oh, she loved to play the victim. But it was all an act until the end, when she got what she deserved. She gotta be the victim for real."

Margie stopped ranting only long enough to rinse a kettle and precariously set it on top of the others in the dish rack. "Of course a man doesn't wanna marry a helpless woman. No, sir-ree. He wants a strong, hard-workin' wife, but a helpless woman can really get his motor runnin', especially when he's older or not thinkin' straight."

I cautiously interjected. "You're being awfully cynical, aren't you?"

She dismissed my remark with a wave of her soapy fingers. "I'm not cynical. I just don't believe in lookin' at life through rose-colored glasses. They distort the view."

She knocked the water taps closed, dried her hands with a clean towel, and swung it over her shoulder in place of the dirty one, which she tossed into a bucket. "Take Ole and Lena, for instance." She lifted a stack of mismatched dinner plates from a nearby shelf.

"Want some help?"

She considered me for what felt like eternity. She wasn't about to make this easy. I'd implied her recently deceased brother was a murderer, and she was going to make me pay.

"Margie," I said, resolving to ease the tension by seeking immediate absolution. "I'm sorry. I guess I just got caught up in your story."

Her eyes lingered on me before she acknowledged, "Well, I suppose we all get carried away at times."

The corners of her mouth ticked upward in what I hoped was the beginning of a smile. "Yah," she uttered, "go ahead and put these on the counter there. It'll serve as our buffet table tonight."

I exhaled in relief. My apology had been accepted, at least to some degree, and that made me feel a whole lot better. As I said, I needed to get along with Margie to finish my job. But more than that, I'd developed warm feelings toward her and didn't want her angry with me.

Nevertheless, my opinion of her brother hadn't changed. I was one-hundred-percent certain he was a murderer. Margie just didn't need to know that. Yep, some things were better left unsaid, a rule of journalism I'd always had trouble following. But, hey, I was trying.

Handing me the stack of plates, Margie repeated herself. "Take Ole and Lena, for instance. No two people ever loved each other more."

She stared off into the distance. "Years ago, Lena would sometimes take supper to Ole in the field, and she'd come back with her hair all messed up and her clothes all disheveled. I'd tease her, and she'd get so embarrassed."

She refocused on me. "But it wasn't all fun and games. Lena worked hard both here and on the farm. And Ole expected no less." A few loose hairs fell against her eyelashes and twitched with each blink. "She was his best beet truck driver, don't ya know."

She grabbed a plastic bin of silverware and carted it to the counter. "When it's time to harvest beets, ya need to work 'round the clock to get 'em out of the ground fast. And one of the toughest jobs is drivin' a fully loaded truck through a field at night after a rain. Ya gotta avoid the wet patches, or the truck will sink so deep in gumbo you'll need a tractor to pull it out. Now, that takes time, and ya don't have time, so ya can't get stuck. Lena never did." Her smile was now unmistakable. "She just knew where to drive."

Margie ambled back to the prep table. "My point is that Ole and Lena truly loved each other. They shared dreams and worked hard to make 'em come true. Yet, look what happened. Ole turned fifty and got down on himself. The tramp saw her openin' and did her 'woe is me' routine, knowin' he'd wanna help. And after he did, she thanked him by callin' him her 'hero' and encouragin' him to join her in the horizontal rumba."

She opened the recipe box and retrieved something from behind one set of index cards. "See this picture? It's Ole and Lena not quite six years ago, just before things went bad." She handed me the photograph. It was wrinkled along the sides, but the center, where Ole and Lena stood in front of the café, remained undamaged.

In the picture, Ole was tall and lanky, his hair fine and light, like his sister's. Lena, on the other hand, was dark and tiny. She only reached Ole's chest but didn't seem overpowered by him. No, they stood side by side, his muscular arm draped over her shoulder, and they appeared very happy.

As I stared at the photo, I found myself wanting to ask a question. Not wishing to ignite any more controversy, I carefully searched for my words.

Margie took note. "So what's goin' on in that brain of yours now?"

Because my search wasn't over, I didn't reply.

"Oh, for land sake," she exclaimed, "speak your peace. It's bad for your digestion to hold things in. Say what ya want. I promise I won't bite your head off."

She winked, putting me at ease enough to talk, even though I wasn't certain how to ask what I wanted to know. "I just don't understand how . . . I don't get . . ." I paused and then tried again. "Well, um . . . Margie, why did Ole have an affair in the first place? He really didn't throw his life away simply because he turned fifty, did he?"

Margie appeared to give my question thoughtful consideration. "I guess I'm not positive. But it's not unusual for people to get frustrated when they reach a certain age—a milestone age—and see they haven't accomplished everythin' they set out to do." She rested her forearms on the table. "Some blame their families and turn mean. Others, like Ole, run from themselves and their so-called failures with the help of booze or a tramp or both." She stood up ramrod straight again. "Dr. Phil actually had a show about that very thing not too long ago."

I returned the photograph to her. "What did Ole ever fail to accomplish?"

"I'm . . . not . . . quite sure." She spaced her words out, as if using the time between them to come up with an explanation—even after all these years—for what had happened to her brother. "He made a decent livin' at farmin' but didn't seem all that fulfilled by it. He spent lots of time tinkerin', though nothin' big ever came of it." Margie stared past me. "I guess he didn't realize 'til it was too late that he was pretty successful anyways."

"How so?"

"Well, he had a devoted wife. He also had family and friends who loved him." She tucked the picture back into the box.

"Margie?" I momentarily wavered. "Do you ever regret not marrying?"

She closed the lid. "I'm not the most religious person in the world, but I believe God has a plan for each of us, and for some reason, his plan for me didn't include that." She rested for a beat. "His plan for Ole and Lena clearly did, though. That's why I don't feel bad about what happened to Samantha. She got what she deserved for interferin' with God's intentions."

That seemed kind of harsh, but I let it go. And after a moment, Margie switched topics.

"Ya know," she said, "I was with Lena the night before she died." Her voice had changed. It was lower and a bit mournful. "She'd been feelin' bad for nearly a month but thought it was nothin' more than a flu bug that wouldn't go away. I wasn't so sure.

"Ya see, Lena was always outgoin', but she'd turned inward, like folks do when they're gravely ill. She was lettin' life pass her by, not noticin' much and carin' about even less." Margie folded her arms across her chest, tucking them under her breasts. "She got so she'd hardly talk, but for some reason, that night she insisted on visitin', so that's what we did.

"After a while, we got 'round to the subject of Ole, of course, and we must have gabbed about him for darn near an hour." She hugged herself tightly. "Lena told me he'd stopped by to urge her to see the doctor. He said he was gonna make an appointment for himself too. He wanted to find out why he'd done what he did. He said the affair was like a dream to him, nothin' but a bad dream." Margie's eyes filled with tears, and she blinked them away.

"He also asked her to go out to dinner with him sometime. Not surprisingly, that got me goin' about them gettin' back together, but Lena warned me to 'slow down.'" Margie sniffled. "I didn't. I guess I couldn't. I told her that when two people are together for a long time, they're bound to hurt each other, so they better learn to forgive. That's when she gave me one of those 'don't push it' looks. She said she wasn't even sure why Ole wanted her back. Did he suddenly realize he still loved her? If so, how did that happen? Accordin' to her, nothin' had changed since he left. Or was life with Samantha just too darn lonely? Is that why he finally walked out on her? Ya see, when Ole and Samantha were together, no one in town wanted much to do with either of 'em, considerin' what they'd done to his family there.

"Yah, I probably should of said more." She sounded so melancholy. "But I simply told her that Ole loved her and only her. That they were meant to be together. Though that didn't ease her mind. She said she was tormented by the thought of him livin' with her again but wishin' he was with Samantha. She told me she knew that life on the farm with her was all about hard work, while life with Samantha was only about havin' a good time. Then she confided that most of all, she couldn't stand the idea of him makin' love to her but imaginin' himself with that tramp."

Margie dropped her gaze. "Oh, I've probably gone and said too much again. That there is pretty personal stuff."

Retreating to her recipe box, Margie studied one particular group of recipes. When she came upon the card she wanted, she pulled it from the box and slid it across the table. "Before I left Lena's house that night, I made some Tuna Noodle Hot Dish. It's a good hot dish for folks who don't feel well 'cause it's not too greasy or spicy."

Chapter Eight

WITH HER FOREARM, Margie wiped sweat from her brow. "Yah, I probably should of said more to Lena. I'd just read an article about infidelity and was gonna tell her about it, but she was so tired I decided to wait for another day."

Margie busied herself with a paper towel, wiping cheese crumbs and water spots off the stainless-steel prep table. "The psychologist who wrote the piece argued that divorce is much harder on kids than previously thought. So he suggested that when a woman has trouble forgivin' her 'unfaithful husband,' she should try instead to forgive the 'father of her children.' A bit corny, I know."

"Children?" I echoed. "Ole and Lena had children?"

Margie registered shock. "Yah, I told ya that."

"No, you didn't."

"Oh, gosh, I'm pretty sure I did."

"No, you told me your sister, Vivian, and her husband, Vern, had a daughter."

"And my brother, Ole, and Lena had children of their own."

"No—"

"But I'm almost positive I told ya about Buford and Buddy, Ole and Lena's twin boys."

"You mentioned their names, but you never said they were Ole and Lena's kids."

Margie dropped her head and groaned, "For cryin' out loud, I swear I'm losin' my mind. As I get older, my brain cells seem to die off as fast as my fat cells multiply." She patted the little muffin top that spilled over the waistband of her jeans. Then she pulled a slip of paper from her pocket. "This here's my checklist. I've done a million of these suppers, but if I don't check everything off . . . Well, a few months back, I cooked for two hundred at a funeral and forgot to put coffee in the coffee makers. We ended up with nothin' to drink 'cept hot water, if ya can imagine that."

"You get two hundred people for a funeral?"

"Sometimes more. When the former mayor died, five hundred folks showed up. They came from all over. Yeah, we end up pretty close around here, if for no other reason than body heat in the winter."

Margie snickered as she skimmed the checklist. Afterward, she shoved it back in her pocket and headed for the rear of the kitchen. "Oh, I was gonna tell ya about the kids." Reaching for several bags of dinner rolls from the top shelf of a large, painted cupboard, she informed me that when Lena died, the twins had a year left of high school, so they moved in with Vern and Vivian."

She hustled to the counter and dumped the rolls into napkin-lined baskets. "While my sister can really frost my buns, she's always been good to those kids. She'd do anythin' for 'em." A gentleness colored her words, which I found heartwarming in light of how she'd spoken earlier about her sister. "I reckon it's because Vivian had trouble havin' children of her own. She had a couple miscarriages, and Little Val barely survived. She only weighed a pound and a half at birth, and it was touch and go for a long while after that." Margie closed her eyes, no doubt wishing away those memories.

"What about Ole? Where was he when Lena passed away?"

Margie's shoulders drooped. "For the love of Jesus, did I forget to tell ya that too?" She shook her head. "When he left the tramp, he moved into an old trailer house out on Vern's farm. And after Lena died and the boys went to live with Vivian and Vern, Ole decided to stay right there, close by, in that same trailer.

"From then on, the twins let him farm with 'em whenever he was sober, though they didn't have to. See, Lena got everythin' in the divorce, includin' the house and all the land. And followin' her death, it all went to the kids." Several seconds ticked by. "Ole didn't want any of it anyways. He wouldn't take so much as a dime in the divorce." Her face turned smug. "He was shacked up with Samantha at the time, and I bet that made her mad enough to drown puppies."

Margie crossed the room and retrieved several serving trays from on top of the refrigerator. After delivering them to the work station, she headed to the freezer, where she collected an array of colorful tins. Barely balancing them, she wobbled back to the prep table and let them slide from her arms, metal clattering against metal.

"Want some help?"

"Well, if it's no bother, ya can take the bars from these canisters and arrange 'em on the platters." She hurried back to the freezer and picked out more tins. "When you're done, put the platters at the end of the counter. I'll get ya the recipes later.

As I yanked the frost-covered tops off the metal containers, the scent of chocolate, vanilla, and mint curled through the air. I was in heaven.

"Yah, Buford and Buddy are good boys." Margie emptied another armload of canisters, and like the others, they clanged like cymbals as they hit the table. "They're naturals, ya know."

"Naturals?" Concentrating was difficult, not because of the noise but because of all the sweet-smelling treats.

"Natural farmers." Margie returned to the cupboard and grabbed a giant electric coffee maker. She carried it to the sink and filled it with water, speaking only after she'd closed the tap. "Ya see, some kids stay on the farm 'cause they're too darn lazy or scared to try anythin' else. But Buford and Buddy stayed because they truly love farmin'. Always have." She twisted a metal cylinder into the pot, poured far too little Folgers in it, and cracked a couple eggs on top of the grounds. Scandinavian coffee. I'd heard about it but had never seen it made.

"When they were toddlers, Lena would take 'em to the field whenever they got crabby. There, she'd put 'em in the tractor with Ole, and they'd calm right down. Rather than fussin', they'd watch out the window as their pa drove down one row and up the next.

More often than not, before a single round was complete, they'd be fast asleep, one on each of his knees. If he moved 'em, they'd wake up and cry some more, so he'd just let 'em be. Like I said, they're natural farmers. It's in their blood."

She cleared some counter space for the coffee maker and plugged it in. "When Ole was drinkin', their Uncle Vern worked with 'em, even after he lost his arm. And a year ago, when they finished the agriculture program at the university in Crookston, they moved back into their parents' house and took over the entire farm operation. Accordin' to Vern, they're doin' a darn good job too."

Margie asked me to fill a large drink dispenser with homemade lemonade. And while I poured the liquid into the yellow, Igloo container, she told me about the twins' sister. "Her name's Rosa. She's four years older than the boys. She was in her last year at Moorhead State when her ma died."

Some time slipped by before Margie whispered, "She found her, don't ya know." She then held back, as if unsure she wanted to tell the story. But in the end, she did just that.

"Ya see, shortly after leavin' Lena's house that last night, I called Rosa to let her know how worried I was about her ma. She said she'd come home after class the followin' day. The twins were gone, so Rosa and Lena would be alone, which Rosa thought might be good since she wanted to convince her ma to go to the doctor.

"Anyways, when she got to the farm, she couldn't find Lena anywheres. Her car was parked out front, but there was no sign of her. Naturally, Rosa called her cell phone but got no answer. Now that wasn't all that unusual because Lena was always leavin' her phone one place or another. But it was kind of odd she wasn't just sittin' there in the kitchen, waitin' for her daughter, considerin' how much she loved her visits." A smile made an effort to take shape but faltered.

"Rosa checked the barn, the Quonset, even the shop. But nothin'. So she headed upstairs. Lena was hardly ever up there durin' the day, but Rosa had run out of ideas. Anyways, she knocked on her ma's bedroom door. Again, no answer. For some reason, though, she opened it and stepped inside. And that's when she saw her—poor, sweet Lena—lying in bed. She'd been dead since mornin'." Anguish filled Margie's voice. "The picture I showed ya earlier—the one with her and Ole in front of the café—was clutched in her hands." A few tears ran down Margie's cheeks, and she rubbed them away.

"Rosa dropped out of college and, like her brothers, moved in with Vivian and Vern. At their house, she had her cousin, Little Val. They've always been close." She struggled to keep an even tenor. "She also spent lots of time with Ole. Yah, that girl always understood her pa way better than her brothers did." She paused. "Then a year and a half later, when she was ready, she went back and finished her degree. Now she teaches vocal music in Hallock, which isn't such a bad job."

Margie again pulled the checklist from her pocket. She acted as if she were reviewing it, but I suspected she was hiding behind it until able to compose herself. Once she had, she crumpled the paper and tossed it in a nearby trash bin.

"Ya might meet all three of 'em tonight." She cleared her throat. "Well, probably not Rosa. She doesn't do much socializin'. She used to be so bubbly, but that all changed followin' the mess with her folks." Margie placed her hands on her hips. "More damage caused by that tramp." When certain she'd made her point, she added, "But if she does show up, you'll recognize her right away. She looks just like her ma, only taller."

"And the boys?"

"Well, they may be twins, but ya won't have any trouble tellin' 'em apart now that Buford burnt his head."

I must have appeared befuddled because she said, "Oh, my, let me tell ya about that." She stole a glimpse at the school-house clock that hung high above the sink. "Ya see," she began, the sparkle returning to her eyes, "a few weeks back, Buford and Buddy had some friends over for a catfish cookout. Catfish make real good eatin'. Ever had 'em?"

I nodded in the negative.

"Well, they're not hard to fillet. Ya just need a sharp knife and a little know-how. And ya can catch all ya want right over there."

She bobbed her head to the west, toward the Red River. "Yah, the twins never go far without their fishin' rods or their fillet knives.

"Anyways, Buford was grillin' over a campfire, which I guess wasn't burnin' hot enough to suit him, so he squirted it with lighter fluid. Well, from what I understand, he still wasn't satisfied, so he went ahead and threw the whole darn can in. Yah, he actually tossed the can itself right into the flames." She grimaced.

"Now he insists he was ignorant of the fact that the can had fluid left in it, but I told him later he was ignorant of far more than that. Accordin' to Buddy, the second the can hit the flames—POOF—a fireball erupted, and when the smoke cleared, there stood Buford minus his eyelashes, eyebrows, and most of his hair.

"The doctor says he'll be fine, but he's darn lucky he wasn't seriously hurt." She clicked her tongue in disapproval. "He claims he hadn't been drinkin' much, but I don't believe him. Sometimes he drinks way too . . ." She narrowed her eyes. "Well, let's just say that if he doesn't start usin' his head, he may as well have been born with two asses.

"I suppose, though, boys will be boys. Plus, we've all had some fun with the fiasco." She drew her lips back into a timid smile while pointing to a homemade sign on the wall that read, "For blackened catfish, contact Burnt Buford, at 1-800-YOU-FOOL."

"That reminds me." She sifted through the recipe cards. "Ya oughtta write down the recipe for Buford's favorite bar. I baked some for him the day after the catfish incident. They're Blondies, meanin' they're nothin' more than blonde brownies with chocolate chips, but Buford loves 'em all the same."

Chapter Nine

THE CAFÉ DOOR OPENED and in walked a woman with a husky build. She strutted to the kitchen. "Hi, Margie." She reached for a mug from a shelf above the sink and wheeled back around. "You must be Emerald Malloy. I'm Barbara Jean Jenson, but everyone calls me Barbie."

Barbie looked to be about ten years younger than Margie. But unlike Margie, she wore lots of makeup, including berry eye shadow and maroon lipstick. She also had a deep, tanning-bed tan and hair dyed henna red, cut short, and spiked with gel. A gaudy, gold chain hung from her neck, resting on a white, spandex, tank top that struggled to conceal her large breasts. The chain secured purple-rimmed eye glasses. Sunglasses, framed in pink, were perched on top of her head. Amazon Barbie.

"I told Barbie you'd be here," Margie informed me. "I thought ya might enjoy talkin' to her. She's the editor of our local paper, *The Enterprise*, but used to write news in the Twin Cities."

Since the fresh coffee wasn't ready, Barbie filled her mug with the last of the lunch-time brew and made tracks to the end of the counter, where the bars were waiting. "I wrote for the St. Paul paper a long time ago," she said. "A hell of a long time ago. It's been almost twenty years."

"You two should sit," Margie suggested. "I have to throw together a few more hot dishes."

Barbie selected two frosted pumpkin squares and motioned me to a booth. "I've only got a few minutes, but definitely, let's talk."

We sat down, and she immediately asked, "Do you know Stan Trendell? He was an up-and-coming reporter at your paper when I was at the one in St. Paul."

I rested my glass of lemonade on the table. "I don't know him personally, but I certainly know of him." He was one of our most popular columnists.

Barbie unfolded her napkin, laid it on the table, and placed her Pumpkin Bars, side by side, on top of it. "We were competitors back then, but I liked him and really admired his work. I had a feeling he'd make it big. Whenever I'm in the Cities, we get together."

I was bewildered, a fact not lost on the newspaper lady, as evidenced by her giggle. "I know what you're thinking." She flipped her hands, palms up. "How in the hell did she go from writing for a daily metropolitan newspaper to being the editor of a weekly way up here?"

"Well . . ."

"I was raised here. I got my bachelor's degree at the University of North Dakota in Grand Forks and moved to Minneapolis to get my master's in journalism at the U of M. While there, I wrote for the college paper, and the folks at the St. Paul paper liked what they read." She picked up one of her bars and took a bite. "I ended up working for them for nearly ten years." She talked with her hands, and her Pumpkin Bar went along for the ride.

"What made you come back here?"

"My parents began having trouble getting around. Either someone had to start checking in on them every day, or they had to sell their home. I couldn't stand the thought of them selling, so when my husband got the chance to become the school band director in Hallock, we packed up the kids and moved north." Barbie waved her hands. "We didn't expect to stay long. My husband grew up in L.A. and didn't think he could tolerate living way up here more than a few years. But in the end, he liked it. Now my parents are long gone, the kids have flown the coop, yet we're still here."

"But it's so . . . desolate."

Barbie scowled. "You call it desolate. I consider it serene."

I'd insulted her. "I'm sorry, I didn't mean to—"

"I agree, it's remote. That's why we travel. Remember, we live here. We're not trapped here." A lipstick grin eked across her face.

"Well, sometimes during January and February, we are." She flailed her arms. "Just kidding. Just kidding. I wouldn't live anywhere else. There's a real sense of community here." She looked to be thinking about something. "You know, I have more friends here than I did in Minneapolis. And it's an eclectic group. Yep, up here, if the town doctor only wants to hang out with other doctors, he'll end up pretty damn lonely."

Barbie polished off her first bar. "One of my best friends is a retired member of Congress. He lives down the road and splits his time between practicing law and managing his family's hog farm. When some other friends got married last spring, he not only drew up their prenup, he slaughtered and roasted the pig for the wedding reception. These people are multi-faceted. Shit, they have to be because there's so few of them."

I mentioned I'd met the local banker, who, I understood, also managed the VFW.

"And he makes a mean margarita," Barbie replied. "But then again, don't all bankers?"

With a laugh, she started in on her second bar, while I sipped lemonade and mulled over how someone like Barbie, discernibly intelligent and talented and undeniably full of spirit, could cope in this environment. She called it serene, but it *was* desolate. The closest Starbucks, Target, and movie theater were sixty miles away. How did she do it? I had to find out.

"Barbie, although the people here seem really nice, I can't help but ask how on earth . . ." That didn't come out right. "It's just that these towns are so small . . ." Still not right. I didn't want to offend her again. "Barbie, don't you miss . . . um . . . well, don't you miss the concerts, the plays, the intellectual stimulation of city life?"

She frantically waved her hands, as if erasing my concerns. "Like I said, we're not trapped here. And when we lived in Minneapolis, we didn't do much anyway." She rested her elbows on the table and pressed her fingertips together. Her nails were short and painted a brilliant red. "Of course we always threatened to 'trip the light fantastic.'" She emphasized the phrase with air quotes. "But when we were younger, we didn't have the money, and when we got older, we didn't have the energy. Hell, most nights we were too tired for sex. I swear I got pregnant the last two times only because of our mattress. It sagged in the middle, and we regularly ended up on top of each other whether we wanted to be or not." She raised her eyes to the heavens like an innocent cherub, but I doubted there was anything innocent about her.

"Tell me." I truly wanted to have a serious discussion. "What changed when you moved back here?"

"Well, first off, we got a new mattress." So much for serious. "And second, I came to realize that the Twin Cities didn't have the market cornered on intellectual discourse. Some of the debates around my neighbor's campfire in Hallock are downright eye opening." She stuck her nose in the air and fluttered her eyelashes with exaggeration. "And if it's culture you want, my husband and Margie's niece direct some of the finest school musicals you'll ever see."

I raised my hands. "I give up! I don't know what I was thinking. Clearly this place is a cultural Mecca, full of Renaissance people."

"Precisely, so why do you live in the Cities?"

"Huh?" The question threw me. "I guess because that's where I landed a job."

"So you're there by default?"

"Default? I'm not sure I'd say—"

"Besides your job, why'd you move there? Family? Friends? True love?"

"Hardly." Her words reverberated in my head. Did I really live in Minneapolis by "default"? That sounded terrible, as if I were taking the path of least resistance, letting life happen to me rather than designing it myself. I wasn't doing that, was I?

"Damn, girl," she went on to holler, "you should move here!"

"What?"

She reached out and grabbed my wrists. "Move here!" She pleaded in mock desperation. "You've got no stake in Minneapolis. And you could make a difference up here."

"What would I do?"

She let go of my arms and wiggled her fingers as if typing. "Write! Work for me. I could use the help. The woman who covers sports for me now pens romance novels on the side."

"What's wrong with that?"

"I end up with articles about boys' basketball with lines like, 'His body glistened with the sweat of desire as his throbbing loins pressed against the man he was guarding.'"

I snickered, but before I could speak, she was on to a new subject. "Do you own a home?"

"Huh?" I needed to think faster to keep up. "No, and I probably never will. You may not remember, but journalists in the Twin Cities get paid crap."

"Well, up here you can get a house for free."

"Really?"

"Nah, I'm just shittin' you. But you can buy one for less than the cost of a new car." She stopped to let that tidbit of information sink in. "I know someone who recently bought a cute, two-bedroom, one-bath, for under $25,000." She leaned across the table and whispered, "You may find this hard to believe, but there's not a big demand for housing in these parts."

As she sat back, she lifted the glasses from her ample chest and peered through the retro, cat-eye lenses to read the time on her Betty Boop watch. "Oh, hell, I've gotta go. I have a paper to put to bed." She shimmied seductively before sliding from the booth, and I followed suit, except for the shimmying seductively part.

Standing, she extended her hand. "It was great to meet you, and if you get a chance, say hello to Stan for me."

Without taking a breath, she hollered toward the kitchen. "Hey, Margie, I tried." Then to me, she said by way of explanation, "I'm always after people to move up here. I don't want these little towns to die." She paused. "Did I mention we have a lot of rich, single, farmers?"

While shaking my head, pretending exasperation, I realized just how tired I truly was. "Do you make that same sale's pitch to every visitor?" As soon as the words left my mouth, I knew they sounded petty. I had no desire to live in Kennedy, so I wasn't sure why it irritated me that Barbie had asked others to make the move, but it did, though I wasn't proud of it. "Sorry. I think my long drive has caught up to me. I'm pooped, and I'm getting crabby."

"Well, I meant it. If you ever need a change of pace, I could use the help. I'm not as young as I look." She fluttered her lashes. "I should start training someone to take over for me."

She peeled a few dollar bills from the pocket of her tight, denim capris and tossed them on the table.

"But why me? You don't even know if I can write."

From another pocket, she retrieved a business card and placed it in my hand, folding my fingers over it. "Honestly? Because you're here. Besides, you wouldn't be working where you're working if you couldn't write." She winked. "And you'd be surprised what I know about you."

That baffled me, but I was too worn out to engage in more banter.

"Now," she added, "I have to skedaddle. I need to get back to my office and finish an article about wind farms. Some locals want one built here."

I tucked my hair behind my ears. "A reasonable request if this afternoon's breeze was any indication."

"Yeah, it clips along like that most days. There's nothing to slow it down. No trees. No hills." She gently patted the wine-colored spikes on top of her head. "Before I moved back, my hair would actually lie flat."

Shifting gears yet again, she hollered, "Hey, Margie, I left you some money on the table."

"Okay, kiddo. Ya comin' back later?"

"Only if I get my work done." Eyeing me, she said in a voice still loud enough for Margie to hear, "It sure would be nice if I had someone to help me."

Margie chuckled knowingly as Barbie wrapped the remainder of her pumpkin square in her napkin and started for the door, her flip-flops snapping against the bottoms of her feet.

When just about there, she twirled back around. "Oh, damn, I almost forgot, I have to finish a story about a meth-lab bust too. I'll need more nourishment."

"You have a lot of those?"

"Nah," she answered, hurrying to the counter. "We don't have much crime of any kind."

The murder immediately came to mind. "What about Samantha Berg?"

Barbie's eyes practically bugged out of her head before she recovered enough to say, "That really didn't amount to much."

"But the FBI was called in."

"And no one was arrested." Trying hard to act nonchalant, she exaggerated her perusal of the bar selection.

"Which means the murderer is still around, right?"

"Not necessarily." She ended up picking out two more pumpkin squares and adding them to her napkin.

"Huh?" The door to my brain slowly opened to another possibility. "Do you think Samantha Berg was killed by someone just passing through? Is that what you're saying?"

Barbie drew back her shoulders and lifted her chin. "I'm saying the matter's closed. I'm saying it's not worth discussing."

She was miffed with me again. "Sorry. I only asked because—"

"Listen, Samantha caused a lot of people pain, including members of one of this town's oldest families. I'm not suggesting she deserved to die, but neither the police nor the FBI could figure out who killed her, so just drop it." She spun toward the exit. "Now I have to go." And with that, she strutted from the building.

Stunned, my mouth actually hanging open, I watched as she crossed the highway to her SUV.

"Yah, that girl's a corker," Margie said, joining me. "She's a one-woman Chamber of Commerce. She loves these towns, and while she jokes a lot, she's dead serious about keepin' 'em goin'. She won't let anythin' stand in her way."

Handing me another recipe card from the box, she added, "Ya may not have noticed, but Barbie likes my Pumpkin Bars. Ya might wanna jot down the recipe." She stopped for a beat. "Ya might also wanna close your mouth before ya swallow a fly."

Chapter Ten

Kennedy, Minnesota, has no motels, but Margie keeps two guest rooms, with attached baths, above the café, "just in case." I guess my visit qualified as one of those "cases."

I grabbed my overnight bag from my car and headed upstairs to freshen up before the benefit. I was wiped out from my drive, greasy from the time spent in Margie's kitchen, and frustrated by my visit with Tundra Barbie.

I undressed and climbed into the shower. The soft water ran down my back, relaxing my muscles and washing my tension down the drain. I soaped up, rinsed off, and toweled dry. Then I flopped on the bed. I had a full evening ahead of me and knew a rest, even a ten-minute one, would do me good.

I woke to Kris Kristofferson. Not literally of course. Rather, I woke to his music, specifically, his rendition of "Me and Bobby McGee." The song had made its way from the restaurant downstairs up through the floorboards. "Freedom's just another word for nothing left to lose . . ."

Squinting at the clock-radio on the dresser, I saw that my ten-minute rest had stretched into a thirty-minute nap. I contemplated rising but was too comfortable to make any sudden moves and remained curled crossways on the double bed, one towel wrapped around my head, another around my torso. "And nothin' ain't worth nothin' but it's free."

From that vantage point, I studied the room. It was similar to the one I had when I was a little girl. The bed was crowned with a white, iron headboard and covered in a colorful, patchwork quilt that smelled fresh, as if recently brought in from the clothes line. Next to the door, a green drop-leaf table straddled two wooden chairs, and on the opposite wall, the antique low-boy dresser stood alone. The furniture pieces and colors weren't identical to those in my old room, but the style was the same, as was the music wafting through the floor. "She's lookin' for the home I hope she'll find."

I was weaned on country rock. My parents were passionate about country dancing. Every Saturday night they joined their dance group down at the American Legion, where they perfected old moves and tried out new ones. During the week, they practiced at home, often persuading me, their only child, to join in.

Our house was always filled with the sounds of Kris Kristofferson and Willie Nelson. And while many kids undoubtedly hated that music, if for no reason than their parents liked it, I always enjoyed it. And I still feel connected to it. Probably because my folks died when I was young, and that music helps me stay close to them, or at least their memory.

When Kristofferson faded away, my thoughts shifted from days gone by to earlier that day and my conversation with Barbie. She'd said that Samantha Berg's murder didn't amount to much. It wasn't worth talking about. But how often did a journalist speak that way about an unsolved homicide, especially one committed in a place where murder must hardly ever occur?

Pondering that, I rose and got dressed, tugging on a pair of blue jeans and slipping into a paisley, button-down, sleeveless blouse. I followed with a half-hearted attempt at brushing my hair. While not wet, it was terribly tangled from the wind outside and being wrapped in a towel for both my shower and my nap.

As I yanked at the snarls, I reminded myself that my assignment didn't include writing about an old murder case, even if it would be far more exciting than a story about a day in the life of a small-town café owner—a story that most likely would never see print.

Setting my brush on the dresser, I swiped on some mascara and lip gloss. I don't wear much makeup, but I try to highlight my lips and eyes. They're my best features, and to my way of thinking, drawing attention to them limits focus on my frizzy, red mane.

I'd have preferred my hair be silky and Irish-setter red, but it wasn't. It was curly and flame colored, prompting my dad to nickname me "Torch" when I was a kid. No one else dared call me that, but he loved the moniker, and I loved him, so he got away with it. And now that he was gone, I'd probably never do anything differently with my hair.

I shoved the makeup tubes back into my bag and pulled out my phone. No messages, not even from my editor. His apparent lack of interest annoyed me, which, in turn, drove me to speculate what he and the other big shots at the paper would do if I returned with a story about an old murder case.

I tossed the phone onto the bed. If I did something extraordinary, like actually solve the crime, they'd have to take notice. Hell, they'd have to give me a by-line. What choice would they have? And if my story was good—and it would be—they'd be obliged to move me from the "Food" section to real news, in spite of my lack of experience. If they didn't, I'd quit and head over to one of the other papers no doubt vying for my talent.

I stared at my mirrored image and whispered, "This could be your big break, Emme." I glanced at my phone and back at my reflection. "But you don't want anyone calling your editor and telling him that you're nosing around for something other than recipes, so you'll have to be discreet." I looked doubtful. "Wait a minute, you can be discreet." I splayed my hands on top of the dresser. "In fact, keep working on your real assignment, and then no one, not even Margie, will catch on to the story you're truly after."

I leaned against the dresser and gazed intently at my image. "Solving this case won't be hard. It's surprising it hasn't been done already." I wrinkled my face in concentration. "I suppose people just get too close to a situation sometimes to see it clearly."

I drew myself up to my full height. "Even though everyone around here seems to be an expert with a knife, Ole Johnson is the most logical suspect. He lost everything—his family and his farm—

because of Samantha. And there's no stronger motive for murder than that.

"Now, Emme, just unearth a little more information and answer a few more questions, such as why Ole Johnson wasn't ever arrested, and you'll be ready to write a story so good it'll knock the argyle socks right off your editor's gout-swollen feet."

I gave myself a determined look. "You can do this." I spread my legs and put my hands to my hips, imitating Wonder Woman. "You're going to do this." I pumped my fist into the air. "And it's going to be big!"

* * *

My super-hero impersonation was cut short by some shouting outside, which I felt compelled to check out. Hurrying to the bedroom window for a quick look-see, I spotted the two old-timers from earlier that day in the café. They had replaced their overalls and long-sleeve work shirts with blue jeans and short-sleeve plaid shirts but still donned the same caps.

They were hollering to a portly, middle-aged man with short legs. He was sliding out of a white service van. The sign on the side of the van read, "Swenson's Sewer Works: Your Sh** Is My Bread and Butter." Once on the ground, he adjusted the waistband of his jeans, half hidden beneath his beer belly, and extended his hand to John Deere.

I cringed. Did he come straight from work or go home first to wash up?

With their hellos out of the way, the three men waddled across the highway, briefly stopping to greet a young woman who ran past them in the opposite direction. She was clad in shorts and a dirty tee-shirt, her long, dark hair blowing in the wind. She carried a shovel among some other garden tools. And after pitching them into the bed of a restored, 1950s pickup, she gave the guys a quick wave before climbing into the truck and taking off.

I followed suit. Only I took off for the café downstairs, thoughts of hot dish competing with those of homicide. While eager to begin my investigation, I also was excited to try Margie's Tater-Tot Hot Dish as well as something she called Cheeseburger Hot Dish.

Yes, I was looking forward to everything I thought the evening held in store for me, from home cooking to intrigue. But I was woefully ignorant as to what truly lay ahead.

Part Two
Boil the Noodles

Chapter Eleven

Entering the café, I spotted Margie, still dressed in her Hot Dish Heaven tee-shirt and blue jeans. She was crouched in a corner, consoling the two little girls who'd been in for ice cream. They were rubbing their eyes, as if they'd been crying.

I also saw John Deere, his friend, and the sewer guy shuffle through the doorway. They stopped to hug a middle-aged, fragile-looking woman with alabaster skin and a colorful scarf tied around her bald head. She held a bouquet of white daisies and blue delphiniums.

Across from her, several men, their sunburns ending where their tee-shirt sleeves began, formed a buffet line along the counter, now chock full of hot dishes, salad, dinner rolls, and bars. The men were accompanied by a smattering of blonde kids, all of them surrounded by elderly people with clouds of gray hair. There were so many gray clouds, in fact, I half expected rain.

My stomach gnawed at me, apparently trying to convince me to eat straightaway, but I needed no convincing. Famished and determined to get my food before the sewer guy, I forged ahead, side-stepping a pair of shrunken-up, stooped-over women, deciding it would be rude to hurdle them, no matter how close to the ground they stood or how quickly I wanted to eat.

I was just about there, my eyes glued on what would be my place in the buffet line, when, out of nowhere, the Anderson sisters stepped in front of me. I pulled up just short of plowing them over.

"Hello there. Nice to see ya again," one of them said, after which the other two chimed in with, "Yah, we're back, just like we promised."

I caught my breath and offered a fake smile. It was the best I could do. Keep in mind, they were standing between me and my dinner. There was Henrietta, the mother hen, the oldest and largest of the three; Harriet, whose moustache was undoubtedly the envy of every boy in town; and tiny, elfin Hester.

"See what I won at bingo." Henrietta pulled a plastic bag of cucumbers from the large canvas purse hanging from her shoulder.

Not sure whether a prize of cucumbers warranted congratulations or condolences, I remained mum.

Harriet, however, knew exactly what to say. "It ain't fair. She's too lucky. She always wins the best prizes."

Still unsure how to respond, I merely stated, "Oh, I'll bet you'll win next time."

To that, Harriet replied, her voice filled with yearning, "I can only hope and pray. Ya see, the cucumbers in my garden turned out just terrible this year."

As shocking as this might sound, I really didn't care about Harriet's cucumbers. Yes, I wanted to talk to her and her sisters. They were Ole's aunts and probably knew something about Samantha Berg's death. But at that moment, I was in no condition to carry on a decent conversation, much less conduct an interrogation. I needed food, so I suggested they join me in line.

Little Hester eagerly accepted my invitation. "Oh, for sure," she said. "But let's get goin.' Ya don't wanna be slow to eat at one of these things. Everythin' gets too picked over."

Henrietta agreed, reciting the poor food choices left for the "slow pokes" at the last community dinner. The tale led all three ladies—large, medium, and small—to hobble ever faster to the counter, with me bringing up the rear.

I pulled a twenty-dollar bill from my pants' pocket, slid it through the slit in the plastic ice cream bucket that served as the donation jar, and stared at the ladies. They hadn't contributed a thing.

Seeing me eye them, they eyed each other until, finally, they retrieved their coin purses from their large shoulder bags and picked through change. Choosing a few dimes and quarters, they dropped them into the pail and, with indignant huffs, snatched their plates and stepped in behind me.

I began my culinary journey with a serving of Cheeseburger Hot Dish and another of Pizza Hot Dish before spying my favorite, Tater-Tot Hot Dish. Not wasting a second, I helped myself to a large spoonful of that, heavy on the tots. The pleasant aroma triggered a reverie of Saturdays during my childhood, my dad and me sitting at the kitchen table, playing Kings on the Corners, my favorite card game, while Mom served up our hot-dish lunch nearby.

Feeling all warm and fuzzy inside, I tucked that memory away and strolled on down the line. I added a dinner roll but stopped when I got to the Jell-O. I don't like Jell-O. I don't like any food that wiggles after it was prepared. Orange Jell-O with marshmallows. Red Jell-O with bananas. I didn't want any but feared I'd be asked if I'd tried at least one, so I scooped up a small amount of something that appeared to be—and hopefully was—more Cool Whip than Jell-O.

While shaking the pink concoction onto my plate, I noticed the steady stream of people now entering the building. I'd planned to do some serious eating, and for that, I needed to be seated, so I quickly claimed my silverware and a cup of freshly brewed coffee and scanned the room for a spot to squat. Spying an empty booth in the far corner, I turned to inform my elderly companions, only to find them still way back in line. I considered waiting for them, but my hunger and desire to rest my rear won out.

Promising to track them down later, I wove through the burgeoning crowd, dodging elbows and beer bellies while struggling to keep my plate and cup upright. My moves were tentative, accompanied by a low, monotone chant of, "Pardon me. So sorry. Excuse me." My chant was accompanied by another fake smile. What can I say? Genuine charm is difficult when near faint from hunger.

Reaching the booth, I settled down and dug in. Pizza Hot Dish first. Cheeseburger Hot Dish after that. Both were delicious, yet I knew I was only using them to tease my taste buds, and when I couldn't hold out any longer, I devoured the object of my afternoon fantasies—Tater-Tot Hot Dish. I savored every bite, soft moans of delight actually escaping my lips. Okay, that was a little embarrassing.

Later, with my stomach full, I strained to see the desserts on the counter, but from where I sat, I couldn't tell a Lemon Treat from a Date Bar. What I could tell, however, was that the Anderson ladies were still dawdling in line, even though everyone who'd accompanied us along the buffet route was seated and eating.

Curious, I thought, until I realized what the old girls were really doing. I blinked to make sure my eyes weren't deceiving me. They weren't. The Anderson sisters were pilfering food.

That's right. In addition to filling their plates, they were stuffing hot dish, dinner rolls, and dessert bars into zip-lock freezer bags partially concealed in their big purses. Little Hester was even trying to smuggle Jell-O, but discreetly spooning that into a half-hidden plastic bag was proving difficult.

"How despicable," I muttered under my breath. "How reprehensible. How . . . funny!"

Sure, it was wrong of me to think that way, but I couldn't help myself. There was something darkly amusing about a trio of elderly, prim-and-proper-looking women stealing food from a benefit dinner. And while no one else appeared taken by the scene, I couldn't tear my eyes away. Were these three Kennedy's biggest criminals? Its most notorious gang? True, they didn't sport traditional gang colors or tattoos, but they did dress alike, in gingham house frocks and black orthopedic shoes.

Of course I was being silly, but given what was playing out in front of me, silly seemed appropriate, prompting me to go with it until a hand squeezed my shoulder and startled the silliness right out of me. I'm pretty sure I catapulted a foot before jerking around to discover Margie laughing at how she'd made me jump.

After patting me on the back, she motioned to her elderly aunts. "They do that all the time. Everyone knows and simply ignores 'em."

I smoothed the front of my shirt, doing my best to downplay that my heart had relocated to my throat. "Well," I uttered with a dry swallow, "at least I now understand why they didn't want to be last in line."

Margie snickered and passed me a few more cards. "These are the recipes for the rest of what's up there. I didn't have time to make everythin'. Father Daley helped me out some."

The recipe on top looked to be for the pink stuff on my plate. I meant to read it over but again got distracted by the Anderson sisters.

Emme, do you really want to ask them about Ole? It was a voice from inside my head. Yeah, that's right. Sometimes I hear voices. The whole therapy thing makes much more sense now, doesn't it?

With their shoulder bags already bulging, they shoveled in more food.

Emme, look what they're doing. They're absolutely nuts. Can you trust anything they say?

If I didn't talk to them, though, I'd be done as an investigative reporter before I even got started. Margie wasn't going to volunteer anything about Ole. She liked him too much. Neither was the newspaper editor. And I didn't know anyone else.

A glob of Jell-O fell out of Hester's bag and splattered on the floor. As she kicked at the slimy mess, my confidence in the women as information sources grew shakier, and before long, it was as shaky as the pink stuff on my plate.

Chapter Twelve

"Now, Emme," Margie said, waving to a man in a short-sleeve sheriff's uniform, "I want you to meet someone."

The guy steered toward us, and I took a visual inventory. I had to. I was a reporter—a trained observer. What's more, he was hot. Tall, no less than six-three, and well built. My guess? Around thirty. His eyes were dark brown, his hair a shade lighter and unruly, making for an interesting look on a cop.

"This here is Deputy Randy Ryden," Margie explained when he reached my booth. "He's from the Twin Cities too. Randy, this is Emerald Malloy, the reporter I told ya about."

"Glad to meet you." The deputy tipped his head, his hands otherwise occupied, a cup of coffee in one, a plate piled high with food in the other. "It's getting crowded in here. Mind if I join you?"

"No, not at all." I took another bite of Pizza Hot Dish. "Sit down."

While Deputy Ryden sidled in across from me and laid out his silverware, Margie excused herself, claiming she had to check on things in the kitchen.

"Margie tells me you're writing a story about her." The deputy raised his eyes to find me using my fork to break a string of cheese that stretched from my plate to my mouth. He smiled . . . or was it a smirk?

I felt myself blush. Then I got perturbed. I don't like anyone—cute or not—judging my manners. It's my biggest pet peeve.

I put my fork down and tore the string apart with my fingers. “Yep.” I defiantly sucked the cheese into my mouth. “I’m gathering Margie’s favorite recipes and writing about her life as a rural café owner.”

He grabbed his own fork—overhand—and pushed hot dish onto it with his free thumb. No mistake about it, he was mocking me. I’d been nice enough to share my booth, and he was repaying me by making fun of how I ate. What a jerk!

Determined to teach him a lesson, I consumed my remaining tater-tots without saying a word. But as I munched, I had to admit that while not talking, I still was gawking.

Well, not exactly gawking. It was more like examining him on the sly. Whenever he looked elsewhere, I checked him out. I attempted to discern if his eyes were chestnut brown with flecks of green or chestnut brown with flecks of gold. No matter, they were striking. And his mouth was the kind featured in toothpaste ads. His lips were full, his teeth, brilliantly white and perfectly straight.

He grinned, the corners of his eyes crinkling all sexy-like, and heat instantly rose along the nape of my neck, making me regret that I’d opted for coffee instead of water. I couldn’t very well cool off by pouring hot coffee down my shirt.

He stuffed his mouth with hot dish and wolfed down a roll. Another smile split his face, and my stomach did a somersault. I reminded my stomach that the guy was making fun of me, and that it needed to hold steady on my behalf.

He stabbed another clump of hot dish, aimed it at his mouth, and as he parted his lips, our eyes met and held. A double somersault. My stomach wasn’t a very good listener.

Perhaps he isn’t mocking you, Emme. It was another one of the voices inside my head. *Perhaps he, too, is just a messy eater.*

A second voice piped up. *Or perhaps you’re making excuses for him because he’s so good looking you want to get to know him, no matter if he’s nice or not.*

Unwilling to accept I was that shallow—after all my therapy—I went with the first voice and the whole bad-manners thing. And for reasons not worth discussing, that motivated me to give him another chance.

My intention was to inquire about Samantha Berg. Now that I'd seen what the Anderson sisters were truly made of—stolen buffet food for the most part—I assumed I'd be better off obtaining information about her murder from area law enforcement. But at the moment, I didn't think very highly of them either. Remember, Ole was obviously guilty but was never arrested. Still, I'd ask Deputy Ryden what I wanted to know. And I'd do it patiently, like a good reporter should. I'd even make some small talk first.

I opened my mouth only to clamp it shut again. My mind, it seemed, was stuck in neutral. I couldn't think of anything to say. And that wasn't like me. Usually, I was quite chatty. Yeah, I know, hard to believe. But there I was, self-conscious and tongue-tied.

Not sure what to do, I stooped to eavesdropping in hopes of hearing something that would ease my brain and my mouth back into gear. First, I caught a snippet about the snowmobiles sold by Arctic Cat in Thief River, but that was no help. Since I'd never ridden a snowmobile, a conversation focused on them wouldn't go anywhere, no pun intended. Next, I heard two women debating the ethics of an indigent lady who had used money donated by a local church for "necessities" to have her breasts enhanced. "Don't be too quick to judge," one of the women said in response to the other's claim that a boob job was never a necessity, "God works in mysterious ways."

I believe it was then I got angry—with myself. Other folks were obviously quite comfortable discussing whatever the hell popped into their heads, so why was I so nervous? It made no sense. And I was going to put an end to it. "Deputy Ryden," I began, "did you say you were from the Cities?"

The deputy cleared his throat. "Well, I've lived here more than six years, but since I wasn't born here, the locals consider me 'from the Cities.'"

I was baffled. "But if you weren't born here, how on earth did you end up here?"

He shot me a look of indignation.

Flustered, I tried to clarify myself. "I didn't mean . . . It's just that people who live in these tiny towns usually have some connection to them. They generally don't move to them voluntarily. I mean . . ." Concluding I was only making matters worse, I closed my mouth.

The deputy tilted his head in amusement. "Growing up, my brother and I spent summers here on our grandparents' farm."

"Oh, so you're one of those kids."

He appeared confused, and I attempted another explanation. "I always dreamed of spending time with grandparents in the country. I just don't have any. I mean I had some. But I never knew them. Well, um . . . they died." This wasn't going well.

"So did mine." He switched utensils, filling his spoon with green Jell-O garnished with shredded carrots. "Die, I mean." He shuttled the green goop into his mouth.

As he chewed or did whatever was done with Jell-O, I silently questioned how he could eat that stuff. Then I questioned God. No, not about the Jell-O. That would have to wait for another time. Presently, I only wanted to know why Deputy Ryden got to live out my childhood fantasy, while I had to live my life.

Not that my life was bad. But I was only thirteen when my parents died, which really sucked. According to the police, their car skidded across a patch of ice on a freeway overpass in Minneapolis. It smashed through the guardrail and plunged into the icy Mississippi. They were killed instantly, leaving a gaping hole in my heart.

I moved in with my mom's only sister and her husband, where I stayed until I graduated from high school. He was a doctor at the Mayo Clinic, and she, a corporate executive. They were decent but stuffy.

"Family time" at their house was limited to dinner, served precisely at eight. At the table, they corrected my manners ad nauseum, everything from how I sat to the way I held my fork and chewed my food. The criticism may have been warranted, but it drove me crazy. Thankfully, by nine, I was in my bedroom, listening to my parents' favorite music or reading novels about kids fortunate enough to live with loving grandparents in the country.

As those memories faded, I dug deep for something else to say. "What did you do in the Cities?"

"After college and the police academy, I was a cop there for three years." He consumed another clump of hot dish, either washing it down or mixing it with his coffee.

"What made you leave?"

"I got tired of arresting the same guys over and over, only to see them out again the next day. And I like to hunt. Up here I can do that practically right outside my back door."

"You don't mind being an outsider?" Fortunately, the questions were forming more easily.

"Folks around here are pretty nice." He flashed a perfect smile, and I quivered. That damn air conditioning! "Sure, a few people consider themselves better than everyone else," he conceded, "but most understand that in the big picture, none of us is . . ."

He motioned toward an obese man who reminded me of bread dough left too long to rise in the pan. He wore a Minnesota Wild cap and tried in vain to look important while speaking louder than necessary into his cell phone. The sewer guy stood behind him, mocking him with charade-like gestures. "See the man over there on the phone?" the deputy asked. "The one in front of Shitty? Now, he's a real prick."

I eyed the guy, from his puffy face to his black socks and sandal-clad feet. "How so?"

"Well, among other things, he claims to be a descendant of the first president."

My gaze made its way back to the deputy. "Washington?"

"No. Before him."

I stared blankly, moving Deputy Ryden to enlighten me. "Washington was the first president under the Constitution. Before that, the country was governed by the Articles of Confederation. The first president under the Articles was John Hanson, supposedly that guy's great-great-great-grandfather or something."

"And you know all this because . . . ?"

He paused, his fork midway to his mouth. "We're not idiots. We may live in the sticks, but we have schools and books and—"

"I didn't mean—"

"And that guy, John Hanson, writes lots of editorials advocating that American history classes be changed to recognize his ancestor and namesake as the true first president." He emptied his fork into his mouth.

"He's serious?"

"Uh-huh."

While the deputy put away more food, I did my best to digest what he'd already said. "What do the other folks around here think?"

He cleared his throat. "Most Scandinavians are humble. They don't like a lot of attention. They'd prefer he shut up." He again readied his fork with hot dish. "Behind his back, they call him Mr. President." He grinned broadly, his eyes sparkling with mischief.

No doubt about it, I'd been wrong about Deputy Ryden. He was one of the good guys. I'd experienced so few of them over the past few years, I just didn't recognize him at first. True, he had poor table manners, but honestly, that just gave us something in common. Besides, he deserved major props for being the first guy in nearly a year to ask to join me for dinner. Okay, he only did so because the café was crowded, but let's not split hairs. He asked.

A year? Had it really been a year since Boo-Boo?

Yes, his name was Boo-Boo, so without a doubt, I should have known better.

I met him shortly after moving back to Minnesota. He briefly played for the Minnesota Twins and ran around with a big guy called Yogi, like the cartoon bear, not the baseball legend.

Within a few weeks, I was positive it was love. I spent almost everything I earned on "date" clothes and called in sick and missed deadlines just to be with him. One Saturday morning I even maxed out a credit card to fly to Chicago, where the Twins were playing a three-game series with the White Sox. I wanted to surprise him, and I did. I also surprised the two blonde bimbos (or is it bimbi?) in bed with him.

Returning home, I buried myself in work, started therapy, and swore off men. Unlike Margie, I couldn't imagine forgiving a guy for cheating, no matter the circumstances. Truth is, my world had always been black and white. Rules existed—expressed or implied—and we lived by them or suffered the consequences. End of discussion. Oh, how things had changed!

Shaking my thoughts loose, I discovered my gaze was still trained on Randy Ryden. But since I was paying a therapist $150 an hour to teach me how to remain guy-free—at least for the time being—I shifted my attention to my plate, aiming to give my noodles the consideration they deserved.

It was no use. I couldn't eat. As goofy as this might sound, I only hungered for witty remarks that would impress the good deputy. Just one problem. I couldn't think of any. The only lines I conjured up were two Boo-Boo had used on me the night we met. One went something like, I seem to have lost my phone number. May I borrow yours? And the other was, I'm new in town, so could I get directions . . . to your house?

When Boo-Boo said them, I thought they were funny and sweet. But now, following nearly a year of counseling . . . Well, let's just say that for the deputy, I wanted to go with something a little less revolting. I settled for, "Don't you find police work here pretty boring compared to what you did in Minneapolis?"

The deputy smiled. Were those dimples? Another quiver, and this time I didn't even attempt to fool myself. It wasn't the air conditioning making me tingle.

"I like my job," he replied, "but it's not the only thing that's important to me. Anyhow, on occasion, we bust a meth lab or catch someone crossing the border from Canada with a car full of weed. And there's always petty theft."

I made a show of nodding toward the Anderson sisters.

The deputy chuckled. "You caught their act, huh?" He leaned his elbows on the table and laced his fingers in front of his chin. "A few years ago I found them in here during the middle of the night. Harriet had pried the back door open with a crowbar. She claimed they were getting ready for a church luncheon, but they were just stealing food. Nonetheless, Margie insisted we drop the whole thing. She said her aunts apparently got a thrill sneaking around, and at their ages, they should be allowed to get their thrills any way they can." He raised his coffee cup. "So that's what they do when they're not watching everyone else's business from their windows."

"Well, I bet you appreciate the extra eyes." My voice was lilting. I'd succumbed to the flirt in me. Not a good sign. I was an inept flirt. It almost always ended badly. "Surely they make your job easier."

"No, not really. And don't call me Shirley." He smirked as he raised his cup.

"Seriously, don't you feel stifled here? Don't you want to be . . . stimulated?"

Deputy Ryden almost choked on his coffee. "Why? What did you have in mind?"

I gasped. *Oh, my God, did I just say that?* Being a redhead, I blush easily, and, at that moment, I was positive my face was as red as a baboon's ass. I felt like one too. "I meant stimulated professionally."

"Oh." He feigned disappointment. "As I said, we get an interesting case now and then."

I dropped my chin and peered at the index card in front of me. It was a recipe for "regular" Jell-O salad. I made an effort to read through it, anything to avoid thinking about what I'd just said. But I couldn't stay focused—and only partly because no one can maintain interest in Jell-O for more than a few seconds.

Chapter Thirteen

W*HY DIDN'T YOU ASK THE DEPUTY about Samantha Berg right away?* It was yet another voice from inside my head.

Because, I thought I'd first put the guy at ease with some idle chit-chat.

But if you would have asked about Samantha Berg right off the bat, you wouldn't have humiliated yourself.

That's probably true, but I wanted to engage in a little small talk before broaching the subject of murder.

Well, I think small talk's overrated.

And I think that falls in the category of "information you should have shared earlier."

Why? You wouldn't have listened anyway. You never do.

Huh? What's that?

"Deputy Ryden," I said, tired of arguing with myself, "were you working up here when Samantha Berg went missing?"

The deputy blinked, apparently thrown by my directness. "How did you hear about that?"

"Margie told me."

"Oh." He used another roll to mop tomato sauce from his plate. "Margie likes to talk." He bit the roll in half.

"Well, did you know her?" *Stay focused. And whatever you do, don't flirt!*

"Yeah." The deputy answered around the food in his mouth. "I knew her."

"And you worked the case?"

"The FBI led the murder investigation."

"But you were assigned to it too, weren't you?"

"Yeah." He spoke cautiously, as if concerned about where the conversation was headed.

"And you local cops handled the missing person's case, right?"

He shoved the rest of the roll in his mouth. "The FBI only got involved after her body was recovered."

His face then took on the look of someone with something important on his mind. But when it became clear he wasn't going to share it with me, I plowed ahead. "So how long was she missing?"

He stuck another forkful of food in his mouth. With his cheeks stuffed, he could only mumble, "A couple months."

"She was gone a couple of months, and you couldn't find her?"

He swallowed hard and frowned.

"Sorry," I uttered. "Sometimes I'm not very tactful."

He wiped the corners of his mouth with his thumb and index finger. "You just don't understand. We didn't start looking for her right away."

"Why not? Didn't she have worried family?"

"Nope. Contrary to what you said earlier, people don't always have ties to the little towns they live in. Samantha, for instance, had no connection at all to Kennedy. She just moved here from North Dakota about a dozen years ago."

"How come?"

He shrugged. "She told some folks she was hiding from an abusive boyfriend. Others heard she was starting over after her husband walked out when their kid got sick."

I scooted forward, not sure I'd heard right over the chorus of laughter coming from the women in the booth behind me. "She had a kid?"

"Uh-huh. He was twelve or so when they arrived. He's now grown and long gone."

"What was wrong with him?"

"Asthma or something. Nothing serious."

"So?" I said, urging him to continue.

"So, her stories didn't check out." He shifted in his seat, and the vinyl rustled beneath him. "There was a boyfriend but no record of violence. And her husband divorced her but not without fighting for custody of the kid. He said she only wanted the boy for the child support."

"Sounds like she had trouble telling the truth."

"You could say that." His delivery was flat, void of inflection. He definitely wanted to drop the subject, but I wasn't ready to let it go. Don't forget, this was my story—my career—we were talking about.

My conscience immediately slapped me alongside the head. *It's not always all about you, Emme. You're not the center of the universe, you know. In this case, there was a dead woman too. You may want to keep that in mind.*

Appropriately chastised, I stated more self-righteously than I had any right to, "Even if she was a liar, Samantha Berg deserved to have her murder solved."

The deputy set his fork on his plate. "No one said otherwise. But it's hard to get people, even good people, to tell what they know about a crime they view as a community service."

"She was disliked that much?"

He rubbed his hands down the sides of his face. "She wasn't very nice. You might say her moral compass was broken."

"But she must have had some good traits. Everybody does."

"You really think so?"

"Don't you?"

He again shuffled in his seat, and for a second time, the vinyl responded with a groan. I suspected he wanted to do the same. But instead, he chose to speak. "I guess it's possible that everyone's born good, but shit happens. And while that makes some folks wiser, it turns others into assholes."

"And Samantha Berg was one of the latter?"

"Her kid wouldn't even come back to claim her body. What does that tell you?"

I had no answer.

"It doesn't matter anyhow." The deputy's eyes flickered at his near-empty plate. "Even if the kid had been around—or had cared at all—we wouldn't have started our investigation any sooner than we did."

"Why not?"

He stabbed his final forkful of Pizza Hot Dish. "Samantha took off all the time, sometimes for a week or more."

"Without telling anyone?"

"Yep, even when her kid was young."

"Really?" What kind of mother would do that? I pictured my own mom. She'd spent almost all her free time with me and my dad. She called us the three musketeers. She never would have left me voluntarily.

"That's why we didn't think much about her being gone at first." His words yanked me back from thoughts best left buried with my parents. "Then by the time we began our search, evidence was scarce."

"But you must have found some clues."

Even as that sentence tripped over my tongue, I knew it sounded incredulous—so incredulous it prompted the deputy to serve up another frown and me another apology. "Sorry, like I said, I'm not very tactful. That's probably why I cover food, not people."

"Exactly, you cover food, so why the interest in Samantha? She wasn't a chef."

I vacillated. While a part of me wanted to share my story idea, another was convinced I should hold my tongue since it wasn't an offical assignment. In the end, part two won out. "I'm merely fascinated by the case. And since Margie's too busy right now to talk to me about cooking—"

"You're killing time with me."

"Something like that," I fudged. "Now humor me. Tell me what you know."

"Well, that's not much." His eyes softened like dollops of chocolate pudding. "And I'd much rather talk about you." His voice had turned shy. "Are you . . . are you single?"

Again I felt self-conscious, though now I was also craving chocolate pudding. "Yeah, I'm single."

"And how did you wind up in the armpit of the state? Lose a bet?"

I laughed nervously. "I thought you liked this place."

"I do, but you're a city girl."

"Not really. I spent my early childhood in a small town. Not this small, mind you. We actually had a zip code." It was his turn to laugh. "And as I said before, when I was a kid, I dreamed of visiting the country. I dreamed of a bucolic life."

He rested his forearms on the table and fingered his napkin. "But now you're all grown up and live in Minneapolis. You work for a major newspaper and love the excitement of city life."

"Well, I work for a major newspaper. Let's leave it at that."

"Oh, no. We can't 'leave it at that.'" He drummed his fingers on the table. "The way I read the situation, Emerald Malloy, you're after something—something far beyond recipes." More drumming. "Yeah, I suspect you hope to score a big story while you're here in town—a story that will propel you from writing about food to what?" He squinted at me. "Hard news?"

My shoulders hitched. "I never said that."

"Not in so many words. But that's why you're asking about Samantha, isn't it?"

With insight like that, he should have solved the murder long ago. But being polite, I didn't point that out. "I find the case interesting. Nothing more."

I thought I sounded convincing, but the deputy's eyes conveyed disbelief in the whole "nothing more" thing.

As for me? Well, even if, deep down, I was rattled by the guy's perceptiveness, on the surface, where I normally hung out, I was too enamored with him to give it much thought.

Chapter Fourteen

I PICKED AT THE PINK WIGGLING mass on my plate. I was anxious again but couldn't get a fix on why. Yeah, the deputy was probably on to me, but I didn't get the impression he'd try to stop me from making inquiries about the murder. Nor would he complain to my editor. Deputy Ryden was his own man. I was pretty sure of that.

I poked at the Jell-O some more as the jitters wreaked havoc on my stomach. Throughout the day, I'd also been doubting my skills as a writer, but that couldn't have prompted my current angst either. I regularly bashed my professional capabilities. Usually daily between brushing my teeth and ordering my morning coffee. On bad days, I could stretch it out till noon. No, these nerves were caused by something else.

I put my spoon down. Then it struck me. The source of my agitation. Earlier, Deputy Ryden had voiced what sounded like genuine interest in me. And because the guys in my past were rarely sincere, his words had apparently awakened my feelings of vulnerability. Yep, even after all my therapy, my vulnerabilities tended to be light sleepers.

Relationship insecurities had definitely caused me a number of problems over the years. Case in point, Boo-Boo. But I was working with my therapist on those personal issues. And now I'd stumbled upon an opportunity to improve my professional life. If I could put aside my skill-related doubts and concentrate on unraveling the Samantha Berg murder mystery, I could possibly go from "glorified gopher" to full-fledged investigative reporter. I could become "somebody" at the paper and in the news community. And that would go a long way toward boosting my confidence in my personal life as well, wouldn't it?

"So," I said to the deputy, "are you going to tell me more about Samantha's death?"

He sighed. "I'll say it again, there's not much to tell."

"Oh, come on. You must have some information. Why won't you share it?"

He held his hands up in defeat. "Well, I suppose I can talk about what's on the public record."

"Including what exactly?"

He shifted in his seat. "Oh, for one, we know Samantha was at home before she disappeared because—"

"How do you know that?"

He sighed again, evidently unimpressed by my enthusiasm. "Jim, the guy who runs the VFW, called her right after eight. He asked her to fill in for him behind the bar. He'd met someone online and wanted to go out. Samantha said she'd do it at ten o'clock, when the Hallmark movie she was watching got over. But she never showed up."

"And you didn't find any clues at her house?"

"Nope. No sign of struggle. No peculiar fingerprints."

"What about on her body? Any clues there?"

"No. None."

"But she was naked when she was discovered, which means—"

"She was partially naked. Her clothes got ripped away by the ice and the debris in the river. And before you ask, there was no evidence of sexual assault."

That aside, a number of questions dangled from my brain. Most related to Ole, though a few pertained to other possible murder scenarios. But since I was certain Ole was the culprit, I didn't believe any of them to be credible. Even so, the words of my graduate school advisor kept me from dismissing them outright.

"Explore all possibilities," he'd routinely instructed me and my classmates, "even those you doubt. Ask questions and seek opinions, especially from experts. And always obtain corroboration. Then, and only then, disclose your findings. That's what serious, contemplative journalists do."

It seemed like overkill to me. Again, no pun intended. I knew the identity of the murderer and wanted to let the deputy know I knew. But more than that, I wanted to be considered a "serious" journalist. So I asked what I was supposed to ask, pointless as it seemed. "Deputy Ryden, is it conceivable that Samantha Berg was abducted on her way to the bar? By a stranger? Someone just passing through town?"

The deputy wiped his mouth with the back of his closed fist. "Call me Randy."

"Well, Randy? What do you think?"

Again, he sighed. He did that a lot.

"Samantha lived out back," he said, "in a small rental house on the other side of the alley, twenty yards from the rear entrance of the bar. There'd be no reason for a stranger to be back there. But if some guy was, he would have been spotted. People from town use the alley all the time." He took a three-beat rest. "And if she'd been grabbed, Jim and the folks in the bar would have heard her scream. No band was playing that night. The place was quiet. And Samantha had a big mouth. Yet no one heard a thing."

I propped my elbows on the table and rested my chin on my palms as I mulled over his remarks. See? I could also be a "contemplative" journalist. "What if the guy stabbed her right away? From behind? Then she wouldn't have had a chance to scream." I was doing my utmost to remain open minded—or at least give that impression.

"She faced her killer. We know that from the tests done on her chest wound. As for the blood? Someone would have noticed it that night or right away the next morning."

"Not if it got covered by the snow."

He rolled his eyes. "A killer's not going to stab someone and stop to shovel snow over the blood."

I shot him a cold, hard look. He deserved no less for being rude. "I meant it might have snowed later in the evening. Or the wind may have picked up and caused the snow to drift."

The corners of his mouth drooped. "Sorry about that. You're right, it did snow, but we only got a dusting. And while the wind regularly blows hard up here, it wasn't strong enough that night to move all the snow necessary to cover the blood that would have flowed from that wound. It was a nasty one."

I tried to maintain my glower. He'd been rude, and I didn't want to let him off the hook too easily. But when it came to eyes, I was no match for Randy Ryden. His eyes were hypnotizing. At that precise moment, they had me imagining I was swimming in a pool of melted chocolate. And it's damn hard to glower while floating in chocolate. "Well, um . . ." I stuttered, "is it possible she was murdered elsewhere?"

Unlike me, the deputy spoke without sputtering. "It's possible. Even probable. We just don't have any evidence along those lines."

The deputy then put his coffee cup to his lips, providing me the opportunity to take control of the conversation. And for that, I was thankful. Because I'd become increasingly distracted by the man, I prayed that by talking more about the case, I'd avoid going completely ga-ga over him.

"Deputy Ryden . . . I mean Randy, based on what you said, the person who killed Samantha Berg must have been someone who didn't prompt her to scream. Someone she left with voluntarily and on the spur of the moment." I made an effort to read him, but it wasn't easy. He didn't give much up. Though after a few minutes, I thought I saw a flicker of what I'd hoped to find. "That's it, isn't it? I was right!"

He set his cup down. "What do you mean, you were right?"

I folded my hands studiously. "Well, to my way of thinking, Samantha Berg was killed by someone she knew well. Someone with ties to both her and Lena Johnson. That makes the most sense given she disappeared exactly one year to the day after Lena's death."

He raked his top teeth over his bottom lip. "If that's what you suspected, why all these questions?"

"Just covering my bases."

He smiled a lopsided smile, as if he couldn't help himself. "Well, most likely, you're right, Sherlock. But since no one's been arrested, let's move on."

"No! Not yet." Sure, I had to be cautious. I didn't want him any more suspicious about what I was up to than he already was. But questions remained, the most important being, did Ole Johnson kill Samantha Berg? While I knew the answer, I still needed verification.

Granted, the deputy was unlikely to come right out and finger Ole given that he and his police buddies never even arrested him, which raised a bunch of other questions. But they would have to wait. First thing's first.

I fiddled with my napkin as I deliberated my approach. What was the best way to get the deputy to verify my murder theory?

The longer I thought about it, the more convinced I became—or the more I convinced myself—that I'd have the greatest chance of obtaining the affirmation I sought if I took a circuitous route. Certainly the road less traveled for me—the woman with an expressway between her brain and her mouth—but what the hell. "Tell me, Randy, do you have any theories of your own about Samantha Berg's death?"

He squirmed. "It doesn't really matter what I think."

I dropped my napkin and sat up straight. "Yes, it does. Please tell me. I'd really like to know." I was being extremely professional, and for that, I gave myself a couple mental pats on the back.

"Like I said, my personal opinion doesn't matter."

"Oh, but it does."

"No, it doesn't."

"Yes, it does. So please tell me. Pretty please. Pretty please with sugar on it" I clasped my hand over my mouth. *Pretty please with sugar on it? Did I just say that? Ugh!*

The deputy leaned back and, with his lips twisted in amusement, stretched his arms high above his head.

I was terribly embarrassed. Yet, when he lowered his arms, I still managed to admire how nicely his beefy shoulders filled out his uniform. Double ugh!

"We never had more than a handful of suspects."

"Such as?" I squeaked out, my throat now tight with shame. At least I assumed it was shame. Although it may have been something else, like lusty desire. That sometimes made my throat tight too.

The deputy failed to answer me. Rather, he snatched one of two different bars from the edge of his plate, bit into it, and licked his lips. "Mmm, these are good. You should try them."

My throat just about closed up completely. Yep, it was desire, all right. And it forced me to cut to the chase. If I wanted to be regarded as a serious journalist, I couldn't wait for this guy to disclose what he knew about the case. Our lazy back-and-forth allowed too much down time—time for him to lick his lips and the devil in me to concoct all kinds of ideas—some of them real doozies. At present, for instance, it was trying to convince me to climb over the table and jump the nice officer's bones.

"Okay . . . um. Well, um . . . I'll start." I coughed in an effort to clear my hormone-clogged throat. "Ole Johnson . . . Well, he . . . um . . . seems to be the most logical suspect."

Deputy Ryden didn't utter a word, choosing instead to give all his interest to his Halfway Bar.

I knew it was a Halfway Bar because I'd asked Margie about them when I was arranging the dessert platters. She'd pointed out that while a Halfway Bar was similar to a Blondie, a Halfway Bar was topped with a brown-sugar meringue.

His looked moist and delicious. And when he popped the last of it into his mouth, I couldn't help but wonder which would taste better, the bar or the man?

Okay. Okay. As a professional, I was—and no doubt remain—a work in progress.

Chapter Fifteen

Deputy Ryden glanced around the room, greeting folks with a slight nod of his head or lift of his finger. If the number of smiles he received in return were any indication, the people of Kennedy liked him just fine, even if they didn't consider him one of their own.

Following his hellos, he turned back to me and said, "The night Samantha Berg disappeared Ole was covering for Margie here in the café."

"He could do that? The way he drank?"

"He wasn't drinking then. He quit following some problem at the fair and didn't start again until after Samantha went missing."

"Don't you find that suspicious?"

The deputy started in on his second dessert selection, a Special-K Bar. "What I'm trying to tell you is that Ole had an alibi." He worked his treat into his cheek. "Samantha vanished sometime after Jim talked to her but before he checked to see why she didn't show up at the bar."

My mouth went dry. "And Ole?"

"He was here in the café all evening—until close to eleven."

"Oh." I swear I heard the sound of my new-found career as a top-notch investigative journalist getting flushed down the toilet.

"Don't be disappointed. He was a nice guy."

"I'm sure he was." I inhaled a shaky breath. "It's just that when Margie told me about the murder, I might have implied . . . um . . . that Ole was the most logical suspect."

"You said that?"

I rearranged my silverware. "Well, not in those exact words." Specifically, I moved my spoon over a fraction of an inch. "But based on what she told me . . ."

The deputy leaned forward, touched my hands, and a bolt of electricity shot up my arm. "That's not how you make friends, Emerald."

I dropped my fork. "Very funny." Not much of a retort, but I wasn't in the mood for creative thinking. What's more, Deputy Ryden's touch had not only shocked my hand, it had short-circuited my brain. It felt like forever before I could say anything at all, and then it was only to repeat myself. "You're sure you can account for Ole?"

The deputy relaxed against the back of the booth. "Most of the night, he was playing cards with those three." He motioned to John Deere, his friend, and Shitty. "And they're as honest as the winter nights up here are long."

Frustration washed over me, and the deputy took note. "Sorry, I hope Ole's innocence won't dampen your enthusiasm for the news business."

What a smart-ass! A very handsome smart-ass, but a smart-ass nonetheless.

He lowered his head and peered into my eyes. "You don't take teasing very well, do you?"

Since the question was rhetorical, I didn't answer.

"Next," he continued, "you'll probably accuse the Anderson sisters of the crime because they can wield a crowbar. At least the older two can."

He was having a lot of fun at my expense, and I didn't appreciate it. Usually I was a pretty good sport, but disappointment had taken its toll on my disposition.

"And you, Deputy Ryden, can be a pain in the butt."

A smile played around his lips. "I guess I can be, especially when I'd rather be talking about something else—like you."

Nice recovery. That's what I said in the solitude of my brain. Out loud, I merely promised to "end the inquisition" if he answered "one last question."

He pinched the bridge of his nose between his thumb and forefinger. I imagined he was debating whether to stay or run for the hills, which, given the local landscape, would have been far, far away. "Okay," he eventually said, opting for the former, at least for the moment, "what's your 'last' question?"

I sat up straight. "If Ole Johnson didn't kill Samantha Berg, who did?"

I wanted to believe I had asked solely out of concern for the deceased. But I knew my own desperation played a role too. When I thought Ole was guilty, I felt as if I were on my way, professionally speaking. Admittedly, I was moving in the wrong direction, but at least I was moving. Having experienced that, I wasn't crazy about returning to a job that revolved around food and recipes but didn't look to be leading anywhere else anytime soon. Nor did I want to wait for my editor to decide when I was ready for a decent assignment. I had a good story right here. And I was determined to pursue it.

Yes, from this point forward, I was going to take control of my life. I wasn't going to leave it to chance or allow someone else to dictate it. Barbie's words had niggled at me. And I'd come to a decision. I would no longer "live by default." I'd live my life on my terms. And I'd start now.

The deputy laid his hands, palms down, on the table. "I've told you about a hundred times, Emerald, no one ever got arrested."

"I know, I know." His evasiveness was beginning to wear on me. "But you must have some ideas. What do you think? Was it Jim, the man who discovered Samantha missing? Do you think he killed her?"

"No. He was back from her house in less than two minutes, madder than hell that she'd taken off after promising to sub for him. And he showed no sign of a struggle."

"Well, I'm certain it was someone who could handle a knife and, considering the date, someone with ties to both Samantha and Lena. So what do you think? Was it Margie?"

I hated to offer her up. She was my host, and I really liked her. But I had no choice. Because of her prowess with kitchen knives and her hatred for Samantha, she was a potential murder suspect, and I was intent on hunting down the murderer, whomever it might be. I had to. For the sake of my career. I stopped, knowing I was forgetting something but having no idea what. One second passed and then another before it came to me. Justice. That's right. I was seeking justice too.

"Emerald, it doesn't matter what I think," the deputy said in response to my insistence.

"Oh, come on."

He restlessly moved about in the booth. "No, I'm not going to say anything more."

"Why?"

His face was a picture of irritation. "Why is this so important to you?"

"Because . . ." I stopped short, warning myself to calm down. I was coming on too strong. I was on the verge of saying too much about my plans. "I just want to know what happened. That's all. So tell me. You must have some suspicions." I thought I'd recovered nicely.

For his part, the deputy parted his lips, but this time, rather than speaking, he stared at me in silence. Then, after several moments, he set his jaw and exhaled heavily through his nose, his nostrils flaring slightly.

Feeling a new tension in the air, I encouraged my gaze beyond our table as I sipped the cold remains of my coffee.

I was pretty sure time stood still before he spoke again. "Yeah, Emerald, I guess I have some suspicions." Alerted by the sound of my name, I turned to him as he added, "And they're all about you."

I bristled. "Me?"

He jabbed his finger in my direction. "You may be fooling Margie, but you're not fooling me. You're far too nosy to be here just to write about food. You're chasing a story about the murder too. I can feel it. So why don't you come clean with me?"

Nosy? I'd often been accused of being nosy, but that didn't make it any easier to hear, especially coming from this guy. Did I mention I kind of liked him? Beyond that, "nosy" was an ugly word. I much preferred "inquisitive."

"I don't understand you or that newspaper editor of yours," I huffed. "There's an unsolved murder here, yet neither of you will talk about it."

The deputy leaned across the table. "You spoke to Barbie about this?"

I recoiled. Even sitting down, he was an imposing figure. Still, I pushed myself to say, "I tried, but she only told me that the case didn't amount to much."

"Well, she was right. Nothing's ever come of it."

"But it's murder!" I'd planned to use an inside voice, but it didn't work out that way. My volume rose proportionately to my frustration, and in the end, I shrieked.

Everyone in the place stared at me slack-jawed. And while the deputy, like the others, remained mum, the corners of his mouth twitched as if he were about to laugh.

Anger simmered just beneath the surface of my skin. *He better not laugh at me!*

I was about to say something out loud to that effect when a dispatcher broke in over the deputy's radio. The message, delivered amid static, was incomprehensible to me, although Deputy Ryden seemed to understand it just fine. He listened while rubbing a gouge in the table. And after he signed off, he announced, "I've gotta go."

My heart sank to somewhere in the vicinity of my knees. Yes, I was irritated with him for being tight-lipped about the murder. And, no, I didn't like that he'd second-guessed my motives for being in town. Even so, I was smitten and wanted him to stay. Yeah, I know, pitiful. But what can I say? "We haven't finished—"

"I have to get back to work. There's been an accident."

He pulled himself from the booth and adjusted his belt. It was loaded down with an array of law enforcement tools, everything from a gun and a flashlight to a taser and that damn radio. "As far as Samantha Berg's murder is concerned, like I said, no one's been charged."

"And that's it?" I wasn't sure if I was referring to what he'd just said about the murder or the abrupt end to our time together. Either way, I felt rebuffed. I heard it in my voice.

He must have heard it too because some kindness found its way into his tone. "Hopefully, I'll get to stop back later. If not, I've enjoyed meeting you." The line of his mouth morphed into a devilish grin. "Even if I don't know what to make of you."

My breath caught in my throat. What? He didn't know what to make of me? I was totally dumbfounded by him!

Well, I guess not totally. As I watched his backside angle around one table, then another, I knew one thing for sure—I very much enjoyed the view.

That did it! I definitely had to start dating again. And soon!

* * *

AFTER DEPUTY RYDEN LEFT, I slumped into the corner of my booth and languished there, thinking about Ole. How could I've been so wrong? He was the obvious killer—at least before I'd learned all the facts. I slumped a little farther.

Oh, well. I suppose there was no point in dwelling on my missteps. I'd just have to keep moving forward, one foot in front of the other, until I found the real culprit. And I would find him—or her.

Yeah, right. Deputy Ryden wasn't the country bumpkin cop I'd expected him to be. And if he and the FBI couldn't solve the case, what made me think I could? This wasn't some television show where murder investigations were neatly wrapped up in sixty minutes minus commercials. This was real life.

And speaking of real life, Emme, Randy Ryden entered and exited yours in less than an hour, and that has to be a record, even for you.

"Now wait a minute," I muttered to the offending voice in my head. "I'm a good and deserving person." That's what my therapist taught me to say in response to feelings of inadequacy. She called it positive self-talk. And while I thought it was kind of hokey, and I wasn't very good at it, I did it anyway. "Don't beat yourself up," I added, as likewise trained. "Do something constructive with your energy."

Something constructive? Hell, I was in a café! What was I supposed to do? Dishes?

Dismissing that as a valid option, I dug out my pen and a few index cards and began copying down more Jell-O recipes. I wrote about gelatin packets and boiling water but soon found myself taking stock of my life. I was twenty-six years old and sitting alone on a Friday night in a café on the edge of nowhere, writing down recipes for funeral food. Could I be any more pathetic?

Glancing across the table, I spotted a half-eaten Special-K Bar on the deputy's plate. And it, too, spoke to me. No need to dwell on what it said. Suffice to say, I replied by gobbling it up.

Chapter Sixteen

Because the café was crowded, I surrendered my booth, claimed a couple bars from the buffet table, and headed outside. I thought the fresh air might mend my crummy outlook. The Lemon Bars in hand were merely backup, in case extra help was needed.

The wind had died down, and it wasn't nearly as hot as it had been, so I strolled over to the community garden. It covered the vacant lot between the Senior Center and a dilapidated store front. At present, it was empty. No people milling about, which was just fine with me. I needed some time alone.

A plaque out front read, "The Community Garden: Beautifying Kennedy One Petunia at a Time." It was staked among yellow day lilies that were flanked by purple cone flowers and white daisies. I started down a wood-chip path lined with delphiniums and garden phlox. To my left, multi-colored hollyhocks encircled poles topped with bird houses. On my right, in a bed of pink roses, two wooden benches begged for company. I decided to oblige them.

Taking a seat, I breathed deeply, allowing the garden fragrances in as I peered over the flower tops, across the highway, and past the grain elevator. There, a couple dozen houses were scattered about, each neat but modest. In one yard, a young boy mowed the lawn. In another, an old woman pulled sheets from the clothes line. Beyond the houses, checkerboard fields of wheat and sugar beets stretched across the flat horizon as far as I could see. And other than the muffled sounds of the people in the café and the hum of that lawnmower, I heard nothing. No city busses rumbling or rush-hour cars honking. None of my normal Friday-night sounds.

The quiet should have calmed me and improved my mood. But it didn't. I suppose the gravel that swept across my face, courtesy of an unexpected gust of wind, didn't help matters. Wiping my eyes, I ordered myself to do a couple things: First, stop wasting time asking about Samantha Berg's murder. Second, refrain from taking stock of life again anytime soon.

I bit into a Lemon Bar and longed for a sugar high and the improved disposition that would accompany it. Sugar has always helped with whatever ails me, from PMS to heartache. Another bite. More waiting.

Preoccupied with anticipation, I failed to see the Anderson sisters as they approached. "Yoo-hoo, they called.

I jumped. "Oh, hello."

"We seen ya here," said Henrietta, the oldest, "and we wanted to check on how your visit was goin'."

"Oh, well, it's going fine." No need to share the excruciating details of the mess that was my day, my life. I continued to nibble.

Henrietta backed her broad behind onto the bench opposite mine. And her sisters followed her lead, medium-sized Harriet claiming the middle and tiny Hester settling on the far end. Each then situated her canvas bag of stolen goodies on her lap, in front of her saggy breasts.

"Say now," Henrietta began, wiggling around to get comfy as the bench groaned in protest, "what do ya think of our little town?"

"It's nice," I replied, although I wasn't sure I meant it.

Of course I liked that in a single day here, I'd visited with more people than I had in a month in Minneapolis, where I routinely wasted away evenings and weekends alone in my apartment. Still, I believed that for a successful career, I needed to live in a vibrant, urban community, where important things happened, even if to date, I'd only seen reports of them after the fact on television or in the paper.

"Yah," Henrietta continued, "small towns are great. We live right over there, don't ya know." With a long, spindly finger, she aimed across the alley at a neglected, white, two-story with a wrap-around porch. "It costs more to heat than most houses in town, but it's close to everythin'."

Despite my wretched mood, I had to smile. Margie had mentioned heating bills too. Together the remarks lent credence to my editor's claim that the cost of home heating was the second most popular topic of conversation among elderly Minnesotans. The first? According to him, it was the effect various food had on the digestive tract.

Immediately images flooded my mind of everything the old girls had piled on their plates and packed in their purses at the community dinner. Dreading what they might want to discuss as a result, I searched for something less disgusting we could talk about.

My eyes darted this way and that before coming to rest on the Anderson home. I snapped several mental pictures of it, if for no other reason than to fill my head, leaving absolutely no room for visual impressions of intestinal distress.

The house was large but not as big as those I'd seen in the country. Some of its shingles were curled, and paint was peeling from the porch columns and window frames. The front stoop sat catty-wampus, and the stair railing was reinforced with a single two-by-four wedged against a cinder block. The place definitely needed work. Yet someone had taken the time to erect a sturdy-looking, single-car garage to the left of the house and plant a garden to the right.

The garden butted against a small lot situated directly across the alley from the rear entrance of the VFW. In the middle of the overgrown lot, a bungalow squatted like a disheveled fat lady sitting in tall grass.

Most people would have considered the place "run down." But I viewed it as much more. To me it was a chance to pre-empt any digestive-related prattle that may be in the offing. It also was an opportunity to learn more about Samantha Berg's disappearance and murder.

I know I just got done declaring I'd drop my so-called investigation. But I had more questions, and the tiny, ramshackle house seemed to be begging for answers. On top of that, the sugar from my lemon treat had kicked in, not only raising my spirits but coaxing me into taking another crack at the case. Really, what did I have to lose?

Admittedly, I no longer believed I'd break the case wide open. This wasn't a game of Clue, and evidently, the killer wasn't Ole in the alley with a knife. I also understood that any article I wrote, no matter how good, would unlikely propel me into a prestigious position at the paper. At least not right away. Ideas I had along those lines earlier in the day were unrealistic, fueled by an overactive imagination and frustration with my career. Yet, I was confident I could pen a good summary—the anatomy of a cold case or something along those lines—and even if it never got published, it would further demonstrate to my editor my skills as a writer. And that would be a good thing, right?

Once back in Minneapolis, I'd form the bones of my story by reviewing public records and archived articles. While here in Kennedy, I'd work on the heart of the piece, collecting reflections from the locals who were around at the time. And to begin, I'd interview the Anderson sisters. Yes, they were wacky, but I was smart and confident I could distinguish fact from fancy.

"Hey," I said to the ladies, "is that where Samantha Berg lived?"

Henrietta lifted her sharp, protruding chin in a haughty fashion. "Yah, but how do you know about her?"

Hester, the youngest, didn't wait for me to answer. "She was sittin' with Deputy Ryden in the café. He must of told her."

I eyed the little old lady whose skin was as thin and wrinkled as the tissue stuffed in gift bags. "Actually," I replied, "Margie first told me about her."

"Oh," all three replied in drawn-out unison.

"Yeah, Margie mentioned that Samantha Berg was murdered, but I wish I could learn more." As I'd hoped, Henrietta and Hester exchanged glances that suggested they wouldn't mind providing their insight, so I added, "I suppose you knew her quite well since she lived right next door."

I waited for a response. If I wanted them to open up, I had to allow them to set the pace of our conversation. Not easy for me to do, but I managed.

"Oh, my goodness, no," Henrietta answered after a couple moments that felt much longer, "we didn't know her well at all."

Harriet, the middle sister with the mustache, followed. "She wasn't very friendly, at least not to women. She was plenty friendly to men, though, if ya catch my drift. We seen men over there all the time."

Without thinking, I blurted out, "Men like Ole?"

All three women lowered their eyes, like chickens in search of feed in the dirt.

Shit! I'd once again pressed too hard, too fast.

I had to apologize and was about to do just that when Henrietta, the mother hen, said, "Yah, men like Ole. He was our nephew, don't ya know. Our sister's son, God rest their souls."

And little Hester repeated, "God rest their souls."

Out of respect, I observed a moment of silence. Then, reminding myself to engage my brain before my mouth, I spoke with as much care as I could muster. "Well, with your close ties to Ole, you must have been . . . um . . . upset when authorities questioned him about Samantha Berg's death."

To my astonishment, Henrietta lifted her head and responded in a full-throated voice, "Oh, not at all. They talked to lots of folks. I'm sure Margie told ya they called on her a half dozen times, which made no sense at all."

"No sense whatsoever," little Hester echoed.

"Why?" I wanted to know. "Margie doesn't hide her hatred for Samantha Berg."

Hester agreed. "But she didn't kill her." She shifted in her seat, careful not to upset her big purse. It stood tall on her lap, concealing the lower half of her tiny face. "She didn't have 'opportunity,' and when it comes to murder, ya need 'opportunity' as well as 'motive.'"

If only I'd kept that in mind earlier in the day.

Little Hester went on, her mouth hidden behind her bag, her flickering, pale-blue eyes, the only visible sign she was speaking. "See, the night Samantha disappeared, Margie was curlin' at the women's bonspiel in Drayton. That's where the beet plant's located. Just on the other side of the Red River. They host a lot of bonspiels. And they always have pretty good food and prizes." She stole a breath. "Anyhow, Margie's team won, and the trophies were awarded between eight-thirty and nine. She was there for the ceremony as well as the pictures and party that followed. So, in the end, the FBI concluded she couldn't of committed the murder. But it took those agents a half dozen interviews with her before makin' that determination. Very disheartenin'. I'd assumed they'd be better at their jobs."

She adjusted her shoulder bag, and I wondered how the Jell-O was holding up. That question was quickly shoved aside, however, by more pertinent ones, including, who in the hell killed Samantha Berg? And why wasn't he—or she—ever arrested?

Chapter Seventeen

"Miss Malloy, do you curl?" Henrietta asked.

"Call me Emme, and no, I never have." I bit into my other Lemon Bar.

"Oh, my, you should try it. Us three, along with our sister, Hortense, God rest her soul, used to curl all the time. It's a good way to pass the long winters. And if I do say so myself, we were pretty fair at it. We actually took second at nationals back in the '70s." She shifted her dentures with her tongue. "We don't curl anymore, of course. We don't go out much at all durin' the winter. It's just way too cold."

I knew very little about curling. Even so, I had a hard time imagining the old birds perched in front of me being proficient at the game. While they were much younger during the 1970s, I still envisioned them hunched over, sliding across the ice in belted house frocks and comfortable shoes, fiercely trying to sweep their rocks onto victory as they clutched bags full of food stolen from the concession stand. Amusing myself with those images, I finished my bar.

Meanwhile, Henrietta and little Hester exchanged knowing glances, those wordless conversations shared by people who'd been together a long time.

When done, Hester asked, "Well, um . . . Emme, what do ya think about this here garden?"

From Henrietta's scowl, I gathered it wasn't the question she had wanted or expected her youngest sister to pose.

"It's pretty," I answered blandly, sucking all traces of lemon flavoring from my forefinger and thumb.

"Yah, Rosa really outdone herself this year."

"Rosa?" That piqued my curiosity. "You mean Ole and Lena's Rosa?"

"Yah, but how do ya know about her?"

"Well, Margie told me."

Hairy Harriet sat up straight or as straight as her curved back would allow. "Did she also tell ya I helped Rosa start that garden? It was a tribute to Lena, her ma, God rest her soul."

"No, she said nothing about that." I dried my fingers on my jeans.

"Then let me," Harriet replied.

Henrietta nudged her. "I'm sure Emme don't wanna hear about the origin of the garden." She drove her point home by squeezing Harriet's arm and staring into her cloudy eyes. "Understand?"

Harriet frowned and pulled at her mustache while sagging against the back of the bench.

I felt sorry for the old girl because, among other things, she was the mustached sister. Not an easy cross to bear, I'm sure. "It's okay," I said before realizing my lips were even moving. "I wouldn't mind learning more about the garden. My mom was an avid gardener, and when I was little, I often helped her."

Henrietta waved her hand like she was shooing mosquitos. "You're just saying that. Ya, it's pretty, but it's just a garden."

I hated to admit it, but she was right. While my heart went out to Harriet, I really didn't want to discuss flowers. Currently, I was far more interested in murder and all things related.

"Now," Henrietta said, "what were we talkin' about?"

Despite Harriet's depressed state, I shifted my attention to her older sister, causing a stab of guilt to pierce my chest, though it didn't hurt bad enough to keep me from answering, "Samantha. We were talking about Samantha Berg. I'm curious as to your take on what happened to her."

"Our take?"

"Yeah, you ladies seem very much in the know." I was proud of how that statement exited my mouth, since, while taking shape in my head, it went something like, *Yeah, according to Deputy Ryden, you three are very nosy, almost as nosy as me.*

"Well, we try," Henrietta responded, her tone implying she knew the full measure of her worth.

"And I understand forensics," little Hester added, informing me of her own importance. "I used to be a science teacher, and I watch a lot of Court TV."

I twisted toward the lady with the translucent skin. "Well then, with your expertise, you must have some definite impressions about Samantha Berg's death. I'm curious to hear them."

"Ya know what they say," Harriet interjected, "curiosity killed the cat."

"Harriet, you shush now," the mother hen scolded before whispering to me, "I ain't sure we should tell ya. With you bein' a reporter and all, it may not be prudent."

I flagged my hand. "I'm here to do a story about food, nothing more." While officially that was true, I crossed my fingers behind my back just the same. "I'm merely interested in what people thought about the whole affair." Not a good choice of words I realized only after I'd spoken.

But I guess it didn't matter. Henrietta jabbered on, evidently not hearing me anyway. "And that ain't the only reason we're leery about talkin'." She stiffly glimpsed over both her shoulders. "Ya see, we think her murderer's still right here."

Now that got me to sit up straight. "Really?"

"Oh, yah."

"And you told the police?"

"Naturally, but they didn't care."

"Didn't care?"

"No." She scratched the waddle of skin that hung from her sharp chin. "Them and the FBI didn't listen to nothing we said."

"Not a thing," Hester repeated. "They just sent us on our way."

"Hmm." Even though the Anderson sisters were loony, it bothered me that the police didn't hear them out. Since most folks in town were reluctant to come forward with information about Samantha Berg, investigators should have eagerly listened to the few who did. Not to mention, these three lived right next door to the murdered woman and may have seen something important. So why did the police give them the brush-off?

I was stumped. I couldn't figure it out until I recalled Margie saying that Ole started drinking again after Samantha disappeared because he felt bad that the people in town were ambivalent about finding her. Initially, I didn't buy it, convinced Ole drank for one reason alone—to drown the memory of killing the woman. But now, after learning of his innocence, I had to reconsider his claim.

Perhaps he was right. Perhaps no one in Kennedy really cared if Samantha was ever found. After she went missing, she may not have been missed enough by any one person to ensure a thorough investigation. Sure, there was Ole. But from the sound of it, he wasn't in any shape most of the time to champion anyone's cause. No, Samantha's lack of friends and family, along with her lowly standing in the community, may have led the townspeople and the cops to do little to solve her murder.

The prospect disturbed me. I had definite ideas about death, born of my own experience and pain. In my book, death always required answers. In every case, no matter the circumstances, the identities of the perpetrators, as well as the motivation for their actions, had to be exposed. It was the only way to ensure they'd pay for their wrongdoing. It was the only way to make sense out of something so senseless. That was my creed. At least it was back then.

I inhaled deeply, filling myself with resolve. Of course, now that I'd gotten to know Deputy Ryden, I didn't want to believe he and his colleagues were bad at their jobs. Then again, it really didn't matter what I wanted. As a journalist, I had an obligation to write stories based on facts, setting aside my personal feelings. And even if this story ended up being nothing more than a recap of the investigation to date, I couldn't—and wouldn't—gloss over shoddy police work.

At the same time, I didn't want to jump to any more conclusions. No, I wouldn't do that again. It wasn't fair to anyone. And it made me look like a fool. This time I'd be more diligent. This time I'd dig deeper for answers. And the garden seemed like the perfect place to start.

"Ladies," I said to the Anderson sisters, "tell me everything you know about the disappearance and death of Samantha Berg. I really want to hear it."

"Well," the little sister replied, catching a few strands of her mousy-gray hair, escapees from the thin bun that sat atop her head, "if ya really wanna know." She carefully tucked the loose hair behind her ears and extended her brittle-looking hands to grasp the handles of her canvas bag.

In my mind, I made a rolling motion with my own hand, signaling her to get on with it, but in reality, I said and did nothing, leaving her to move at her own pace—her own excruciatingly slow pace.

She inched forward to the end of the bench and dropped her mouth open, only to snap it shut again, reminding me of an old turtle. She then released her grip, allowing her big purse to tilt unclasped in my direction.

I expected Jell-O and dessert bars to spill all over the ground, creating a banquet for the neighborhood ants and squirrels. But nothing tumbled out except the unpleasant odor of sun-heated cream of mushroom soup mixed with cherry gelatin. It emanated from partially open plastic bags and filled my nose. No further need to wonder how the Jell-O was holding up.

"Well," little Hester uttered, seemingly unfazed by the stench, "we think Samantha Berg was killed by . . . Vern Olson."

My nose instinctively wrinkled from the smell. "Vern Olson?"

Hester's expression suggested she fully appreciated my apparent disdain for the man. "My feelin's exactly." She wrinkled her nose too. "He's Margie's brother-in-law. He's married to Vivian, her sister, our niece."

"You mean the guy with one arm?"

"Oh, you've met him?" She again took hold of the woven handles of her bag and, in doing so, closed the top, sealing off much of the pungent smell.

"No, I haven't met him." I'd been holding my breath without realizing it. "But Margie told me about his accident." I gulped fresh air.

"Well, he still had two arms when Samantha died," the little lady said, "and we think he used both of 'em to kill her and throw her body into the river."

Oh, this was getting good. Now that I could breathe again, I only wished I had something more to eat.

Chapter Eighteen

"WHY DO YOU BELIEVE VERN OLSON killed Samantha Berg?"

The mother hen answered me. "We seen him at her house the night she disappeared."

"And that ain't the first time," Harriet added, "if ya know what I mean."

Forming a "T" with my hands, I motioned for a time out. "Are you suggesting something was going on between the two of them?"

Before Harriet could respond, Henrietta squeezed her hairy sister's arm in another less-than-subtle attempt to silence her. The oldest of the three women then said, "Misbehavior of that sort runs in his family. Always has."

Harriet nevertheless piped up, "And ya know what they say, 'The apple don't fall far from the tree.'"

"Did you tell the police you saw him there?"

"Oh, yah."

I raised a finger. "But let me guess. They weren't interested. They wouldn't listen."

"No, they listened." Henrietta patted the gray sausage curls that covered her head. "But afterwards, they told us they already knew. See, Vern regularly went over there. The police said it was to tell Samantha to leave Rosa alone."

"Why? Did she harass Rosa?"

"Oh, yah, she enjoyed gettin' after both Rosa and Lena. She didn't like that Ole walked out on her, 'cause she was used to doin' all the dumpin'. So when he left, she got back at him by tormentin' the two of 'em."

"And he didn't stop her?"

"Well, he had a hard time believin' Samantha would do such a thing. Anyhow, when Lena was alive, she handled the problem herself."

Henrietta pulled the hem of her dress down after a wisp of wind had lifted it to reveal her nylon tops. They were rolled down to just below her bulging knees. "One night Lena actually went into the 'V' when Samantha was workin', climbed up on stage there, and stopped the band right in the middle of a song. Then she yelled at Samantha that she had better leave Rosa alone."

The old hen peered down her sharp beak, making her pin-prick eyes look even closer set than they truly were. "I guess Samantha hollered back, 'I ain't afraid of you. You're nothin' but a wetback. What ya goin' to do, knife me?'"

Henrietta raised her chin and clicked her dentures in disapproval. "That's when all heck broke loose. Lena jumped off the stage and tackled Samantha, and the two of 'em rolled around on the floor, punchin' and scratchin' till a couple guys pulled Lena off and another four got Samantha under control. Yah, it took four men to get Samantha simmered down. She was a big girl, don't ya know."

Little Hester agreed that Samantha was quite large, but the two sisters disagreed on her exact proportions, sparking a lively debate about the comparative size of the dead woman's rear end. I kept quiet until certain I'd rather fill my ears with dirt than listen to another word. It was at that point that I implored Henrietta to finish her story, which she did, though she appeared somewhat annoyed with me for putting an end to the great ass debate.

"As ya might expect," she said in a matter-of-fact tone, "Samantha wanted to press charges against Lena, but the folks in the bar wouldn't substantiate her story to the police. They said she probably deserved a good beatin', considerin' what she'd done to Lena and her family." She paused, not because she was through talking but because she needed another deep breath to keep going. "For a while after that, she kept clear of Lena and Rosa. Although people said it was the turnin' point for Lena."

"Turning point?"

"Yah, about that time Lena's health started goin' downhill. Before long, she was dead, and Samantha was back to harassin' Rosa."

I interjected, "And that's when Vern began stopping by Samantha's house to warn her to behave." It was more of a statement than a question.

"Supposedly," Henrietta replied, to which Harriet added, "But ya don't get after someone by cavortin' with 'em."

My shoulders jerked involuntarily. "You mean Vern and Samantha were 'cavorting' the night she disappeared, and the police didn't think anything—"

The mother hen again interrupted. "Well, we didn't actually see 'em."

"I did," Harriet insisted.

"After Vern knocked on the door," Henrietta continued, ignoring her sister, "our favorite TV show started. It's the one with that Nancy Grace. It's on every night at nine." She smiled. "Ain't she great?" Henrietta and little Hester took some time for silent adoration of the talk-show host. "Oh, yah, once Nancy Grace got started, Hester and me didn't pay any attention to what was goin' on next door."

"But I did!" Harriet barked, her brows knitted, her eyes turning slightly crazed. "I seen 'em carryin' on right there on the porch. They were all over each other."

"Yah," Henrietta said, still failing to acknowledge her hairy sister or her urgent remarks, "the police said it was just another instance of Vern stoppin' by to tell Samantha to leave Rosa alone, though we don't believe it. See, whenever he was there, he stayed inside way longer than it takes to tell somebody off. And as we said, he comes from bad seed."

"But you didn't actually see them carrying on?"

"No," the youngest sister reluctantly told me. "Samantha always kept her shades drawn."

Harriet took out a mosquito. "I know what they was doin'. It was hanky-panky, and that night it spilled right onto the porch."

"You shush now," Henrietta ordered.

But Harriet wasn't about to be shushed. "Yah, there they were, Carl and Elsa, cavortin' out there in front of God and everybody. Of course it was all her doin'. Carl wanted to get away, but that hussy just kept throwin' herself at him."

Huh? Carl? Elsa? What was she talking about?

Harriet went on jabbering, her untenable words falling ever faster from her mouth until Henrietta again grabbed her arm and squeezed it really hard, as evidenced by the hairy lady's wince. The mother hen then glared at Harriet until she cowered, her spine curling against the back of the bench like a question mark.

When apparently satisfied that Harriet would no longer interrupt, Henrietta proceeded, evidently feeling no need to explain her sister's nonsensical comments or Carl and Elsa's identity. "Oh, yah, even though the police refused to arrest Vern, we're sure he did it. He was Samantha's only visitor that night, and he's the spawn of a scoundrel. To us, it's as plain as the nose on your face. He killed Samantha Berg."

My eyes zeroed in on Henrietta's long, hooked beak. "Why would Vern murder Samantha Berg?"

"We believe him and her were havin' an affair," Henrietta stated, "whether we can prove it or not. We think Samantha threatened to tell his wife, so he got rid of her. Nancy Grace says that kind of thing happens all the time."

With my eyes still locked in on the old lady's honker, I unwittingly replied, "Well, I don't want to stick my nose where it doesn't belong, but—"

Henrietta once more ran over my words with some of her own. "Sure, he got his arm cut off, but he deserves a lot more than that."

"Yah, what goes around, gotta come around," little Hester added in a sing-song voice. "Vern comes from a bad family, and none of his people ever made amends for their wrong doin'. Not until the baler incident."

"But justice demands way more than the loss of one measly arm," Henrietta insisted. "Vern should go to jail too."

"For sure." Hester eyed me intently. "He's the last of the Olson men. If he don't get everythin' that's comin' to him and his, they'll go unpunished, and that wouldn't be right."

I assumed that remark was the "last word" on the subject, although the peace that followed was quickly fractured by Harriet, who whined, "The 'squiters are gettin' me." She flapped her arms. "They're gettin' me bad. Make 'em stop. Make 'em go away."

Henrietta patted her arm. "There, there, now. Settle down." Leaning across her, she added for Hester's benefit alone, "She's been in a terrible state again lately, hasn't she? Not sleepin'. Talkin' nonsense. Actin' crazy one minute, just fine the next. It frustrates me so." She gazed into the distance, her volume dropping to a whisper. "Yeah, it's been a bad one this time for sure." She shook her head and added on a long sigh, "Well, I suppose, we better get her home. And we probably shouldn't dilly-dally."

Little Hester nodded in agreement, sending Henrietta to her feet amid arthritic groans. Hester rose too, positioning her bag of contraband on the bench before fumbling for her sweater. It hung like a cape from her shoulders.

Despite the temperature, still hovering around eighty, Henrietta also donned a white, acrylic sweater for the fifty-yard walk. And a moment later, cloudy-eyed Harriet got up and did the same, seemingly forgetting all about the mosquitoes.

Once all three ladies were buttoned up, I stepped forward to assist Harriet with her bag. While she looked to be the strongest of the three—possibly because of her manly moustache—she emitted such an air of helplessness that my heart actually ached for her.

She mumbled as I secured her bag to her shoulder. Then she studied my face as if she'd never seen me before. Her eyes were devoid of any recognition, although, as I stepped away, they seemed to offer a flitter of awareness. It was just before she cast an accusatory finger at her sisters.

With spittle flying and her short, gray, scarecrow hair shooting out in all directions, she went on to holler at them about something that made absolutely no sense to me. I guess it didn't matter. The tirade was over almost as quickly as it had begun. And her sisters showed little concern about what she'd said.

With a roll of her shoulders, she tottered back in my direction. She looked docile, as if nothing had happened. And after she became fixated on a piece of lint that clung to her dress, the slight tremor of her hands was the only vestige of her outburst. She repeatedly grabbed at the offending fluff until capturing it between her fingers and flinging it into the air.

Appearing satisfied with herself, she proceeded to smooth the wrinkles in her skirt while initiating a new monologue. This one was directed at me, or more accurately, through me, as if I wasn't even there. Her voice was soft and introspective, not at all enraged, as it had been mere moments earlier. And this time I understood every word, which wasn't a good thing, believe me. Her comments, you see, centered on overnight flatulence and the food from the benefit dinner that might cause it.

You heard me right. She recited the names of all the hot dishes she'd eaten, as well as the number of helpings consumed of each, at last settling on Three-Bean Hot Dish. "Yah," she said, "since I had more than my fair share of that one, I reckon I'll be in for a long night."

Now, you may not have picked up on this, but I have a weak stomach. Margie's detailed account of Vern's baler accident almost did me in, and I was certain to be a goner if I had to listen to much more from Harriet. Notwithstanding my compassion for her, I had to get away.

I opened my mouth to offer a quick good-bye but was stopped by Henrietta, who hissed, "Well, speak of the devil."

Yes, I needed to leave. Yet, with those words, that need was eclipsed by curiosity. Not all that uncommon for yours truly, but on this particular night, it would end up costing me dearly.

Not knowing that at the time, however, I followed my natural inclination and tracked Henrietta's eyes across the highway to the gravel lot next to the grain elevator. The area was practically full of vehicles—pickups of every kind, interspersed with SUVs—though no people were around other than a man and woman exiting a black luxury sedan.

The woman was tall and skinny, but something about the deliberate way she moved reminded me of Margie. For his part, the man appeared no different from the other men I'd seen in town, except this guy was awfully thin. No beer belly. None at all. And this guy only had one arm.

"We have to go," Henrietta said. "If ya can get that scoundrel arrested, ya go right ahead. He oughtta be in jail. And by all means, write about him. Tell the whole world what he done. Just don't drag our names into it. Don't forget, we gotta live here."

"I understand." I remained transfixed on the scene across the road, a slight breeze teasing my hair and sending a shiver down my neck. Okay, it probably wasn't the breeze causing my chills. But that's what I told myself because I didn't want to believe it was some kind of errie premonition.

Vern made his way around the car. And joining Vivian, he cupped her elbow and navigated her through the parking lot and across the highway. At the sidewalk, he hurried ahead to open the café door, allowing her to enter without ever breaking her stride.

When they were out of sight, I made a one-eighty turn to find that the Anderson sisters had started down the alley. They wobbled along like a collection of vintage wind-up toys.

They were talking about something, but I couldn't make out exactly what was being said. At one point, though, I thought I heard Harriet warn the other two, "Whatever happens tonight, it's your fault, not mine. Like I told ya before, ya should of stopped me."

Chapter Nineteen

I SLAPPED MY CLEAVAGE and the blood-sucking mosquito chewing away in it. Not being very busty, my target was small, and my aim had to be spot on. Glimpsing down the front of my shirt, I saw that it was. The little pest was squished. I brushed it away but had no allusions of victory. Harriet may have been confused about a lot of things, but she was right about the mosquitoes. They were vicious. No doubt, it was time to go back inside. Yet, I lingered.

While only half visible above the horizon, the sun was massive, much larger than I'd ever seen it before. It was mesmerizing too, stunningly bright, framed in warm, silky ribbons of dusty pink and purple, only the elevator silhouetted against it.

In awe, I gazed to the west until the staccato sound of an old engine redirected my attention.

Down the highway, an antique John Deere tractor came into view. It chugged along, the young man behind the wheel steering into the make-shift parking lot next to the elevator. With gravel popping, he pulled into one of the few remaining open spots. Next, he and his companion, another young man who'd been sitting in a lawn chair in an open trailer towed behind the tractor, jumped to the ground and sauntered over to the café.

As I said, the sky was captivating, but the mosquitoes were attacking with vengeance, so I too headed indoors.

***

Inside Hot Dish Heaven, a few stragglers made their way through the buffet line, while a couple others lingered in booths. I didn't see the tractor boys anywhere and assumed they were in the VFW, where the dance should have been underway. Jim, the banker and bar manager, must have had trouble finding a replacement band, however, because the only music I heard accompanied a female karaoke singer—an atrocious karaoke singer. She was attempting Kris Kristofferson's "Help Me Make It through the Night." But no mistake about it, her need for help was far more immediate.

My eyes swept the room in search of Vern, and though I saw no sign of him, I did spot Vivian. She was standing with Margie in the kitchen, arguing about something. She shook her finger in Margie's face, while Margie stood her ground, fists on hips. From where I was, I couldn't tell what they were saying. To me, the entire exchange was nothing more than angry pantomime.

When Margie noticed me, she took leave of Vivian, who kept right on waving her finger back and forth like a windshield wiper.

"There you are," Margie said, drawing near, two small plates of some type of creamy dish in hand. "I thought ya got lost."

"I was admiring the sunset and the community garden."

"Well, no one here can take credit for the sunset, but we'll argue that durin' the summer, it's the best you'll see anywhere." She stopped for a beat. "The garden's courtesy of Ole and Lena's daughter, Rosa."

"That's what I heard."

"Yeah, I wish ya could of met her. She was in earlier with fresh-cut flowers for our guest of honor. I told her you were upstairs, but she couldn't wait around. I don't know why."

I recalled the young woman I'd seen from the bedroom window. That must have been Rosa.

Margie motioned me to a booth, where we sat opposite each other. "I forgot to put this out," she said, placing the plates on the table. "Ya gotta try it."

She went on about the popularity of the dish, but I paid little attention. As difficult as this might be to believe, I wasn't interested in eating. My stomach was upset, either from all the sweets I'd already consumed or Harriet's ranting about colitis. "Sorry, but—"

"Oh, come on. It's a favorite. It's called Snicker Salad."

Another misnomer. Like most of the so-called salads at the benefit dinner, Snicker Salad shared none of the ingredients of a real salad. No lettuce, no garden greens of any kind. It consisted of nothing other than green apple slices and pieces of Snicker candy bars mixed with Cool Whip. Not that I'm criticizing. The fact is I believe green M&Ms should be classified as vegetables. I'm just saying.

"Please try a bite," Margie pleaded.

I had a hunch she wouldn't give up. I'd have to try a little, so that's what I did. And I had to admit, "this is pretty good."

Only a trace of a smile touched Margie's lips before she switched topics. "Yah, I wish ya could of met Rosa. She's real nice." She nodded at Vivian, who was rushing toward the hallway. "Unlike that one," she huffed. "She's my sister, don't ya know. But she's so mean that even if she deserves to go to hell, the devil will never take her."

I was chewing a candy-bar nugget yet managed to say, "Now wait a minute. I thought you told me that Vivian was great to Ole and Lena's kids. She took them in after Lena died and—"

"For sure she's a good aunt and a decent ma, but she can be a real bear to other folks."

I snatched a final glimpse of the woman before she disappeared. "She doesn't look that tough."

"Don't let her bony body fool ya. She's as tough as leather." Margie speared a couple chunks of cream-covered apple. "Anyways, she's mad as heck at me."

"Why?" I ate a little more, deciding that since Snicker Salad contained fruit, it might have been the healthiest thing I'd eaten all day.

"I didn't tell her you were comin'. I didn't want her to know in case it didn't work out. I'd never hear the end of it. So, she didn't find out you were here until she got here herself a little while ago."

"And that made her angry?"

She raised her eyes to the ceiling, as if she'd find her answer there. "I'm guessin' more jealous than angry. She said I had no business invitin' ya or any other reporter here without talkin' to her first." She slowly pulled the apple pieces off her fork, licking her lips when she was done.

"Why should she care?"

Margie answered amid chomps. "Vivian's self-centered. Like I said, she's probably mad you're not doin' a story about her."

"Could be," I replied, now very curious as to what Vivian knew about Samantha Berg's disappearance and death. "Could be."

Chapter Twenty

THE TRACTOR BOYS PEEKED around the corner, and I pointed them out to Margie.

"They're just the Donaldson brothers," she said. "They're always losin' their drivers' licenses for one reason or another, but since ya don't need a license to operate farm equipment, they get by, though they might be pushin' their luck drivin' on the highway."

As if coming to town by tractor wasn't that unusual and didn't warrant a whole lot of discussion, she dropped the subject by asking, "Now, what were we talkin' about?"

I briefly contemplated pursuing the Donaldson brothers, figuratively speaking only, but decided instead to go in search of more information about Vivian and her possible connection to Samantha Berg's death. In particular, I wanted to find out if she cared enough for her husband, Vern, to help him cover up the murder. But since Margie was extremely sensitive about her family, as I'd discovered earlier in the day, I would have to be cagey with my questions, like I was with Deputy Ryden. Although that didn't work out all that well, did it?

"Margie," I began hesitantly, "your sister and her husband don't have a very good relationship, do they?"

She crimped her brow. "Now why on earth would ya care about that?"

"Well . . . um," I stammered, once more noting that "cagey" just wasn't my thing, "I . . . um . . . I was just wondering."

Margie eyed me with uncertainty but answered anyway. "I suppose they're like most couples married for thirty years."

"Oh," I replied, collecting myself. "Considering what you told me, I assumed they didn't get along."

"Well, like I said, Vivian's one tough cookie." Margie reached for my empty "salad" plate and placed it on top of her own. "But she and Vern have been through more than their share of rough patches, and that's bound to create some kind of bond, right?"

I didn't answer. I was busy mentally banging my head against the wall. Why couldn't I be more tactful? Why was that so difficult for me? One of my professors had routinely reminded me that tact was "getting a point across without stabbing someone in the eye with it." But I, it seemed, often caused near blindness.

"Well, um . . . Margie," I said, taking another shot at it because I was too stubborn to admit defeat, "have Vern and Vivian ever experienced anything that might shatter that bond? Something like . . . um . . . Ole and Lena's problem?"

Margie raised her chin, and with a mix of exasperation and trepidation, I answered her perplexed expression head on. Or more accurately, eye to eye. Why not? Among my tact-related shortcomings was an undeniable inability to make my point subtly. So why pretend? "I mean have Vivian and Vern ever dealt with . . . um . . . infidelity?" I cringed and waited for her to pitch a fit.

Rather than yelling, though, she threw her head back and laughed. "Oh, my goodness, no. Vern likes to tease, but he's no fool. If he ever had an affair, Vivian would kill him or the woman involved or quite possibly both."

"You're . . . um . . . kidding, right?"

She leaned toward me. "No." The sour smell of alcohol laced her breath.

"Now," she added as she rose from the booth, clutching our dirty dishes, "I'll take these to the kitchen. I was nursin' a bottle of wine back there, and I'm gonna get me another glass. Want one?"

Vivian? A killer? It was possible, I suppose. But the killer in this instance? Not likely. It just didn't fit. "Um . . . yeah, I could use some wine."

With a nod, Margie walked away, plates in one hand, silverware in the other.

No, it didn't fit for a number of reasons, and while sitting there by myself, I ticked them off on my fingers:

One, despite any homicidal tendencies that Vivian might harbor, she wouldn't have avenged Lena's death. According to Margie, her sister wasn't the type. When it came to Lena, Margie said Vivian wasn't that nice.

Two, while Vivian may have been inclined to kill Vern, the "other woman," or both if she ever learned of an affair, Margie found the idea of Vern actually having one literally laughable.

Three, even if Vivian had concealed Samantha Berg's murder to save face, or for some other reason, Vern alone did the deed. No one else was seen at the bungalow that night. True, the Anderson sisters were the source of that information, but reportedly, the police confirmed his presence.

Four . . .

My train of thought got derailed by the hollering from down the hall. Several guys in the bar were belting out their version of Shel Silverstein's "Put Another Log on the Fire," and the crowd was getting into it.

> Put another log on the fire. Cook me up some bacon and some beans. Go out to the car and change the tire. Wash my socks and sew my old blue jeans. Come on baby, you can fill my pipe and then go fetch my slippers. And boil me up another pot of tea. Put another log on the fire, babe. Then come and tell me why you're leavin' me.

Margie sang along in a tone-rich, alto voice as she made her way back to me, a tray balanced on one hand. From the tray, she retrieved a plate of Chocolate Caramel Bars and set it on the table before passing me a large coffee mug. "It's wine," she said, as if I'd asked. "Since we don't have a liquor license here in the café, we can't be too obvious."

I sipped. "Tasty."

Margie sat down and nodded toward the bar, where the singers carried on about doing their women wrong. "Don't ever push a woman too far," she warned with a devilish smile.

Images of Vivian, Margie, and Lena dashed across my mind's eye. "No, don't ever push a woman too far," I repeated as a strange sensation bubbled up inside of me—a sensation that felt a lot like admiration.

But how could that be? I liked Margie, but I didn't admire her. She never strayed far enough from home to have her own life, so what was there to admire? As for Lena? She gave up on life. And while Vivian wasn't a murderer herself, she wasn't to be trusted either. Just the same, there must have been something about the trio that resonated with me. Something that stirred my emotions.

I gave it more thought, begrudgingly concluding that I might have mischaracterized the ladies—or at least two of them. Even though I was almost one-hundred percent certain I'd pegged Vivian correctly, I may have erred where Margie and Lena were concerned.

Truth be told, I didn't know Lena or the battles she fought prior to her death, so I had no business assuming she surrendered her life. Perhaps she went down fighting. And Margie? Well, I had to admit she was fiercely independent, strong-willed, and confident. And with all that going for her, she would have enjoyed success regardless of where she lived. Yes, she might have identified with the town of Kennedy, but she didn't let it define her. She was true to herself.

I was in no position to judge anyway. After listening to Barbie's spiel about "living by default," I had plenty of concerns regarding my own life. Yep, throughout my adulthood, I'd been terribly unsure of myself, second-guessing most everything I did.

In fact, prior to pursuing the story about Samantha Berg, the only thing I'd done of late with any real conviction was slash the tires on Boo-Boo's Range Rover. It happened the week after finding him frolicking in bed with those two inflated-breasted, baseball groupies. I got the idea from a country song and the nerve from a bottle of tequila, but I did the deed myself.

To toast the resolve I exhibited on that sole occasion, I downed most of my wine. But amid the coughing jag that followed, I reconciled myself to a few realities: First, I wasn't much of a drinker. And, second, whatever their shortcomings, Margie and Lena were tenacious, even ruthless when necessary. So was Vivian for that matter. Perhaps even more so than the other two. But all three were decidedly tough broads. And that must have been what I appreciated about them. After all, I'd never be a member of any "tough broads club." It wasn't in my nature. At most, I'd be a rare guest, as I was the night I worked over Boo-Boo's car. And between visits, I'd have to settle for just being me, nosy old me.

To that end, when done almost choking to death from guzzling my wine, I asked Margie another question, sticking with the direct approach, the one most suitable for me, even if it occasionally led to vision loss in others. "Margie? How did Vivian and Vern react to Lena's death?"

She licked her lips. "Vivian's always considered herself a cut above the other women in town, especially Lena. She was upset about her death but mostly because of the kids. Vern, on the other hand, was overcome with grief. See, he adored Lena. He loved her like a sister."

Margie proceeded to detail how the people in Kennedy had come to love Lena but none more than Vern.

While listening, I selected a Chocolate Carmel Bar with lots of caramel drizzled on top, conveniently forgetting that only moments earlier I'd ordered myself to forgo any more sweets.

When finished talking, Margie chose one too. "I think these taste great with this wine," she said, swishing the contents of her coffee cup. "But remember, you're supposed to sip wine, not chug it, not even from a mug."

"Yeah, yeah," I uttered for lack of anything better to say. I was ashamed of my poor drinking prowess but not ashamed enough to abstain. I gulped more wine before taking a big bite of the thick, dessert bar.

Margie was right. The bar tasted delicious on the heels of the golden wine—like a chocolate-caramel truffle with kick.

After swallowing, I spoke in a throaty voice, my gullet clogged with rich chocolate. "Did Vern blame Samantha for Lena's death?"

Apparently as amused by my eating as she'd been by my drinking, Margie smiled. "I suppose he blamed Samantha." She stopped to reflect, several emotions passing over her face. "Although he was really mad at Ole too. Not so much over Lena's death as the affair itself."

"Oh?" I sucked caramel from my fingertips.

"Yah, Vern was furious that Ole took up with Samantha in the first place, and he never got over it."

"What makes you say that?"

"Well, after he found out about the affair, he gave up on bein' friends with him."

"Wait a second." My fingers licked clean, I rested my hands in my lap. "I thought you said that when Ole left Samantha, he moved into a trailer out on Vern's farm."

"That's right. Vern helped him out, but they weren't close. Before the affair, they were more like brothers than brothers-in-law. They fished together and bowled and curled. Gosh, they even took a vacation to Alaska together. But after Ole moved in with Samantha, Vern wouldn't hang out with him anymore." She slowly tipped her head from one side to the other. "No, sir-ree, he couldn't stand the thought of Ole bein' with Samantha Berg."

I absently patted my hand against the table, the tapping underscoring a number of questions. I wanted to know why Ole's affair upset Vern so much. Was it only because of his brotherly love for Lena? Or was something else going on?

I stared at what was left of my Chocolate Caramel Bar. I longed to finish it. It tasted great, and as I might have mentioned, I think better when I eat. My editor routinely said I was the type of writer who "likes to chew things over."

But contrary to what I'd assumed earlier, my stomach wasn't eagerly awaiting a "chocolate-caramel truffle with a kick." And now it was upset again and warning me against so much as another nibble. To keep peace, intestinally speaking, I pushed the chocolate treat aside.

Was it truly possible that, once upon a time, Vern had designs of his own on Samantha Berg? Well, that would certainly explain his strong reaction to Ole's affair with her. He was jealous. And when Ole finally put an end to his relationship with the woman, Vern quite possibly began frequenting her house on his own behalf. Allegedly, he went there to stop her from harassing his niece, but maybe he was actually having an affair himself.

But if that were true, why kill her? It couldn't have been in retaliation for Lena's death. He wouldn't have had an affair with her first. That would have been just too creepy. Nor would he have waited an entire year after Lena died to commit the crime. Moreover, he probably would have killed Ole too since Ole was just as much to blame as Samantha for the tryst that resulted in Lena's failing health and ultimate death.

I drew a blank index card from the bottom of the pile and jotted down the recipe for Chocolate Caramel Bars. As I wrote, I grappled with a notion that was lurking around the edges of my consciousness: Stabbing someone, particularly in the heart, was an intimate crime. I recalled that from school. And Deputy Ryden had confirmed that the perpetrator in this case faced Samantha while thrusting the knife—or whatever the weapon was—into her chest. The killer stood close to her, mere inches away. He must have seen the terror in her eyes. Yet, he didn't stop. He couldn't stop. With unbridled anger and overflowing adrenaline, he shoved the weapon through her ribs and lungs and into her heart. "Hmm."

I was in the dark, although slowly, very slowly, understanding dawned on me. The murder of Samantha Berg was personal, an act of passion. There was no other reasonable explanation. And given that, the perpetrator was much more likely to be an enraged lover than a concerned uncle or distraught in-law.

It all made sense. Vern and Samantha were having an affair. They had to be, in spite of Margie's belief that Vern would never do such a thing. And on that fateful night, the two of them were embroiled in a heated argument, quite possibly over Samantha's threat to expose their relationship. Their exchange was emotionally charged. And at some point, Vern lost control, stabbed her, and with both of the hands he had back then, dumped her body in the Red River.

I allowed the air I'd been unknowingly holding to escape my lungs. There it was. Vern's motive as well as his *modus operandi.* I had them both figured out. And that should have provided me with a sense of satisfaction. Which it did. For a second. But that satisfaction was quickly followed by major misgivings. Not about my presumption. I was confident that Vern was the killer. But I didn't like being in agreement with the bag of mixed nuts known as the Anderson sisters. Nope, I didn't like that one bit.

Chapter Twenty-One

Margie unfolded herself from the booth and scuttled to the kitchen, where someone was hollering for help with cleanup. I was about to follow, thinking my head, a bit cloudy from wine and thoughts, might be well served if I moved the rest of my body. But before I could, Vivian slid into Margie's seat.

"Hi, there." She extended her hand and limply shook mine while scrutinizing me with cool detatchment. "I'm Vivian Olson, Margie Johnson's younger sister."

I smiled at how she emphasized the word "younger," although I think she interpreted it as a sign that I was delighted to meet her. And while not "delighted," I was admittedly interested. Remember, I wanted to learn the role she'd played, if any, in covering up Samantha Berg's death.

"I heard you're doin' a story about Margie." She snapped her gum while splaying her hands in front of her face. She looked as if inspecting her manicure was far more interesting than any response I might offer.

"That's right." I attempted to take her all in. It wasn't easy.

Vivian Olson was on the near side of fifty and blonde, her hair helped—and I use that word loosely—with dye that left it all the same dull shade. It was sculpted into a French roll, bangs at rest on her frameless, rectangular glasses. Her eyes were similar to those of her sibling's, but hers were dramatically made up with thick black liner, brown shadow, and lots of mascara. Her facial features, also like her sibling's, were angular, but hers were much sharper, probably because she was rail thin, a condition undoubtedly exacerbated by her cigarette habit. The smell of tobacco clung to her despite a generous use of lilac-scented perfume.

In her arms, she cradled an ivory, satin-covered album, which she placed on the table and opened to the *click-clack* of her red acrylic bracelets. "First of all," she said through a plastic smile, "I, myself, as does everyone else in town . . . Well, we think it's just great about the article 'cause Margie's worked hard these many years to progress this café and also makes good hot dishes and bars among oh so many other things. Not that the food is great, but it's fillin' though some should eat less even if she doesn't charge much and rinses the meat and lets folks take some home for themselves or a party. And there too, I suppose that makes her deservin' and a role model to them that haven't been so blessed by showin' each and every one what opportunities are there if they're willin' to work hard, though the café's not all that busy most of the time, and caterin' is hit and miss. Still, I keep remindin' Marge she has to reach high and really stretch not only her hours but her menu options, not to mention her budget, to grab that there brass star, such as it is."

Huh? My brain must have been malfunctioning. That's all I could figure. Why else would Vivian sound so ridiculous? I hit the side of my head with the heel of my hand in an effort to realign the mental spark plugs that must have been misfiring.

"And sometimes," she proceeded to say in the same screechy voice, only louder now to drown out the clatter of the dishes in the kitchen, "special occasions call for somethin' more special than bars, not that there's anythin' wrong with bars, oh gosh no, but that's where I come in if I'm so blessed to do so, even though I don't work at the café." Her eyes darted around the room, as if she were talking to an audience—an audience partial to Pig-Latin or some other form of gibberish. "See," she said, pointing to the plastic-covered pictures in her album, "I make special-occasion cakes to help shore up the menus for those special occasions and also for other things."

Her voice and speech were quickly becoming too much to bear. If hitting my head had helped, I still would have been banging away. As it was, all I could do was cringe when she opened her mouth again. The grating tone. The complete disregard for syntax.

"Also," she went on to say, "it's an honor for me to be a small part of those special occasions, offerin' best wishes in the best way I know how for those lucky enough to be celebratin' there."

While cracking her gum, she arched her brows and gently rubbed her red, bobble necklace between her thumb and tobacco-stained index finger. It was an obvious attempt at conveying an air of elegance. It failed.

Her cakes, however, were anything but failures. The confirmation cake pictured in her book was decorated like the Bible, complete with gilt-edged pages and a frosting cross emblazoned on the cover. And the retirement cake on the opposite page was shaped like a golf cart, a bag of frosted clubs leaning out the back.

"Mind you," she continued, "these cakes are edible, I'm proud to say, usin' the best ingredients and makin' them in my kitchen, from scratch, to yours."

"Well," I managed to utter, "they certainly are pretty."

She pulled her shoulders back and stuck out her flat chest. She then paged through the album with one skeletal hand while using the other to play with her red, dangle-ball earrings. Directing her remarks to her imaginary audience—the one versed in gibberish—she spoke in circles about basket-weave piping, gum-paste flowers, and tier separators.

"You betcha," she said at some point, "if I'd known you were comin', I would of baked a cake." She cackled. "And, also, I could of gotten together a small picture book to look at and for you to take on back there to the Twin Cities if you were so inclined to present my cakes. As it was, I could only hurry home and grab my big album, as you can see here. Although I have half a mind . . ."

No truer words were ever spoken. I pinched my thigh and reminded myself to be nice.

"Vivian, your cakes are beautiful, but I was assigned to gather recipes for the kind of food served at church functions."

She fluttered her gunked-up, spider-like lashes and cracked her gum some more. Ever since high school, I'd hated gum. And the sound of hers popping put me on edge.

"Well, my cakes are served at all kinds of church functions—weddings, baptisms."

"Vivian, I mean I'm after recipes for the kind of food served at . . . um . . . funerals."

She grinned, and because of her sunken cheeks, the grin truly stretched from ear to ear. "I've done a few funeral cakes too."

She flipped through her album until reaching a page near the back. Then, with a long, pink-painted fingernail, she tapped against a picture of a cake designed like an elaborate marble headstone. The deceased's name as well as the dates of birth and death were etched in black icing.

"These folks, who ordered this cake here, were real proud of the marker they designed for their mother, after dyin' of colon cancer, and wantin' a cake to match." I visualized her—Vivian, not the dead woman—with duct tape over her mouth. But somehow, she kept on talking. "Of course I did my darndest to give it to 'em, balancin' good taste and keepin' that in mind along the way."

She clapped her hands together. "Get it? Good taste? And I'm referrin' to cake?" She cackled again, this time ending with a snort. "If ya want, ya can use that there line in your article."

"Thanks." My right eye began to twitch. "I just don't think my editor will accept cake recipes." I held my eyelid shut with the tip of my finger. "He's more interested in food . . . well, in the kind of food served here tonight."

"Oh." Vivian's shoulders drooped, her plastic smile cracked, and a sharp pain penetrated my chest even though I assured myself I had no reason to feel bad for Vivian Olson. She was the one annoying me, for God's sake. Because of her, my eye was twitching like I was using it to send Morse code. What's more, I didn't need to take pity on someone possibly mixed up in murder. Which reminded me, I had questions to ask.

True, Vivian was unlikely to answer them. And even if she did, I probably wouldn't understand a word she said. Still, I had to ask. And because I'd have a better shot at getting her to drop her guard if she liked me, I weighed my options while pretending to wipe dirt from my jeans.

Cake recipes on the one hand. Information on the other. If I agreed to a few recipes over which I made no publishing decisions anyway—though she didn't need to know that—she might say something pertinent to the case.

The choice seemed obvious. "Vivian, on second thought, e-mail me a few of your favorite recipes, along with some pictures."

She ushered out a sigh. "Well, if you insist."

I pressed another finger against my eyelid.

"Now, what's your e-mail down in the Twin Cities there?" She scrounged in her red glitter bag. "I better jot this down."

Finding a blue Bic, she removed the cap and, with a supposed air of sophistication, repeatedly licked the ball point. That's right. She slobbered all over the ink end of her pen. And because I'd always hated when people chewed on pencils or snapped their gum or drooled over office supplies, I went crazy. Or perhaps it was just the final straw in a big pile of crazy. Whatever the case, I knew I needed to get away before I shoved that pen up her nose and wrapped her gum around her head like a scarf.

Of course I hadn't obtained any answers. Hell, I hadn't even asked my questions. But that didn't matter. I had to go. I was at the end of my rope, and if I didn't leave soon, I'd tie her up with it and toss her in a ditch.

Yeah, yeah. I might have been overreaching. Quite possibly due to the stress of the day. Or perhaps I'd discovered why so few people chose to live in the area. Her name was Vivian.

I pulled a business card from my shirt pocket and pushed it across the table. "All my contact information is right there." I scooted back my chair. "Now, if you'll excuse me, I have to use the restroom, then collect more recipes from Margie."

Vivian carefully placed my card and her pen back in her purse. "Of course." Her tone was business-like, but the clump of red lipstick stuck to her teeth and the blue ink streaked across her upper lip undermined any attempt at looking the part.

I gawked but remained mum.

"It was a pleasure to meet you," she added with no sencerity whatsoever.

Even so, I attempted to smile because it was the right thing to do. But the damn thing kept sliding off my face. So with nothing more than a nod, I rose and steered myself down the hall, toward the bar. I'd catch the bathroom on my return.

* * *

NOW, YOU MIGHT ASSUME I WAS in dire need of an antacid or a strong drink. But I wasn't. What I really wanted was a Chocolate Cherry Brownie. I'd seen Jim, the bartender, grab a tray of them from the café a little earlier. But as I approached the bar, I saw the tray. And it was empty.

"Damn." I'd have to settle for a beer. Not that I dislike beer. I'm Irish after all. My dad often said beer was proof that God loved us and wanted us to be happy. And my dad was very happy on a regular basis. But between you and me, a beer was no Chocolate Cherry Brownie.

Employing my eye tic, I nevertheless signaled Jim for a Finnegan's on tap. At least that's what I hoped I'd signaled for. And after that, I retrieved some money from the pocket of my jeans and reached it across the counter. He just waved it away, telling me with a smile that my money wasn't any good in his place. So, again with my tic, I thanked him and wrapped my fingers around the cool, brown bottle he handed me.

Following a long drink, I played with the drops of moisture running down the glass. At the same time, Vivian's nerve-racking voice and bizarre speech jockeyed for position in my brain. Words couldn't describe my take on either, although shrill and mind-numbing were definite contenders.

Several more gulps and I actually reran a portion of my exchange with the woman. And by the time the mental video had finished playing, I was mulling over a new theory. Was it possible that Samantha Berg got trapped with Vivian somewhere and stabbed herself and jumped into the Red River just to get away? Another gulp of beer. Like I said, it was just a theory.

Chapter Twenty-Two

After emptying my beer, I used the restroom, which was way too ugly to describe, and headed back into the café.

"Hey!" Margie yelled from the same booth we'd previously shared. And like before, I jumped, and she snickered. "You're kind of jittery, aren't ya?"

"Yeah, I guess I am." The result of time spent with your sister.

Sliding in across from her, I noted just two other people in the room. A man and a woman huddled over a table near the entrance.

"Before I forget," Margie said, "Father Daley wants to meet ya, bein' you're Irish and all." She scratched the handle of her coffee cup. This time it appeared to be filled with coffee. "He and Maureen Russell, tonight's guest of honor, are the only Irish folks in these parts."

"Where is he?"

She stopped scratching. "He'll be along shortly." She angled her thumb in the direction of the hallway. "He's playin' cards in the bar."

"What?" I wasn't sure I'd gotten that right. Playing cards in a bar wasn't common behavior for any of the priests I'd known.

"Yah, he says if he didn't come to the 'V' once in a while, he'd never see most of his parishioners." She nodded at her cup. "Want some?"

"Not right now."

Another nod. "Anyways, he was Lena's priest, and there was a time when he and Ole were good friends too." Her smile barely registered, yet it softened her sharp features. "Years ago I'd stop by the farm and find the three of them, Ole, Lena, and Father Daley, in the kitchen, sippin' wine and cookin' up a storm. Ole and the padre golfed and curled together, and they loved to fish." She sighed wistfully. "But it all came to a screeching halt when Ole moved in with the tramp. Father Daley couldn't abide by that."

"Seems odd they were friends in the first place. An Irish-Catholic priest and a Scandinavian-Lutheran farmer. Sounds more like the makings of a bad Ole and Lena joke."

"Well, they were, though some folks, includin' Reverend Swenson, the former Lutheran minister, didn't approve." Margie rested her jaw but only for a second. "Ya know, he confronted Ole in the grocery store in Hallock one day. Warned him it was wrong for him to socialize with a priest and downright sinful to attend mass with Lena and the kids, even if only on special occasions. He said he better change his ways, or by God, he'd be punished." A scowl briefly darkened her face.

"Over the years, I've talked to Father Daley about that. He says he doesn't believe the Lord sees things that way. He doesn't think the Almighty cares what team you're on as long as you're in the game and play by the rules." She bobbed her head to emphasize her point.

"Now, as ya might expect, Ole didn't take kindly to Reverend Swenson's remarks and told him so in no uncertain terms. Not surprisingly, Reverend Swenson wasn't used to people talkin' to him that way and got real mad and made a nasty comment about Lena." Margie's thin lips stretched like a taut rubber band. "Well, of course, Ole couldn't stand for that, and he up and punched the Reverend. That's right. He punched that albino-looking, sanctimonious jerk smack dab in the jaw, sendin' him backwards into the fresh fruit display." She shook her head as if she still couldn't believe it had ever happened.

"Accordin' to Bob, the butcher, when Reverend Swenson got up off the floor, his entire black suit was covered with squished raspberries and strawberries. He even had berries in his white hair and beard. I guess it was quite a sight. But the funniest part was that Bob spent the rest of the day askin' everyone who came in the store, 'What's black and white, and red all over? Reverend Swenson in the berry display, down aisle three.'" She slapped the table. I jumped. And she shook her head some more.

"Not long after, Reverend Swenson got transferred to some church in Iowa, and we got ourselves a new minister, Reverend Pearson. He's not very outgoin', but he's a decent guy, and he and Father Daley have become great friends.

"When Ole died, Reverend Pearson invited Father Daley to perform the funeral with him, so it ended up bein' one of those ecumenical services. But, ya know, it was nice anyways." She sounded shocked. "And followin' the ceremony, we buried Ole right next to Lena." She pressed her finger into her cheek, like people sometimes do when they're mulling over something. "I suppose that means, in a way, they're back together again."

Now, that must have been a revelation because it led Margie to do some silent reflection, which left me with nothing to do except listen to the karaoke music from down the hall. Two women were attempting to do justice to Waylon Jenning's "Good Hearted Woman," but justice was not served, although I'm certain more drinks were. Anything to deaden the senses, particularly that of hearing.

"Margie, I take it Jim didn't find a band?" I rubbed my temples to stave off the headache that was threatening.

"Last I heard, he was still workin' on it." She made the comment while signaling to a robust man, no doubt Father Daley.

The guy appeared to be in his late sixties. He was dressed in black slacks and a black shirt, a religious collar partially concealed behind his double chin. Doing the two-step to the karaoke music, he danced his way solo across the floor, moving quite gracefully considering his size, his age, and the warped hardwood beneath his feet.

As he drew near, he rolled his shadowed eyes and twisted his fat finger in his ear. "Those Lindgrin girls sure can sing, can't they?" He was boisterous. I sensed he came by it naturally. And sarcasm dripped from every word.

Margie laughed. "Father Daley, this here is Emerald Malloy, the reporter who's gatherin' recipes for the paper."

"It's always a pleasure to meet someone with roots in the homeland." With his left hand, he removed a toothpick from the corner of his mouth. With his right, he reached for my hand and brushed the back of it with a kiss. "Especially one as pretty as you."

"Watch out," Margie warned as I felt my cheeks flush. "He's full of blarney."

The priest groused, "She's a reporter. I'm sure she can distinguish blarney from sincerity."

Margie agreed. "And that's why she'll remain leery of you."

Father Daley's laugh rang out, and the couple near the entrance turned our way, but he didn't seem to care.

"Hey," he said to Margie, leaning over the back of her booth. "I've got a new Ole and Lena joke for you."

"Oh, no." Margie craned her neck so he could see her pained expression, but he paid it no mind.

"Aye, and this one has a religious theme."

She dropped her head and closed her eyes. "Since I'm guessin' there's no way to keep ya from tellin' it, go ahead and get it over with."

The priest chuckled as he combed his thick fingers through his curly, salt-and-pepper hair. "Okay now, ya see," he began, glancing between Margie and me, "Ole and Lena spent every night readin'. And while Lena read lots of books, Ole only read da Bible." He employed an outrageous Scandinavian accent—one that made the guy with the John Deere hat sound like a graduate of elocution class. "So one night Lena said, 'Eh, Ole, why do ya read da Bible but nothin' else?' And Ole answered, ''Cause da Bible holds da answers to all tings.'" The priest continued to slide his eyes between the two of us. "Now Lena wasn't sure she believed dat, so she said, 'If dat's true, Ole, den what does da Bible say about PMS?' Well, Ole thumbed through da Good Book till he found da passage he wanted, and den he said, 'On da subject of PMS, Lena, da Bible says, and Mary rode Joseph's ass all da way to Jerusalem.'"

Father Daley roared with laughter, while Margie drooped in her seat and teasingly scolded, "And you're supposed to be a man of God."

"Now I don't care who you are," the priest fired back, his jowls jiggling, "that there was funny." He replanted his toothpick between his lips and shot a look my way, evidently in search of support.

I had none to offer. Until that moment, my contact with members of the clergy had been limited to the priests I'd encountered during my time in parochial school. And all of them were stodgy. I had no idea how to act around one who played cards, hung out in bars, and told PMS jokes. No idea at all.

"Tell me, lass," he proceeded to say, speaking through my thoughts, "you really didn't drive all the way up here just to get recipes from this old crow, did you?"

Margie wacked his hand.

"Well, Father, my editor wants hot dish recipes, and what better place to get them than Hot Dish Heaven?"

"I suppose." A curious expression enveloped his face. "But I'm sure you could have found some much closer to the Cities."

Margie jumped in. "None as good as mine."

The corners of the priest's mouth twitched with a smile, yet his eyes remained fixed on mine, causing anxiety to swirl around inside of me. He looked to be straining to get a peek at my soul, but for what purpose, I wasn't sure.

Did he also question the reason for my visit? Did he too suspect I was up to no good? Or was he after something more priestly, like the date I last attended mass? My heart immediately skipped a beat, and I rushed to speak, determined to keep him from strolling down that thorny path.

"My editor thinks dishes common to rural Minnesota would be of interest to our readers." You see, it had been a while since I'd darkened the doorway of any church, but he didn't need to know that. "Most of our subscribers live around the Twin Cities, although we have some in greater Minnesota too. And many of our city readers grew up in rural Minnesota and remain connected to it." I was rambling, but I couldn't stop. I was running interference for my soul. "My boss thought they'd enjoy recipes for the food they grew up with. Food like hot dish, bars, and Jell-O."

"Jell-O" must have been the magic word because as soon as I said it, the priest shifted his focus back to Margie. "I didn't think most people would even cross the street for Jell-O." He struggled to keep a straight face.

"Say now!" Margie held up her index finger in warning. "A heckuva lot of people enjoy my Jell-O. My pistachio's a favorite."

The priest chortled, and I should have felt relieved. Apparently, I had just dodged a bullet—in a spiritual sense—if that's even possible. Still, anxiety continued to swirl inside of me like butterflies caught in a net.

Why did Father Daley unsettle me so? Did I sense he disliked or mistrusted me? Or was it just that he was an unusual priest, and for me, departures from the norm bred discomfort?

I guess the "cause" didn't really matter. The "effect" remained the same. Whenever uncomfortable, I chattered incessantly, especially if there was nothing to stuff into my mouth. And eyeballing the room, I didn't spot a thing. "Yeah, my editor wants recipes," I reiterated, knowing my mouth was about to run amuck, and there wasn't a damn thing I could do about it. "So that's what I'm here to do. Get recipes. And if I can, a story—"

The priest cut me off. "A story? A story about what?"

Margie glanced up at him. "Yours truly."

"No, really," he said, his features reflecting an expression I couldn't quite read, "what kind of story are you after?"

"Hey!" Margie exclaimed, "I'm interestin' enough to be the subject of a story."

"Of course you are," he replied dismissively before shooting me a hard-edged glance that, despite the heat in the room, chilled me to the bone.

Chapter Twenty-Three

EMME, YOU'RE BEING PARANOID.

It was another voice from inside my head. Yeah, I know, I have a lot of them. Sometimes it's like a damn convention in there. And while I generally ignore them, I decided I should listen to this one. As I said, my wariness of Father Daley likely had little to do with him and lots to do with my previous interactions with priests.

For the most part, those experiences revolved around scraping gum from the bottom of desks, the favorite after-school punishment for whatever infractions were committed by the students at Saint Mary of the Lakes Catholic High School. Yes, gum scraping had given rise to my general disregard for clergy as well as my immense disdain for gum. And while an aversion to gum chewing wouldn't pose a problem on this night, an inability to converse with a priest just might.

Because my time with Vivian had been a complete bust and Margie was unlikely to provide any dirt on her brother-in-law, I wanted to get a scoop or two from his partner at cards. True, I couldn't ask any tough questions in front of Margie. For them, I'd have to call on the priest when my host was otherwise occupied. But whether now or later, I was certain I'd have more success if Father Daley thought of me in a positive light. So I had to tamp down my clergy-related biases and be on my best behavior.

I opened my mouth, but my voice faltered. Questioning a priest was going to be harder than I'd expected.

And why is that, Emme? Could it be because you plan to lie?

That's one of the reasons I usually disregard the voices in my head. They're hypersensitive. I wasn't going to lie. I was merely going to limit what I shared. I had to. I couldn't very well say, "Hey, Father, I believe your friend Vern is a murderer, and I want the low-down on him and the crime so I can write a newspaper article. So cough it up." No, I couldn't say that.

I opened my mouth once more. Still nothing. Not good. Not good at all. I needed information. And if I couldn't get it from Father Daley . . .

It took several moments for me to consider my options but only one to choose the coward's way out. "Margie," I said, turning away from the priest and toward my congenial—and talkative—host, "I was visiting with your aunts earlier tonight. And if I'm not mistaken, they don't care for your brother-in-law very much, do they?"

Out of the corner of my eye, I saw Father Daley rock back on his heels. "Why?" he asked sharply. "What did they say about Vern?"

Margie slapped the table. "Emme, you better watch out!" She looked about ready to burst. "Don't speak poorly of Vern with his number-one defender standin' next to you. He might damn ya to hell or purgatory or some such place."

"Oh, come on," Father Daley groaned, gently wrapping his knuckles against the side of Margie's head, "you like him too."

"Yah," she acknowledged with a chuckle, "but I doubt anybody thinks as highly of him as you. Not even Vivian."

The priest bit down on his toothpick and talked between his clenched teeth. "Well, that's not saying much. Vivian doesn't think very highly of anyone."

"Father, be careful," Margie warned. "You're treadin' on shaky ground there."

The priest held up his hands and backed up a pace. "It's just that the guy's had some tough times, and he's come through them amazingly well. We all could take a lesson from him, Vivian included."

The priest smiled. "He's also the worst card player I know. I can't begin to count all the money I've won off him over the years. If nothing else, I've got to love him for that."

Father Daley skidded his eyes in my direction. "Now, what did those old crows say about him?"

"Well, um . . . ," I stammered, not sure how to reply. I was prepared for the priest to be Vern's card-playing buddy, but I wasn't expecting him to be president of the guy's fan club. "Not anything specific really."

First, you skip mass, Emme. Now, you lie to a priest.

I mentally ordered the little voice in my head to stuff a sock in it.

At the same time, Margie explained, "My aunts hate Vern, which is sad since their feelin's actually have nothin' whatsoever to do with him."

I sat up straight, avoiding Father Daley's gaze. My middle school teacher, Sister Helen, had claimed that priests could spot a lie merely by looking in a person's eyes. I never believed her, but this man's eyes were so piercing I didn't want to take a chance.

Instead, I watched Margie as she wiggled around in an attempt to get comfortable. And once she was, she squared her shoulders and rested her folded hands on the table. I'd been with her for less than a day, yet I knew those actions meant just one thing. Margie Johnson was about to tell a story. And I was deeply grateful for the distraction.

"Vern's dad, Carl, left my aunt Harriet at the altar darn near seventy years ago," she said. "Harriet's the middle sister. The one who looks like she just ate a lemon. The one with the hairy upper lip."

I nodded.

"Anyways, accordin' to the story my ma used to tell, everyone was at the church for the weddin'. It's the church in the country. The one with the tall steeple. Ya must of passed it on your way into town."

Again I nodded, recalling the small, white church with the adjacent cemetery, where women tended flowers on the graves.

"Well, like I said, everyone was there 'cept Carl, the groom. He was late, real late, and Harriet was beside herself with worry. She didn't let on, though. No sir-ree. She just sat on the steps of the altar in her weddin' dress and stared at the door."

Margie pulled a wayward strand of hair away from her face and twisted it around her finger, clearly dragging out the narrative for effect. "Finally, there was some commotion outside, and Harriet got all excited. She started goin' on to the guests about how Carl's car must of got stuck in the snow, but he was there now, so the ceremony would get underway shortly. Yet, when the church doors opened, Carl was nowhere in sight. Only his best friend, Donald Donaldson, stood there in the foyer."

Margie bent toward me and spoke in a soft, confidential voice. "He's the Donaldson brothers' great grandpa, don't ya know. He must be ninety-five by now, but believe it or not, he still gets around. He drives a golf cart all over town. And I mean all over—the right side of the street, the left side."

She settled back against the booth. "Anyways, Donald went ahead and told everyone that Carl had eloped the night before with Elsa Erickson. Yah, that's what he did, all right. He recited the story as if it was nothin' more than the daily commodities' report."

Annoyance puckered Margie's lips. "That man's got no sense. Never has. I swear he could be in a crowded bus headed straight for the river, and he'd waste time bitchin' about where he was goin' to sit."

I gave that some thought while Margie continued. "Naturally, Harriet was devastated. Elsa moved onto the Olson farm with Carl. That's the farm Vern operates now. And Aunt Harriet and her two unmarried sisters went on livin' with their folks, my grandparents, on the farm next door. That's the place the twins own.

"Well, wouldn't ya know, about nine months later, maybe a little less, Elsa gave birth to Vern, and twenty-five years after that, Vern and Vivian got married in that very same church. But neither Harriet nor those other two would go near the place, even though Vivian's their niece, their own sister's daughter, and Carl and Elsa were long dead."

Margie again leaned across the table, this time speaking in a conspiratorial tone. "They got killed by a tornado. It picked 'em up and threw 'em darn near a hundred yards." She bent her head to one side. "Carl landed in the cemetery behind the church. And that's the God's honest truth. Some folks found it sorta creepy, but most reckoned it was fittin' since he was the tightest man in the county and would of appreciated the savin's on the hearse."

I had nothing to say to that.

"Anyways, my aunts wouldn't go to the weddin', and to this day, they bear only ill will toward Vern."

The priest steepled his fingers. "So the moral of the story is you can't put any stock in what those old ladies say." He shifted his toothpick from one side of his mouth to the other. "They're so bitter and spiteful they could alienate a saint."

"But mostly they're just confused," Margie countered. "Harriet in particular. She never got over Carl. Ma said she was always moody and, at times, eccentric, but after that whole weddin' mess, she got a lot worse. Now she's so bad that sometimes she has trouble tellin' what's real and what's not. I don't know if it's Alzheimer's or dementia or . . . Well, whatever it is, it causes her to live part time in a make-believe world."

"Inhabited by Carl and Elsa?" I asked.

"Ya got a peek at that?"

"Yeah, just a peek."

"It happens sometimes." Her shoulders stooped slightly, a burden obviously weighing her down. "More often again lately."

Margie's expression cycled from sad to frustrated before she changed the subject altogether. "Hey, Father, Rosa was in earlier. She gave Maureen some flowers from the garden. I told her to stay and meet Emme, but she said she couldn't wait around.

"Uff-dah, she was crabby." Margie shook her head. "Ya know she made the little Nelson girls cry this afternoon. Hollered at them for diggin' in the wrong place in the community garden, if ya can imagine that."

"I'm sorry I missed her," the priest replied. "I can't remember the last time I saw her."

Margie winked at me. "Father Daley likes to keep tabs on Ole and Lena's kids."

"That's right." He wadded up a napkin and shot it like a basketball, aiming for but missing Margie's coffee mug. "Though that gets harder and harder to do."

"See, he was the twins' high school hockey coach," Margie explained, "so he used to see 'em almost every day. Plus, years ago,

Rosa played organ and sang at the Catholic Church in Hallock. But when she went off to college, she gave all that up."

The priest took over. "Now she's back, but I can't get her to come to mass very often, much less sing or play when she does." He rubbed the upper deck of his double chin. "And as far as the twins are concerned, well let's just say I'm concerned."

"Oh, come now," Margie squawked, "they're good boys. They just take after the Lutheran side of the family. We aren't very consistent about our church goin' either."

Margie clearly had a soft spot in her heart for Father Daley. It was evident by her tone, a combination of thoughtfulness and playfulness, no doubt meant to show she cared while, at the same time, raising the man's spirits through a little teasing.

And it worked. The priest flicked his finger against Margie's shoulder and joked, "Well, you Lutherans are just a bunch of heathens."

Margie's lips hinted at a grin. "Don't ya have a poker game to get back to, Saint Daley?"

"Yeah," he answered, glimpsing down the hallway. "I suppose I should go. I'm sure those poor souls are just itching for me to take their money."

"Hold on a minute," Margie said, clutching the priest's forearm. "Before ya leave, I wanna make sure it was okay that I gave Emme your recipe for Irish Hot Dish."

"Of course. With her ancestry, she'll actually appreciate it, unlike you folks."

His tone was jovial and his smile pleasant, causing guilt to simmer inside of me for having mistrusted him. Being an errant Catholic, however, I was accustomed to the sensation. It was a lot like acid reflux.

"Keep in mind," the priest followed up by saying, "if you're article about Margie ends up lacking—and it probably will—you can always write about me."

"Yah, 'cause nothin' is more excitin' than a story about a priest," Margie teased.

Father Daley bit his upper lip in an apparent attempt to stifle his amusement. "Yes, Emerald, my lass"—He spoke with a fake Irish brogue—"you could write about the life of an Irish-Catholic priest forced to minister to a community of Scandinavian Lutherans. Tell your readers about the poor mass attendance and the dreadful St. Patrick's Day parades."

"If I had a beer," Margie jokingly whimpered, "I'd cry in it."

"But, believe me," he added, sans the accent, "there's nothing here beyond that story or the one you're writing about this old crow." He hooked his thumb in Margie's direction. "No, there's nothing else worth reporting about from Kennedy."

He peered at me, his eyes unnerving. "And whatever you do," his voice equally unsettling, "don't give a whit of credence to any if the cockamamie stories the Anderson sisters might tell you, especially about Vern."

He leaned forward, and I slunk back.

"A few years ago," he continued, "there was a homicide here, and those three actually started a rumor that Vern had committed it."

"That's not quite right." Margie worked her jaw. "They reported he was at Samantha's house the night she disappeared. Which was true."

"Those old scallywags insinuated a whole lot more, and you know it." Father Daley's gaze only brushed Margie's face before returning to mine. "Because of them, Vern was subjected to countless interrogations. His home was searched. So was his car. It got so bad he voluntarily took a polygraph just to get the cops off his back. Sure, it proved what we knew all along—that he was innocent—but it took a lot out of the guy. Thank God he's resilient."

"What did you say?" I needed him to repeat himself because I couldn't believe my ears.

"He's resilient."

"No, before that."

"I said Vern was innocent. He had absolutely nothing to do with that woman's death."

He went on talking, but I didn't hear a thing except the pounding of my heart. It grew louder in direct proportion to my anger. Soon I was so livid I was certain that both the priest and Margie could hear every furious beat. Those old bitties had used me! They'd accused Vern of murder, knowing he was innocent. And they'd used me!

My thoughts were scattered, and I knew I had to gather them up. To think clearly, I also had to set my emotions aside. But I couldn't. Three stale nuts had lied about Vern previously, and now they had done it again. Only this time, they'd involved me!

Spots jumped in front of my eyes, and I could only stare at Father Daley until they faded. I had questions for him, and when my eyes finally cleared and my pulse returned to a more natural rhythm, I opened my mouth to ask them. But all attempts at speech failed. I'd been struck dumb yet again. Or, more accurately, I'd been dumb for a while—at least since meeting the Anderson sisters.

I inhaled deeply, exhaled slowly, and waited. At last, when I could think straight, I first considered what I wanted to do to the Anderson sisters. No point in going into details. And, after that, I focused on how calculating the old ladies were.

Following Samantha Berg's death, they must have dangled Vern in front of law enforcement. And when the cops refused to bite, they had no choice but to wait. Three years later, when I came to town, the old girls cast him out again, this time, in my direction. They wiggled their lines but didn't overplay them. If anything, they held back some. "Emme, we don't know if it would be prudent to say who we think killed Samantha." Yep, they held back just enough to convince me they were on to something.

But did they really dislike Vern and his family so much that they wanted him arrested for a crime he didn't commit? Apparently so. And if they couldn't get him arrested, did they truly hope to get a damning newspaper article published about him? Evidently. And who was the fool who was supposed to make all that happen? Well, that would be me.

I gritted my teeth. I was enraged and mortified at the same time. The plunge from dogged conviction to abject humiliation had been swift but anything but painless. The fact is both my chest and my feelings hurt something awful.

"But you deserve it," I mumbled. "You can be such a guppy at times!" I leaned back and stared down at my Size 10 feet while pulling at my orange hair. Guppy, hell, I was a damn clown fish!

Part Three

Combine the Meat and Noodles and Mix in the Soup and Seasonings

Chapter Twenty-Four

After Father Daley returned to the bar, Margie and I sat alone in our booth in the cafe. We didn't say much. Margie knew nothing about my theory regarding Vern, so she wasn't upset with me for suspecting him of murder. She was simply quiet.

As for me? Well, I was still smarting from being bamboozled by the Anderson sisters. I didn't want to believe that three old ladies had taken me for a ride. But I guess they had. I saw no evidence of anyone else in the car.

I longed to hold the old girls accountable for everything that had happened, though I knew I had to assume some of the blame. The people of Kennedy had been nice to me. Yet I had wasted no time accusing them, one after another, of being murderers, accessories after the fact, or otherwise in cahoots. Margie was my host, for God's sake, but even that hadn't stopped me from offering her up as a suspect. Yep, I too was responsible for what had happened and how lousy I felt. No doubt about it, self-awareness can be a bitch.

For years, I had dreamed of becoming a big-time investigative reporter. And when I came to Kennedy, I got my chance, only to discover I wasn't any good at it. Or more to the point, I wasn't any good at mistrusting people. And that posed a problem since mistrust—or, at a minimum, cynicism—seemed to be a job requirement. And in all probability, my deficit in that regard had led me to get sucked in by the Anderson sisters.

Yep, just one more addition to the list of "Investigative Skills I Lack." I could pencil it in right below "patience." As I said before, my deficiency in that area undoubtedly explained my earlier rush to judgment regarding Ole.

I shuffled in my seat, attempting to refrain from sliding any farther into the funk developing like quicksand all around me. Believing in people and being spontaneous weren't bad traits. I tossed that line around in my head as if it were a tow rope, meant to pull me back from the brink of despair. It didn't work. The rope must have snapped.

Overtaken by melancholy and out of similes to describe how I felt, I sought relief by doing what I do best. Or, rather, second best. I chased my worries away. Of course I would have preferred to bury them under a mountain of brownies, but I didn't spot any or possess the emotional strength to go in search of them. So, instead, I settled for banishing all negative thoughts. That's right, Scarlett O'Hara had nothing on me. Well, nothing other than a plantation, two guys who loved her, and an eighteen-inch waist.

With my heart riding low in my chest, I distracted myself with the signs on the wall above my booth. The first, crudely written in thick, black marker, advertised a local farmer's need for truck drivers for the upcoming beet harvest. Perhaps I'd quit journalism, learn to drive a truck, and apply for the job. But what about after harvest? Then what?

I moved on, noting I wasn't much of a Scarlett O'Hara.

The next sign, professionally produced, displayed red letters against a multi-colored background. It announced that the County Center for the Arts was to present *The Sound of Music* the following week.

I hated *The Sound of Music.* I saw the movie for the first and only time while attending Our Lady of Perpetual Light Middle School, where Sister Grace was my music teacher and idol.

She was intelligent and beautiful and very godly. In my opinion back then, she was the epitome of sisterhood and the antitheses of Julie Andrews's movie character, who went so far as to break her vows just to marry Mr. Von Trapp. And Margie thought Samantha Berg was a tramp!

I stared at the poster. Maybe I should join a convent. Then I wouldn't have to worry about a career or romance. I'd simply do whatever I was told and take lots of cold showers.

Yeah, like that would work. More than likely there wouldn't be enough well water for all the showers I'd need. And on my first day, Mother Superior would probably issue an order, and I'd ask a bunch of questions and end up in trouble, just like in high school.

In truth, I really didn't do anything terribly wrong in high school. Mostly, I just questioned things—a lot. When I was younger, my parents encouraged it. But after I got older and my folks were no longer around, my curiosity was often seen as annoying. At times, extremely annoying.

On second thought, perhaps I'd be better off establishing my own convent. Then I could dig an extra deep well and wouldn't have to take orders from anyone else. Yeah, I could buy a cheap house here in Kennedy and call it "Our Lady of the Arctic."

The bar erupted in cheers, putting an end to my tongue-in-cheek musing. Two men had begun to sing Mac Davis's "Oh, Lord, It's Hard to Be Humble," prompting Margie to set her cup on the table, a look of unexpected delight on her face. "Buford and Buddy must be here," she said. "That's their theme song, ya might say." She eased from the booth and brushed the front of her tee-shirt. "Come on. Let's go watch 'em."

Not waiting for a response, she hurried toward the hall, and I had no choice but to angle from my seat and trail after her.

* * *

WE PASSED TWO BATHROOMS and a coatroom before entering a banquet room reminiscent of a church basement. Like the hallway, the banquet room was paneled in faux wood, with florescent lights hanging from the dingy, acoustical-tiled ceiling. At the back, adults sat around long tables, alternating between eating and scolding their children. For the most part, the kids disregarded what they were being told in favor of pushing metal folding chairs across the vinyl floor and spilling paper cups of lemonade. Up front, Buddy and Buford sang on a slightly elevated stage, while three young women watched starry-eyed from a small, hardwood dance floor that flowed into the bar.

Margie mouthed that the young man stage right was Buddy, and the other was Buford, though her help with identification wasn't necessary. Buddy had a shock of wavy, dark hair with thick eyebrows to match, while Buford was evidently attempting to hide his bald head beneath a faded, purple, Minnesota Vikings' baseball cap. As for the scaly patches of burnt skin on his cheeks or his lack of eyebrows? Well, there was no hiding that. Yes, for the time being anyhow, Buddy was movie-star handsome, while Buford had a face only a mother or, in this case, an aunt could love.

Appearances aside, the twins were equal in their enthusiasm. Both sang with gusto. "Oh, Lord, it's hard to be humble, when you're perfect in every way. I can't wait to look in the mirror 'cause I get better lookin' each day." That last line led the women in front of the stage and most of the folks bellied up to the bar to cheer wildly until Buford removed his cap and bowed. When the noise died down, the duo sang on, their voices surprisingly full and controlled. "To know me is to love me. I must be one hell of a man." And nearly everyone in the place joined in for the refrain, "Oh, Lord, it's hard to be humble, but I'm doing the best that I can."

As the boys moved on to the second verse, I let my eyes stray. While in the bar earlier, I'd been on a mission to calm my nerves after "visiting" with Vivian. A daunting task. As a result, I hadn't paid any attention to my surroundings. But now I saw that the bar was a cavernous place, punctuated only by the light fixture above the pool table and the neon beer signs affixed to the dark, wood walls. It also smelled of stale beer and cigarettes.

Smoking has been banned in Minnesota bars and restaurants for years, but I suspected the "V" wasn't very strict about enforcement. Or maybe it was, but smoke from the past had penetrated the walls and furnishings so deeply that the place would always smell like . . . well, a bar.

My gaze came to rest on John Deere, his pal, and Shitty, the three of them perched on stools along the glossy, L-shaped counter, their feet resting on a tarnished, brass rail. They were visiting with Jim, the banker/VFW manager/bartender, who was far too busy mixing drinks and opening beer bottles to add much to the conversation.

On the short end of the counter, a woman sat alone and spoke to no one as she added to the pile of discarded pull tabs in front of her. My thoughts turned to the little Nelson girls, and a lump of disgust lodged in my throat. I looked away.

The Donaldson brothers were on the opposite end of the room, one of them hunched over the pool table, racking the balls for their next game. Behind them, Father Daley sat at a table shrouded in darkness. He was playing cards with three guys I couldn't make out. And next to him stood an odd-looking character. It took some squinting on my part, but I finally recognized the "character" as the life-size, wooden, Precious Moments' minister Margie had told me about. The one her sister, Vivian, had made for Little Val's wedding.

I pointed out my find, leading Margie to bend her head in my direction. She then raised her voice above the din to say, "Father Daley jokes that they're friends. He brings him out of the coatroom whenever he's here." She lifted her head only to angle it toward me again. "The wooden bride and groom are still in there." She nodded toward the coatroom. "Before the night's through, they'll be arranged in all kinds of positions, some of which would even make Dr. Ruth blush. All courtesy of Buddy and Buford."

I chuckled, noting I felt a whole lot better. Sure, I'd been played for a fool by the Anderson sisters, but it wasn't the end of the world. Yes, they'd hurt my pride. And, yes, I now was fully aware that the career of my dreams would never be anything more than that—a dream not to be realized. But the day could have turned out a whole lot worse. I could have gone public with my suspicions regarding Vern. That would have really sucked. That would have been downright God-awful.

In my head, I kicked myself in the ass—not an easy feat. *Don't be so melodramatic, Emme.* It was one of the tougher voices in my head. *You never really wanted to be an investigative journalist anyway. You merely convinced yourself you 'should' be one. But it's time you stop allowing the disappointments of your past to dictate your future. There are lots of jobs out there. Meaningful jobs. Some even in the news business. You'll find one. And until then, you can keep copying down recipes. It's not so bad.* Shitty stood nearby. *It's got to be better than cleaning sewers.* And with that, the voice fell silent, leaving me amazed by its perceptiveness.

As for the twins, they finished their performance to a rousing ovation before Margie caught their attention and urged them over with a wag of her finger.

By my calculation, the guys were twenty-two or twenty-three and lean but hard-bodied, most likely from physical labor out on the farm. Buddy wore a light-blue denim work shirt, slightly fitted but untucked, the sleeves rolled up to his elbows. Burnt Buford was dressed in a white cotton henley. Both had barbed-wire tattoos around the midpoints of their left forearms and leather boots that peeked out from beneath their faded jeans. As I said, Buford wasn't much to look at, but Buddy was handsome enough to help me and every other woman on the planet forget our troubles for more than a night.

"Hi, Margie," Buddy said as Buford greeted his aunt with a mere bob of his head. Both men then locked eyes with me, the stranger in town.

"Boys, I want you to meet Emerald Malloy. She's a reporter from the Minneapolis paper. She's here to write about me and my recipes."

"That's cool," Buford replied, blinking his lashless eyes at his aunt. "You're going to make the paper without cutting off a limb or anything."

"Oh, stop that," Margie scolded with very little conviction.

Buddy dismissed his aunt and his brother with a shake of his head and then shook my hand. His touch sent a chill up my arm, but he didn't seem to notice, so I pretended I didn't either. He simply went on to introduce himself and his burnt brother by saying, "Buford's nice enough. But if he invites you to join him for a barbecue, you may want to decline."

I giggled. That's right. I giggled. "I've heard a lot about you two from your aunt, but she failed to tell me what incredible entertainers you are." Yep, even when down on myself and out of sorts, I can rally long enough to flirt. Troubling but true.

"Well, we do what we have to," Buddy answered, and his burnt brother added, "And I have to get me a beer. My throat's parched."

Margie stiffened and glared.

And that, in turn, led me to take a shot at lightening what I thought might quickly turn into a tense situation. As I said earlier, I don't handle conflict very well. It causes me distress. And I didn't need any more distress. "Um . . . I noticed you guys have groupies." I nodded at the young women who'd been watching the twins up close during their performance. At present, they were lurking in a nearby corner. "Are your girlfriends among them?"

Buddy canted his head, "Doubt it. Last I saw, Buford's girlfriend was sprawled out on the closet floor. She'd sprung a leak and was pretty much deflated."

"Oh, bite me," Buford growled.

And Margie scolded, "Enough!" Her voice was kind of frosty for August. "Now tell me, have you two eaten?"

"That's where we're headed right now," Buddy replied. From his tone, I gathered this was a common line of questioning, and he knew exactly how to respond. "Jim has a roaster full of Wild Rice Hot Dish behind the bar, and we're on our way to get some."

"Along with a beer," Buford added wryly, snapping and popping his fingers against the palm of his hand. "My throat's so dry I swear it's been on fire."

With a groan, Buddy back-handed his brother before asking me, "You hanging around for a while?"

"Yeah, I'll be here all night."

"Good." Buddy flashed me a half smile.

It was one of those crooked, sexy, bad-boy smiles, which should have appealed to me. I was usually drawn to bad boys. Remember Boo-Boo? But this time, I reacted differently. This time I felt a rumble of unease inside of me. At least I thought it was unease.

"That's real good," Buddy repeated. "Maybe we can dance later."

More rumbling. It was unease all right. "Um . . . maybe." I gulped down an amassing sense of dread and scanned the room for an out. Buddy Johnson was extremely handsome, and I loved to dance, but I didn't want to dance with him. My instincts were advising me against it. And while I normally dismissed my instincts, I felt bound to listen to them in this instance.

That's right. For the second time in a day, I was going along with my common sense. Maybe all my therapy was at last paying off. Maybe my emotions were beginning to catch up to my intellect. One could only hope.

But this wasn't the time for speculation. I was busy. I was on a mission. I was intent on finding an excuse so I wouldn't need to spend one-on-one time with Buddy Johnson.

Another peek at him, though, and I reconsidered. Dark, sun-kissed skin and a strong, chiseled jaw. Not to mention, a small cleft in his chin, undoubtedly a mark made by God to signify some of his better work. So tell me again, why shouldn't I want to be alone with him?

The rumbling, a little voice from inside my head reminded me. *The rumbling.*

Oh, yeah. I turned away and pressed my eyes into action, permitting them to rest only after they'd accomplished their mission of finding me a way out of my current predicament. They circled the room once, then twice, finally perching on the empty stage. "Just one problem," I said to Buddy, my finger pointed at the vacant platform, "no band." I did my best to convey an air of disappointment, but it was difficult given I was filled with relief. "Sorry."

He merely offered up another devil-may-care grin. "No need to apologize, Emerald." Motioning to the back door, he added with a wink, "Here comes the band now."

The door squeaked open, and a sense of foreboding welled up in my chest. "Oh, how lucky for us," I replied with as much enthusiasm as a cat in a room full of rockers. It was one of my dad's favorite sayings, but not even invoking his memory made me feel any better.

Chapter Twenty-Five

SEVERAL PEOPLE BUMPED THROUGH the back door of the bar. They carried instrument cases, drums, and audio equipment.

"Well, I'll be," Margie said, "that's Little Val and Wally's band. They must be fillin' in tonight."

As the musicians meandered toward the stage, I noticed a young, dark-haired woman lugging a giant, encased, bass fiddle. "Is that . . . ?"

"Yah," Margie replied, "that's Rosa. And the blonde with the baby bump is Little Val."

She went on to inform me that the man with the pinwheel bald spot and the Adam's apple that looked like he'd swallowed the fruit whole was Wally, Little Val's husband. The older guy with the nickel-gray pony tail, carting the bass drum, was Tom, the high school band director and husband to Barbie, the newspaper editor. And while the last guy looked familiar, I couldn't place him until Margie reminded me that he was the mayor. I'd met him in the café when I first arrived in town. She explained that in addition to his civic duties, he played guitar in the band and, during the day, worked as an accountant.

After Buddy assured me he'd be back later—much to my chargin—the twins made a beeline for the bar. And about that same time, Barbie lumbered in, the door slamming behind her. She was weighted down by a bulky, black amplifier. It teetered in her arms until her husband came to her aid.

Pawning the piece of equipment off on him, she surveyed the place and ultimately proceeded in our direction.

Someone then hollered for Margie from the hallway, leading her to return to the café after assuring me she'd be back in a "jiffy." Now, I've never known the length of a "jiffy" but was positive that under the circumstances, it was way too long for my liking, regardless of its measure. Considering how my earlier conversation with Barbie had ended, I had no desire to be alone with her again, no matter the length of time.

"Hello," Barbie said, finger combing her spiked, cranberry hair.

Without pause, I replied, "Margie was called away but should be right back."

"Well, I'm glad I caught you alone. I wanted to apologize." Barbie clasped her hands together, her eyes remorseful looking, like those of a basset hound, a makeup-wearing basset hound. "I'm sorry I snapped at you this afternoon. It was rude of me." She waved her arms for emphasis. "It's just that when drumming up businesses and new residents for this area, I espouse the virtues of small-town living, high among them, the low crime rate. Talk of that murder undercuts my sales pitch."

I was impressed by her candor. "I understand. I was only curious." Okay, I wasn't as forthcoming. Big deal. "I'm sure you can appreciate that, you being a journalist too."

A slight nod suggested she did. "For quite some time after Samantha Berg's body was discovered, I hounded everyone with questions." She shifted her weight from one foot to the other, her flip-flops still in place, her toenails painted the same dark red as her fingernails. "But after a while, I saw what my questions and the police investigation were doing to these folks. They were becoming suspicious of one another. Rumors were flying." She flapped her arms. "It was ugly."

I knew what she meant. In less than a day, I'd become dismayed and disappointed over how I was thinking about the people in this town, and I didn't even know most of them.

"I realize my attitude may seem cold," she acknowledged, "but the case was tearing this place apart, and we can't have that. There's so few of us up here, we have to stick together."

She played with the glasses that hung from the gold chain around her neck, the pair on top of her head earlier now nowhere in sight. "Admittedly, when Samantha first vanished, I didn't feel all that bad. I figured it was merely the cosmos restoring moral order. But after her body was discovered and everyone began finger pointing, I became disheartened. And by the time the police and the FBI finished their initial investigation, I just wanted life to return to normal. Most folks did. That's why we vowed to put the whole mess behind us and move on."

I reflected on that. "If that's true, why did Margie open up about it to me?"

Barbie narrowed her eyes. "Her brother died a few weeks ago. It stirred up a lot of memories and emotions." She tapped her index finger against her maroon-colored lips. "She's working to make sense of everything that happened back then. She's not sure about some of the views she held."

"Really? She was pretty sure of herself when she spoke to me about those days. She made it abundantly clear that she loved Ole and his wife and hated Samantha Berg for coming between them."

Barbie granted me a faint smile. "Well, she certainly wanted Ole and Lena to get back together and live happily ever after. But it wasn't meant to be."

"Because Lena died." I was stating the obvious, but it seemed appropriate.

"That's what Margie would like to believe. But I doubt it would have happened regardless. See, Lena loved Ole, but she told me more than once that love isn't always enough."

"So she was a tough broad too." I meant to keep that comment to myself, but it somehow snuck out.

"I don't know how tough she was." Barbie pinned her gaze on something far away—or maybe long ago. "She died of a broken heart."

Hmm. Margie had said the same thing. And it now caused me to wonder if I'd ever love someone so much that losing him would literally break my heart. My parents probably shared that kind of love. If they hadn't perished together, the survivor may have succumbed to a broken heart. The idea was sweet and, at the same time, disturbing in a Romeo-and-Juliet sort of way. But more than that, it was immaterial since both my parents were already gone.

"Well, let's concentrate on Ole," I suggested, knowing I'd be steadier emotionally if I limited our conversation to subjects that wouldn't instantly remind me of my own parents' demise. "Why did he cheat on Lena in the first place? According to Margie, it was some kind of mid-life crisis. Is that what you think?"

Barbie gnawed on her bottom lip. "It's possible. But I believe it was something else."

"What exactly?"

She continued to bite her lip as if it were lunch. "Well, um . . ." she stammered, "Lena thought Ole might have been . . . um . . . sick."

"Sick? With what?"

Red blotches formed on her neck. "A mental illness of sorts."

"A mental illness that caused him to have an affair?" Skepticism was clearly registered in my voice.

"Of course not." The blotches migrated to her cheeks. "At least not directly. But some of those illnesses can play havoc with a person's judgment. If left unchecked, the results can be devastating."

I wasn't sure if I could buy what she was selling. "Why didn't Margie mention any of this to me?"

She shifted her feet as if part of her wanted to walk away. "She'd never do that. I only knew because Lena and I were friends. She shared her suspicions with me because my husband has the same kind of problem she thought Ole had." She peered at me, apparently attempting to gauge any further reaction on my part. Having no idea what to think, I didn't express anything.

And after leaning against the wall and defensively crossing her arms, she continued. "Mental illness routinely runs in families, and Ole's Aunt Harriet has exhibited symptoms most of her adult life. But back in her younger days, no one went to the doctor for that kind of thing. My mom, who grew up with her, said folks either considered her 'grumpy' or 'wild,' depending on her mood."

The corners of Barbie's eyes crinkled in muted laughter. "Mom used to tell me some outrageous stories." She glanced to her right, then her left, before proceding. "I suppose this really isn't funny, and I shouldn't repeat it, but I can't help myself given how crotchety that old lady is now."

She stepped closer and lowered her voice to a mere whisper. "One time, years ago, when Harriet and her sisters were at the national curling championship, she was really out of control, not thinking right at all." Another glance around the room. "Well, following the awards' ceremony, she stripped naked and streaked across the rink."

Again I imagined the Anderson sisters gliding across a sheet of ice in their sensible black shoes, their bags of stolen goodies hanging from their shoulders. Only this time Harriet was as bare as the day she was born, although her breasts still sagged to her knees, like deflated party balloons, and the wind still whistled through her mustache and . . . I winced.

Barbie grew more reflective. "Then, years later, someone caught her coming out of the former Lutheran minister's parsonage early one morning, her hair and clothes in complete disarray. She was in her early seventies by then, so I guess that really wasn't all that funny." A beat later, she amended that statement. "In fact, it was pretty sad." Another beat. "Yeah, Reverend Swenson was a jerk for taking advantage of her like that."

"Did he know she had issues?"

Barbie arched her penciled brows. "He should have. By that point in her life, Harriet wasn't exactly 'Girls Gone Wild' material. Nope, she was normally quiet. When she wasn't, it was plain to see she wasn't thinking straight."

She wiggled her finger at me. "It happened shortly after we moved back here. Lena talked to Tom and me about it because we had always been open about our own situation."

She unfolded her arms. "Lena was so angry with Reverend Swenson, I thought she was going to hand him his asshole to wear around his neck in place of that religious collar of his."

I shoved that image from my mind, afraid it would otherwise haunt me for days.

"What about Ole?" I asked. "Did Lena ever confront him about his issues?"

"Oh, yeah, but he refused to see a doctor, almost to the day Lena died."

Again Barbie leaned against the wall, this time propping it up with her shoulder. "His sisters weren't any help either. Margie and Vivian made excuses for him. On a few occasions, they even went so far as to blame Lena for the problems in their marriage."

She lifted her chin. "Now don't get me wrong. Lena was no saint. To the contrary. She could be a real hard-ass, especially where Ole was concerned."

I still wasn't sure what to think. Barbie's remarks definitely raised a lot of questions. Some I'd have to ponder. Others I could ask right away. So that's what I did. "Well, how did Margie and Vivian explain Harriet's behavior?"

Barbie twisted her bottom lip while holding it between her thumb and forefinger. "They said Harriet's problem was nothing like Ole's. They blamed Ole's trouble on booze but said Harriet, who's never had a drink in her life, was just plain nuts. They said there's a nut or two in every family."

I had to agree with them on that. From what I'd gathered, Ole had developed a drinking problem during a mid-life crisis, while Harriet had been dealing with psychological issues most of her life. "Well . . ."

Barbie shook her head defiantly in answer to my unspoken skepticism. "I know what I know. And now Margie's wondering about it too."

I wasn't sure what to say. I didn't want to make her angry again. Still, I wasn't one to take stock in arm-chair analysis, which was exactly what she was peddling. Bottom line, Ole was never professionally diagnosed with any type of mental illness. I stopped short as a notion teased my brain. Then again, neither was Harriet. Hmm.

The band was setting up, and among them, Tom, Barbie's husband. I watched as he positioned his drums. I'm not sure what I expected to see, but I didn't spot anything out of the ordinary. He didn't appear any different from anyone else. Not that he would, I suppose.

"How's your husband now?" My curiosity was comingled with confusion regarding a health condition I knew nothing about.

"Oh, he's fine," Barbie waved her hand, as if that would further convince me. "After he decided to take control of his life, he came to Minnesota to dry out. He'd self-prescribed alcohol to treat his other issue, so he ended up with two serious problems." She grimaced.

"Through treatment at Hazelden, he got hooked up with a therapist he still sees once a month. He got sober, began taking his medication faithfully, and went back to school. After he finished his music degree, he got his teaching license.

"That's how I met him. I interviewed him for the university's paper. You know the story: 'Rocker Gives Up Everything for Life Anew.'" She swept the air with her hands like she was reading a banner tied to the back of a plane.

"Rocker?"

"Yeah, he played drums for some well-known bands when he was in California. But the music industry isn't exactly conducive to healthy living."

I gazed at Tom. He was an interesting-looking guy. His face was heavily creased, giving him a tired look, but he smiled easily. He wore a sleeveless tee-shirt, cut-off jeans, and Birkenstock sandals. A peace sign was tattooed on his right arm, near his shoulder, and silver posts dotted his earlobes. "He never resented giving up his old life style?" His arms and legs were thin, although he carried extra weight around his middle. He didn't seem to mind. He munched on a homemade Nut Goodie Bar, another waiting on a napkin on his snare drum.

"If he hadn't changed his life, he'd be in jail right now, or a hospital, or possibly the morgue." Barbie spoke without sentiment. "So no, I don't think he has any regrets."

"Well, I'm glad he got himself straightened out."

"Oh, don't let me give you the wrong impression." Her hands poked at the air like she was groping for the right words. "It . . . um . . . hasn't been easy, and it certainly hasn't been perfect. He's had . . . um . . . his share of set-backs, and he'll struggle with demons the rest of his life." By the expression on her face, I could tell she was pondering something. "Then again, who won't?" She paused, providing time for that philisophical tidbit to take root. "And all things considered, we've done pretty damn well. I like to think the experience has made us better people. More understanding. More forgiving. Less serious."

"Less serious?"

"For sure. If we can't laugh at some of this, we'd cry all day." She glimpsed at the stage, captured her husband's attention, and blew him a kiss.

He flashed her a smile in return. It was a great smile. It originated in his eyes and lit up his entire face.

"I hope I didn't bore you," she went on to say. "Like Margie, I've been thinking a lot about Ole lately. I suppose that's what people do when someone they care about dies before their time. They question things. They wonder if they could have done more."

"Is that what you think? You could have done more?"

She only briefly hesitated. "No. Tom and I did our best. I just have trouble—even to this day—accepting that he ever got involved with that tramp in the first place. God, she was a pig. She's the only person I've ever truly hated."

Barbie picked at her thumbnail, scraping polish from it. "She's the reason Lena died, you know." More scraping. "I miss that woman so much." She sighed heavily. "I swear I cried every day for a year after her death." She looked at me dead on, something she hadn't done much of during our conversation. "Finally, Tom convinced me to do what I could about the situation and then let the rest of it go. So that's what I did."

Chapter Twenty-Six

After Barbie excused herself to grab something to eat, I talked to John Deere and the other guys leaning against the bar. Then I visited the bathroom again. And when I was done in there and back out in the hallway, I noticed the café doors that served as entrance to the coatroom. According to Margie, the Precious Moments bride and groom were on the other side.

I glanced up and down the hall. No one seemed to be watching, so I stepped forward and gently pushed on the swinging doors. Yep, Buford and Buddy had struck again. The wooden figures were on the floor—together in the biblical sense—at least as together as two wooden figures could be. And while I couldn't see the bride's face, I had to admit the groom looked incredibly happy.

Oddly embarrassed, I stepped back and let the doors swing shut. Then once again I scanned the hall. Spotting no one and no one seemingly spotting me, I tugged at my shirt, pushed my hair behind my ears, and nonchalantly shuffled into the café.

As planned, Barbie was there, at the counter, waiting for me. The place was otherwise deserted.

"Margie was just in here," she informed me. "She said Vivian visited with you earlier. Why didn't you tell me?"

"What was I to say?"

We each grabbed a stool, Barbie's butt barely brushing the vinyl before she dug into her dinner, a mish-mash of left-over hot dishes. "Well, how'd it go?"

I checked over both shoulders and spoke quietly. "I didn't talk about it because I didn't want Margie to get angry with me for trashing her sister. But the truth is I had to run away. And even though it's been a while, my head still hurts from listening to her."

Barbie snickered. "Yeah, Vivian has that effect on people. She thinks she sounds smart by speaking like that."

"Well, I think she sounds ridiculous."

"You and me both."

Barbie speared another clump of food. "God, I'm starving. Must be from all the typing I did this afternoon."

"Did you finish your stories?"

"Yeah." She frowned. "No thanks to you."

I rapped her forearm. "You're kind of owlish when you're hungry, aren't you?"

With a glint in her eyes, she returned to her dinner.

I, on the other hand, rewound our previous conversation, stopping when I got to the part where Barbie said that Vivian and Margie blamed Lena for the problems in her marriage to Ole. The remark had been bothering me, like an itch I couldn't quite scratch. To get any relief, I knew I had to ask about it, so I decided to do just that.

"Barbie, in spite of what you told me, I can't imagine Margie and her sister joining forces against anyone, much less Lena. Not the way Margie slams Vivian almost every chance she gets. Which, by the way, I understand perfectly now that I've met Vivian. But anyhow, what's the real deal there?"

Barbie pointed her fork at my nose. "Emme, don't forget, blood's thicker than water. Margie may talk trash about her siblings, but no one else better." She went back to her food.

"Well, I wish I'd known that this afternoon."

"Why? Did you say something bad to Margie about Vivian?"

"Nooo." I drew out the lone syllable. "Not Vivian. Ole."

Barbie looked confused, so I tried to set her straight by explaining how I'd implied to Margie that Ole was the most likely suspect in Samantha Berg's murder case.

She didn't even attempt to hide her amusement. "Margie must really like you or want her story in that paper of yours because she's banned people from the café for far less than that."

"That's not the worst of it." I eyed the room for something sweet. Did I mention that sugar helps to ease the discomfort that routinely accompanies unpleasant conversations? I believe it's a scientific fact. But the only treat I saw teetered on the far side of Barbie's plate. And since I was pretty sure she'd object if I reached in front of her and snatched it away, I went without. "I have a few other confessions to make too." Sweets or no sweets, I had to unburden myself.

"Wait a minute." Barbie raised her hand. "Let me go get Father Daley."

"No!" I yanked her arm down. "I already made an ass out of myself in front of him."

She appeared bemused. "How so?"

"Well, after I learned from Deputy Ryden—"

She slapped her hand against the counter. "Hold on! You met Deputy Frisk Me Please?"

I rolled my eyes. "Margie introduced us. She had him sit with me during dinner because the cafe was so crowded. Or so I thought. I didn't know about the banquet room at the time."

Barbie rested her elbows on the counter, one on each side of her plate, her fingers knitted together in front of her face. "God, I love that woman. Every time I think she's messed things up for me with that big mouth of hers, she goes and does something wonderful. I never even thought of using Randy to entice you into moving here."

I made a pained face. "Don't get too excited. I scared him off. I tend to do that to men. That's why I'm opening a convent."

"A convent?"

"Yep."

Barbie smirked. "Is your love life really that bad?"

"You wouldn't believe . . . But it's more than my personal life. I'm confused about my career too."

I caught her grinning smartly, as if she knew something I didn't. "That's because deep down you want to relocate and work for me. The realization just hasn't made it to your conscious mind yet."

I rolled my eyes again. "Seriously, I thought I had my professional life all figured out, but now . . ." Since there was no easy way to articulate my frustration, I let the words tumble out, hoping they'd fall into some sort of logical order along the way. "After Deputy Ryden told me that Ole had an alibi for the night Samantha was murdered, I decided the killer had to be Vern because that's what Margie's aunts claimed. And while I warned myself not to believe anything they said, I kind of did just that."

"You got taken in by those three?" Barbie rubbed her hands together. "This is just too damn good."

"Stop that! It's not funny."

Her lips took a sympathetic turn, though it was clearly less than genuine, given the smile in her eyes. "Emme, I learned a long time ago you have to take everything those old girls say with a grain a salt. A shot of tequila and a slice of lime aren't bad ideas either."

I heaved air like a slashed tire—Boo-Boo's slashed tires. "And later, when Margie introduced me to Father Daley, I mistrusted him right from the start too. In part because he had such a high opinion of Vern, but also because I'm Catholic but not a very good one."

"So?"

"So that causes me a lot of guilt, which I suspect screws up my intuition and judgment when it comes to things like priests. On top of that, your Father Daley is a rarity."

Without a doubt, Barbie was wrestling with her emotions. It seemed she didn't want to laugh but was having a hard time holding her giggles in check. She repeatedly bit the inside of her cheek, the indentation clearly visible. "You've had a tough day, haven't you?"

There wasn't an ounce of sincerity in her voice, but I didn't care. I was in a lousy mood and willing to take any measure of sympathy, real or manufactured.

"Yeah, well, after Father Daley advised me that the old ladies had once before tried to frame Vern, I felt terrible for what I'd been thinking about him, as well as a bunch of other people. Like you said, it's not good to go around questioning everyone's character. It caused me to question my own. Not something I enjoyed." My shoulders slumped. "That's why I'm done with investigative journalism. Hell, I'm not even sure I want to be a journalist of any kind."

"Hence, the nun talk?"

"I was joking." I thought about it some more. The celibacy thing would be a bummer—a definte bummer. "Yeah, I'm almost positive I was joking."

She patted my shoulder. "Don't be so hard on yourself, Emme." Her tone was now truly consoling. "You don't know these people, so it's not all that strange that you wondered about them. Me on the other hand?" She took a breath so deep it stretched the limits of her spandex tank top. "I grew up with most of them. Even so, when Samantha's body was found, I kept right on thinking that this one or that one was the killer. It was terrible of me." She stopped for a second. "Hell, for a while, I even believed Vivian was the culprit. Of course she wasn't. I guess being a pain in the ass doesn't automatically make you guilty of murder." She threw up her hands. "Who knew?"

Barbie bit into the bar that had been taunting me from the corner of her plate. It was a Seven Layer Bar. I first became acquainted with that particular treat in my youth. My mother made them. They were one of my father's favorites. Another quick look around. Nope, none had miraculously appeared.

"So why'd you suspect Vivian?"

A second big bite and her bar was history. She washed it down with coffee. "She wouldn't account for her whereabouts on the night of Samantha's disappearance." She set her cup back down. "Considering how angry she was with the tramp for wrecking her brother's family and hurting his children, I assumed she'd done her in. But eventually, she owned up to where she'd been."

"Which was?"

She traced the rim of the cup with her finger. "With a guy everyone calls Mr. President."

She definitely knew how to get my attention. "I heard about him. Deputy Ryden pointed him out at dinner."

"Did he tell you that the two of them, that is Vivian and Mr. President, have some kind of thing going, something that's been sparking for years?"

Just when I thought she couldn't surprise me anymore, she did just that. "You mean an affair?"

She shook her entire body, as if having a seizure. "Don't say that. Pictures pop into my head, and I can't get rid of them. Then I can't sleep, which leaves me exhausted and edgy the next day.

"Anyhow, I don't think either of them is interested in sex. It's more of a mutual admiration society. She tells him how wonderful he is, and he reciprocates. She's one of his allies on the school board. She believes that if she helps him pass his President Hanson petition—a whole other story—she'll get to be First Lady or something."

"Really?"

"No, I'm just shittin' you again."

I rolled my eyes, this time all the way to the back of my head. It actually hurt a little. "If there wasn't anything going on between them, why didn't she come clean right away?"

Barbie leaned forward and tented her fingers in front of her chest. "She was scared. Vern hates the guy and doesn't like Vivian anywhere near him. But she finds him so damn irresistible she can't help herself."

I rubbed the corners of my eyes. They seemed okay. But I had to stop with that whole eye-rolling thing. "Were their whereabouts confirmed?"

"Oh, yeah. At the time Samantha disappeared, they were having dinner and drinks in Grafton, about forty minutes from here. When Vern found out, he hit the ceiling."

It was my turn to lean in. "That was hypocritical of him, don't you think? According to the police, he spent a lot of time at Samantha's house. So why shouldn't Vivian—"

"He only went there to demand that she leave Rosa alone. You see, Samantha got a kick out of mocking the girl. And Vern despised her for it. He even threatened her. Because of that, he was the cops' prime suspect when Samantha's body was first discovered. But I never thought he was guilty."

She tilted her chin toward the ceiling and spoke with authority. "If he had killed her, he would have been inconspicuous about it. Yet that night he stopped in the 'V' before going to her house and hung out here in the café afterwards. Those aren't the actions of a guilty man. Still, the cops put him through the wringer." She twisted her lips. "Just goes to show that no good deed goes unpunished. He helped Rosa and ended up paying a hefty price for it."

"But, Barbie, doesn't it bother you that the murder was never solved? Don't you wonder who did it and if they're still around?"

She again ran her finger along the rim of her coffee cup, allowing close to a minute to go by before answering, "I guess I try not to think about it."

I was about to jump all over her for making such a comment but got interrupted by another question. It was posed over a microphone down the hall, in the bar. "Where's Emerald Malloy? Emerald Malloy, our guest from the Twin Cities? Where is she?"

"Who's that?" I asked.

"Well, I believe it's you." Barbie snickered.

"Very funny." My voice was filled with sarcasm. "I mean who's asking?"

"It sounds like Father Daley. And if I'm not mistaken, he'd like you to join him in the bar."

"For what?"

She pushed her plate away. "I don't know. But he's stubborn. If you don't go, he'll just keep hollering."

"How mortifying." I covered my face.

"Oh, go on. See what he wants."

I spread my fingers apart, peeking out between them. "No way. As I said before, he doesn't trust me. I don't think he likes me."

She brushed away my concern along with some of her dessert crumbs. "You're being paranoid. Father Daley's a good guy. He probably just wants to introduce you to everyone."

I wanted to believe her but was afraid. "I don't know."

"Miss Malloy, where are you?" The priest's voice was loud without a microphone. With one, it was booming.

"Oh, come on, I'll go with you."

"Okay. But if he accuses me of having nefarious reasons for being in town, I'll . . ." I let the sentence fade. He was a priest. What was I going to do?

Barbie spun around on her stool. "He won't accuse you of anything 'nefarious.' But we aren't stupid. We all know you'd love to get a story about Samantha Berg's murder while you're here." She got up and headed toward the hallway.

"That's not true." I slid off my stool and trudged after her. "I don't want to be an investigative reporter anymore. I'm not sure I want to be a reporter of any kind. Hell, I may not even stay in the news business."

"Oh, right, I almost forgot," she replied over her shoulder. "You're going to open a convent."

With a laugh, she entered the banquet room and headed for the stage. "Well, come on, Sister Emme, let's go see what Father Daley wants."

Chapter Twenty-Seven

Everyone," Father Daley announced, "in addition to showing our love and support to Maureen Russell, our guest of honor, I'd like you to welcome another Irish lass. She's visiting from the Twin Cities, where she's a newspaper reporter. She's here to write an article about one of our own, Margie Johnson. That's right, isn't it, Emerald? You're here to do a story about Margie?"

I barely nodded, seeking to remain anonymous in a crowd where everyone knew everyone else. Needless to say, all eyes were on me, and for a moment, I contemplated running into the coatroom. I doubted the wooden bride and groom would even notice.

Father Daley continued. "Her name is Emerald Malloy." He waved his arm like a TV pitchman, giving rise to a smattering of applause and a shoulder squeeze from Barbie.

"See, he's just being friendly," she whispered. "You have nothing to worry about. Nothing at all"

I wasn't so sure. His words were pleasant enough, but I thought I heard an ominous undercurrent in his tone. And there was something in his eyes. What? I couldn't tell. Mistrust? Caution? An eyelash?

"With the help of my trusty fife," the priest went on to say, "I'm going to sing a Tom Russell number to Maureen and Emerald. And when I'm done, the band will take over. So here we go, a one and a two and . . ."

Maureen Russell walked up and shook my hand as Father Daley began, "When Irish Girls Grow Up," a folk song about the evils that await innocent Irish farm girls who move to the city. I knew the song because my dad often sang it when I was an adolescent. Afterward, I'd promise to live at home forever, and he'd laugh and pick me up and twirl me around.

In a strong, Irish-tenor voice, Father Daley sang, "Now, Darling, don't go to the city, you'll get lost there in the crowd. All the boys there in the city, they drink and smoke and talk too loud. And the women in the city, they sneak their whiskey from a cup. Oh, isn't it a pity when Irish girls grow up."

I'm not sure if it was the song and the memories it triggered or the fact that I was standing arm in arm with a woman who, by all accounts, was fighting a dreadful disease with great dignity. But something touched me deep inside, and a tear or two rolled down my cheeks.

Barbie nudged me, a tissue in hand. I accepted it and wiped my face as the three of us—Barbie, Maureen Russell, and me—swayed to the music. "Have you heard about the Cooneys, the Russells and Malloys? Their girls all left the farm and went to chase those city boys. Their mothers pray to Mary that the girls won't turn corrupt. Oh, isn't it a pity when Irish girls grow up."

Father Daley played his fife and sang two more verses. And when he was through, he stepped from the stage and joined us.

I thanked him for the "serenade" while silently scolding myself yet again for ever having been suspicious of him.

The priest replied that he was "honored" to sing to us "fine Irish lasses." Then he asked to speak with Maureen privately, and they strolled away, arm in arm.

Meanwhile, the band had begun its next number, a boogie that featured a brief instrumental solo by each member of the group. Wally led off on guitar, followed by Little Val on the keyboard. After that, Rosa took a turn, swiftly sliding her fingers along the bass fiddle, plucking the strings with such intensity that she actually looked possessed by the music.

Unlike Lena, who was reportedly outgoing, Rosa, her daughter, came across as guarded. She played with passion, but it wasn't willingly shared with her audience. Her face remained rigid, her focus entirely on her bass.

Yes, Rosa Johnson was beautiful in an exotic way, yet there was something mysterious about her too. "Rosa's quite a musician," I whispered to Barbie. "She's attractive too." As an afterthought, I added, "She must have lots of guys interested in her."

"That's what you'd expect," Barbie said, "but it's not the case. Deputy Ryden went out with her for a while, but it didn't work out."

I winced, though I thought I hid it well by pretending to scratch my shoulder. Damn afterthoughts!

"She doesn't perform with the band very often," Barbie explained. "I'm surprised she's even here tonight. But I suppose she wanted to be a part of the evening since Maureen was her classroom assistant until she had to quit because of the cancer."

Margie approached us from behind, draping her arms over our shoulders and hanging her head between our own. She dangled three open beer bottles from her hands. "Take one," she instructed, so that's what we did.

I sipped my beer and did my best to downplay what Barbie had just said. I barely knew the deputy, and I'd probably never see him again. So it didn't really matter who he dated. What's more, it sounded like they broke up. He probably turned out to be a jerk. Yeah, most likely, I was lucky he left the café when he did.

While I tried desperately to assure myself of all that, the band transitioned into an up-tempo country song that led folks to the dance floor, among them, burnt Buford and one of the women who'd been mooning over him during his duet with his brother.

I checked the rest of the room, praying that his twin had gone home or had otherwise forgotten all about me. I couldn't get past the uneasiness I felt around him. Nope, I had no desire to be his dance partner, even if the band was really good, as confirmed by my tapping foot and swaying hips. Of course I put the kibosh on my hip action before anyone noticed, but my foot continued to do its thing.

Thankfully, I didn't see Buddy anywhere, although I did spot Father Daley. He was back playing cards, seated next to Vern, with the Precious Moments minister still standing guard. I also saw Vivian and Maureen Russell. They were at a nearby table, paging through Vivian's cake album, while Mr. President sat at the far end of the bar, next to the Nelson girls' mother. He was ogling Vivian. The Donaldson brothers were at the bar too, surrounded by several people who were hollering and exchanging money. Someone yelled something about woodtick races, but I didn't ask for details. I had no desire to know.

I circled back to Barbie and Margie, my head bopping to the music while the steady hum of conversation filled my ears. Notwithstanding the prospect of games involving blood-sucking insects crawling on the bar, near the food, I was having a pretty good time. Well, at least as good as I could expect considering my career plans were pretty much in the shitter, and my prospects—professional and personal—were nil.

Getting depressed all over again, I tried to lose myself in the insistent beat of the drum and the bass guitar. But I guess I didn't try hard enough, because Buddy found me. In fact, he stepped in front of me, mere inches from my face, causing me to yelp.

He shot his hands into the air. "I didn't mean to scare you. I just wanted to know if you were ready to shake a leg?"

My leg was already shaking. The guy certainly made me nervous. But for Margie and Barbie, he prompted an entirely different response. "Oh, go on," they cajoled. "Get on out there. Have some fun."

I had to admit, if only to myself, the song the band was playing was perfect for dancing. The rhythm was pulsating. Sensual even. Still, uncertainty poked at me. Either that or Barbie and Margie were prodding me into the guy's arms. "Oh, go on. Get on out there," they repeated.

"What do you say?" Buddy gestured at the dance floor. "Should we give it a try?"

An internal debate ensued, the cautious me versus the risk taker. Usually caution wins, hands down. But as I said, the band was great, and it had been a long time since I'd done any dancing. The music tempted me, and as others took to the floor, my resistance waned. It wasn't long before desire won out over common sense, and I handed my beer to Margie for safe keeping. No harm in just a dance or two, right?

"Do you swing dance?" Buddy asked as he escorted me to the powder-prepped dance floor.

"Yeah," I answered uncertainly, "but I'm surprised—"

He finished my sentence. "That a farm boy does?"

"I didn't mean—"

"My mom taught us. Music was important to her."

He placed his hand on the small of my back, and I jerked. He expressed bewilderment, and me, embarrassment. "Ticklish," I lied. *Nothing bad can happen while dancing.*

He again settled his hand on my back and tapped out an unhurried beat with his right foot before starting us across the floor. He moved effortlessly, leading me through a series of side steps and back rocks. Soon he integrated more complicated moves, swinging me out and pulling me in, all to the count of six against a four-beat rhythm. "Hey, you aren't half bad," he said.

"Thanks," I dead-panned. "But don't flatter me like that. It'll go to my head."

He laughed, his dark eyes glimmering. "Seriously, where did you learn to dance so well?"

We rocked back and forth. "Music was important to my folks too."

He propelled me into a double turn, twirling me several feet out. I did the "sugar foot" back into his arms, and he uttered, "Damn," in appreciation.

I didn't know what to make of Buddy Johnson. Perhaps I'd misjudged him. Perhaps there was nothing sinister about him after all. I might have simply seen and felt the arrogance and certainty possessed by many handsome and talented men. He certainly was handsome. And he definitely had talent. He could really move! And out there on the dance floor, his moves counted for a lot. As I said, it had been a while since I'd danced with anyone and even longer since I'd danced with anyone who knew what he was doing. Matter of fact, my last good dance partner was Boo-Boo.

Truth be told, Boo-Boo was good at a lot of things. He turned out to be a jerk, but before that, he opened my eyes to a host of new experiences. He even encouraged me to explore my wild side, a side I didn't even know existed until I met him. And guess what? I kind of liked it. Of course, as I discovered that morning in Chicago, Boo-Boo was a little too wild for me.

The band segued into its next song, a blues cover, and those on the dance floor began a sexy version of the electric slide, with Buddy pulling me along until we fell into step behind his brother. Apparently it was Rosa's number to do with as she desired, and she desired to make it her own. Her fingers seduced brooding tones from her bass fiddle, while her voice soulfully caressed the lyrics. Like her or not, Rosa Johnson was a remarkable musician and a beautiful woman, all of which led me to "like her not." *Okay, so I can be petty. Big deal.*

Out on the floor, most of the dancers kept to the standard line-dance moves, but Buddy and Buford put on a show. They substituted the "fan" or a complicated "hitch and slide" whenever possible. And while no one else could follow along, I managed to stay right with them. I mimicked their every move, and before we were through, I even showed off a few of my own.

They were visibly impressed. When the music died, burnt Buford actually slapped my back and gave me an "atta girl." That was just before he began explaining to everyone within earshot the finer points of cooking Egg-Bake Hot Dish. I had no idea why. Nor did I catch much of what he said. His voice frequently got swallowed up by the noise in the room. But I didn't care. I wasn't especially interested in cooking advice from a burnt barbecue anyway.

His dance partner, however, was utterly captivated, or so it seemed. She literally hung on his every word as well as his arm, easing her concentration and her grip only long enough to wave to a young woman who'd sashayed over.

The woman was blonde, buxom, and insistent that Buddy dance with her. When he stole a glance at me, ostensibly to get my reaction, the woman went so far as to step between us, with me getting her rear view. I'd seen better. Not necessarily in my own mirror. But I'd seen better.

Naturally, part of me wanted to tweak her for being so insolent—and having such a nice ass. And I figured the best way to do that was to claim Buddy as my dance partner for the rest of the evening. Yet, I was leery. I didn't want to send him the wrong message. I'd almost convinced myself that my earlier take on him was off base. Almost. But not quite. With my feet once again firmly planted on the ground, that nagging sensation had returned, the one that whispered, *There's something amiss with Buddy Johnson.*

Chapter Twenty-Eight

PRESSING THROUGH THE CROWD, I worked to rid myself of all thoughts of Buddy Johnson. He was a great dancer. But I had to stay clear of him. He was a bad boy. I was positive of that. I just wasn't certain how bad.

I found Margie and Barbie in a dark corner. They'd highjacked a table toward the back of the room. I plopped down on a chair, and Barbie complimented me on my dance moves while Margie handed me my beer.

As I drew a long pull from the bottle, Margie warned, "Now, don't choke." She couldn't disguise her smile. "I know how much trouble ya have handlin' your booze."

With a clunk, I set the bottle down. "You think you're pretty funny, don't you?"

"On occasion," she replied with a snort of laughter. "On occasion."

I fanned my hands in front of my face. "God, it's hot in here."

Barbie leaned forward, a goofy grin on her face. "And it's about to get a whole lot hotter." She nodded toward the door.

Margie and I twisted around to see the object of her focus. It was Deputy Ryden.

Margie splayed her hands on the table. "Do ya hear that, Barbie? I do believe it's our cue to leave?"

"Don't you dare!" I aspired to sound threatening, though I must have fallen short because both women merely chuckled as Barbie waved her arms over her head until she got the deputy's attention and motioned him over.

"What are you doing?" The tone of my voice had changed to an odd mixture of apprehension and anticipation. "I told you what a mess I made out of my dinner with him. I don't think I'm ready to talk to him again."

Barbie ignored me while the deputy closed in on our table. "Hi, Randy," she said, pulling out the empty chair between us. "Take a load off."

"Thanks." He spun the chair around and threw his leg over the seat, like he was mounting a horse. As he sat down, he smiled at me by way of hello.

"Was the accident serious?" I wanted to sound cool and classy, but my voice may have been in "Olive Oyl" range.

"No, not serious at all." He rested his forearms on the back of the chair. "How's everything here?"

Barbie answered for me, an impish look on her face. "The night started off as a slow burn, but I think it's about to heat up."

Margie added something equally ridiculous, causing me to kick her under the table. "Ouch," she whimpered.

"What's wrong?" the deputy asked.

She stammered while shooting me the devil's eye. "Umm, I meant to say, 'shit,' not 'ouch.' Shit! I'm supposed to be gettin' recipes together for Emme here, and I just remembered I'm not done. Oh, shit."

I placed my hand firmly on her forearm. "You told me I had all the recipes you were going to give me." I squeezed her arm to let her know I was on to her.

She slowly pulled free and scraped back her chair. "Yah, but I was wrong. When I was in the kitchen a while ago, I saw a heckuva lot of recipe cards still layin' on the prep table. There's one for a Jell-O salad that's delicious, regardless of what Father Daley might say, and another for Apple Square Bars that are out of this world. Before I forget, I better go get 'em. And when I'm back there, I'll double check that I didn't miss any other good ones. I want ya to have a bunch to choose from for that article of yours."

"Why don't I give you a hand?" Barbie said.

"Okay, let's get a move on."

With bogus exasperation, Barbie shook her head. "Margie, Margie, Margie, how many times do I have to tell you not to end a sentence with a preposition?"

Margie fanned her hand like she was a nineteenth-century southern bell. "Well, pardon me, darlin'," she drawled. "I meant to say, 'Let's get a move on, bitch.'"

Both women fell back in their chairs, laughing and slapping their thighs. If I had to guess, I'd say they had consumed more than a few beers while I was dancing.

When done amusing themselves, Margie wiped her eyes and stood while Barbie said to the deputy in a voice just loud enough to be heard over the music, "You don't mind keeping Emme company, do you? I know you're on duty, but we'll only be a few minutes."

Deputy Ryden glanced at me and then back to Barbie. "Yeah, I can hang around awhile."

"Good." She sprang to her feet, and the two of them hurried away. Well, that wasn't quite true. Barbie hurried. Margie hobbled. And I didn't feel bad about it in the least.

"You don't have to babysit me." I made the statement while pulling a napkin from the dispenser on the table and wiping my face.

The deputy rubbed his thighs. "No problem. I wanted to talk to you anyhow." He bent his head close to mine. "But it's really loud in here. Mind if we go outside?"

Gazing at him, I knew exactly what I wanted to say. After warning myself not to appear too eager, however, I let an appropriate amount of time pass before responding. It was the longest three seconds of my life. "Sure, let's go. I was dancing. And I got really warm. I could use some fresh air."

The deputy twirled his chair around. "Who had you out dancing?"

I rose, leaving my half-empty beer on the table. "Margie's nephew, Buddy Johnson."

"Oh." The deputy's mouth took on a grim set.

For a moment, I considered asking him about it. And for another, I toyed with the idea of sharing my own assessment of Buddy Johnson. But I tossed both ideas aside. After all, what would I say? I have an icky feeling about the guy. It's not based on anything concrete. It's just an icky feeling. Yeah, right.

I steered toward the door, the deputy on my heels, and several pairs of eyes on the two of us. I did my best to ignore the staring by considering what was flitting around in the back of my mind. It was just out of reach, and the more I grabbed at it, the more elusive it became. It was a question. Of that much, I was sure. Big surprise there, I had another question.

I veered around tables, restricting my glances to the door, the floor, and the table legs. Even when the deputy touched my back to usher me around a cluster of folks, sending shivers from my head to my toes, I refrained from looking at him or anyone else. And then it came to me. The question. It was about Rosa Johnson. I wanted to ask the deputy about his relationship with her. I just had to figure out how.

As I stepped outside, I found that night had settled in. The air was cool and filled with the smell of freshly cut grass, while the sky was veiled in northern lights, a pleated curtain of pale colors that repeatedly intensified before floating down to the horizon.

"Aurora Borealis," I stated, taking in the heavenly sight. "I've never seen them in person. Too many lights in the Cities." I dropped my head back. "They're spectacular."

The deputy remained silent until I lifted my head, and our eyes met. "Yeah, very pretty," he replied, making me glad it was dark because my cheeks undoubtedly pinked up after realizing he wasn't referring to the sky. At least I didn't think he was.

Breaking eye contact, he then strolled across the parking lot behind the bar, me stepping alongside him and the gravel crunching beneath our shoes.

"I wanted to talk to you," he said. "I didn't want you to leave town thinking I was a jerk." He paused, possibly to give me a chance to assure him he wasn't, but I remained mum, and soon he heaved an audible sigh. "Well, I guess what I'm trying to say is I'm sorry for being so rough on you at dinner."

"What do you mean?"

"Well, let's just say that the investigation into Samantha Berg's death has been hard on everyone around here. I don't like talking about it. When the subject comes up, I can get kind of grouchy."

He took our walk to the street, seemingly working through something, so I clamped my mouth shut to keep from disturbing him. "You know," he said after we passed the gas station, already closed for the night, "during that time, folks got so they didn't trust anyone around here, including those of us in law enforcement."

The hair on the back of my neck bristled.

"Some acted as if we didn't care about solving the case," he said. "Can you believe that?"

It was more of an indignant statement than question, so I didn't feel it was necessary to answer.

"And others thought we were covering for certain people." He combed his hands through his hair in an unmistakable act of frustration. "Things are finally back to normal, and I'd like them to stay that way." He stopped for a second or two. "That's why I'd rather not talk about it. That's not to say we don't follow up on the new leads we get. We do. We just don't broadcast it. That way folks don't get all riled up."

A couple strolled by, headed in the opposite direction, undoubtedly destined for the bar. Where else? The rest of town was buttoned up tight.

Deputy Ryden greeted them with a mumbled, "Hello," and a dip of his head.

When they were well past, I spoke, determined to say what was on my mind and, in the process, pardon myself for maligning Deputy Ryden and his colleagues for what I had suspected was a lack of dedication. "I don't know about anyone else, but you can't be surprised by my curiosity. I'm a reporter. And if I seemed suspicious of you or you got the impression that I questioned the integrity of your investigation, it's your own fault."

"My fault?" Our walk had become a series of starts and stops, and my remark yielded an immediate halt.

"Yeah. You were so closed-mouthed, what did you expect?"

I knew I was being unfair. I also knew this tactic was effective. I had learned it from Boo-Boo, the master of shifting blame and, thus, easing his own guilty conscience. Whenever I caught him in a lie, he'd turn things around until I was apologizing to him.

"Well, if you think I'm going to tell you that I'm sorry for being closed-mouthed about a police matter, Emerald, you're sorely mistaken."

Evidently, Deputy Ryden didn't understand how this strategy was supposed to work.

"And on top of that," he said, "I think you should be up front with these folks about the story you're writing."

I held up my hands. "I'm not—"

"They're decent. They deserve honesty."

I waved my hands in front of his face. "But I'm not doing a story."

He furrowed his brow. "What?"

"I'm not writing about the murder."

He appeared suspicious. "Really?"

I crossed my heart with my finger. "I swear." A gentle breeze stirred my hair, and I brushed it away from my face. "I'll admit I was planning to. But that was before it became clear that I don't possess the right temperament for investigative reporting. I just don't like questioning people."

His eyebrows shot skyward. And for a second, I thought they might actually rocket right off his face.

"Okay, okay, I like asking questions. But today I realized, or finally acknowledged to myself, I don't like questioning people's integrity."

He began moseying down the street, and I followed. "You don't have to doubt everyone to be an effective investigator," he assured me.

"That may be true, but I can't seem to turn it off. And it makes me feel mean and stupid."

His gaze remained fixed on the road. "Stupid? How?"

I laughed hesitantly. "Remember how I was convinced that Ole had murdered Samantha Berg?" I caught up to him.

"Yeah, I remember."

"Well, he wasn't the only one I suspected."

He tilted his head my way. "And?"

"And I was wrong again and again and again. And I don't like being wrong. It makes me feel stupid."

He looked my way and smiled just enough so I could see the lines that fanned out from the corners of his eyes. They made him look pretty damn sexy. "Well, um . . ." he said, "that probably wouldn't happen so often if you weren't so quick to make judgments." On second thought, maybe he wasn't all that sexy.

"It's not my fault. I can't help it."

He stopped in his tracks, a contrite expression on his face. "What I meant to say is that investigative work requires lots of patience."

"Which I have in short supply. And I can't seem to do anything about it." By giving voice to my biggest character flaw, the deputy had once more opened the tap on my self-pity. But since I didn't want to serve up any more of that than I already had, I searched my mind for something else to talk about.

Shuffling through my thoughts, I came across what he had said about following up on the new leads in Samantha Berg's murder investigation. Even though I was no longer professionally interested in the case, I certainly could appreciate that. And I did. I just didn't get as excited about it as I thought I would—or should.

And why was that? I wasn't sure. But I had an idea—an idea I didn't like very much.

Chapter Twenty-Nine

Deputy Ryden and I passed under a street lamp, its light casting elongated shadows and allowing glimpses of the homes and yards set back from the road. A silhouetted figure moved behind a drawn shade in a narrow two-story, while in the yard next door, a golf cart leaned into a hedge, its wheels hung up on a garden timber. The lawns were landscaped with flowers and a mixture of evergreens and maples, but no trees lined the boulevard, although a honeysuckle vine twisted around a light pole, offering a sweet fragrance as we strolled by.

"So," the deputy said into the comfortable silence that had settled over us, "let's try another subject." He jammed his hands into the pockets of his jeans. "Something more serious. Far more important."

I tensed up, having no idea where he was headed.

"I've been wondering about your name, Emerald. It's different. Where'd it come from?"

I relaxed with a smile. "My folks were part of the Woodstock generation. Real free spirits. They actually met there, at Woodstock, and were inseparable from that point on. Late in life, they decided it would be cool to have a baby and got married shortly before I was born."

I hadn't told that story for a long time and was amazed at how sentimental it made me. My eyes grew misty and my voice shaky. And I could only hope the deputy thought the wobble in my words was due to the cool night air.

"As you probably know, most babies—white babies anyway—are born with blue eyes, but mine were a brilliant green. My mother's midwife, who had chalked up hundreds of deliveries along the Grateful Dead circuit, said she'd never seen anything like it. She insisted it was a sign that couldn't be ignored. So my parents didn't. They named me Emerald."

"You do have nice eyes."

"Thanks."

He stutter-stepped, apparently uncertain whether to stop or keep moving. He chose the latter. "And what do they do for a living, these hippie parents of yours?"

"Well, Mom was a poet, though she earned a living by teaching high school English. Dad was a sculptor and ran a furniture restoration business out of our garage. They're deceased."

"Sorry."

Okay, that was enough. I couldn't talk about them anymore. "So what about your name?"

He squinted at me, closing one eye, looking confused. "Randy?"

"No. Deputy. How did you end up in law enforcement?"

He sniffed in amusement. "Truthfully, I became a cop because, after college, I learned I wasn't good enough to play professional football, and I couldn't stand the idea of working behind a desk. What's more, my older brother assured me that uniforms were chick magnets." He sniffed again. "The way I saw it, I could be a police officer or a fire fighter. I settled on cop because professional fire fighters only work in big cities, and early on, I knew I wanted the option to live in the country."

"And how's it going?"

"I told you before, I like my job."

"No, I mean the chick-magnet thing."

He barked out a laugh. "Not so great. I think my brother might have lied."

There it was. My opening. I could ask about Rosa Johnson. I could say I'd heard he was dating—or had dated—the singer in the band. But I didn't get a chance. I chickened out. Or maybe I just waited too long. In any event, I didn't ask, and he shifted the focus of the conversation to me.

"Now, it's your turn," he said. "What got you interested in journalism?"

"Well, as you so aptly put it, I'm nosy."

He stopped. "I don't think I said—"

"Yes, you did. But don't worry. It wasn't anything I hadn't heard before." We continued down the road. "I've been asking questions all my life. Couple that with my love of writing, and journalism was the logical career choice."

"But there are all kinds of jobs in journalism. Why'd you decide to pursue crime reporting?"

"I never said—"

"Give it a rest, Emerald. I know better. You clearly want to do investigative work."

"Wanted to. Past Tense. Not anymore."

"Well, what got you interested in it initially?"

I shrugged. "I suppose I felt the need to right the world's wrongs."

He peered at me, speaking in an expectant tone, "A mighty tall order for one person, isn't it?"

No doubt, he wanted to hear more, but I didn't have the will to say anything else. I didn't want to explain how, after my folks died, my aunt and uncle sued the state because the guardrail that gave way on the bridge, causing my parents' deaths, was defective and reportedly so for years. Nor did I want to explain how the state dragged out the lawsuit until my aunt and uncle were forced to settle, yet the state refused to take responsibility, insisting the settlement agreement read that while a payout was made, no liability was accepted. And I certainly didn't want to explain how the whole thing ate away at me, particularly after I began using that money for college and graduate school. Or how I decided to aim for a career in solving crimes via journalism in an effort to replace my guilt with a sense of purpose. Or how I convinced myself that by exposing wrongdoing, I'd pay tribute to my folks, who were wronged in the worst possible way and, at the same time, justify my use of blood money. No, I didn't want to explain any of that.

Besides, I wasn't sure what I thought about journalism anymore. I wasn't especially enamored with it. Or with myself for that matter. At some point during the day, I'd come to terms with the fact that I lacked the personality necessary to be a good investigative reporter. I wasn't cynical, tactful, or patient enough. But I continued to struggle with another revelation. One that caused me even more pain. You see, I'd also realized that I wasn't the crusader for justice I imagined myself to be. Yes, there were some chinks in my self-righteous armor.

I'd always believed I was a "truth seeker" because of my parents or because it was a noble endeavor. But today I'd discovered that justice wasn't my primary motivation after all. At least not in this instance. Sure, I may have said the right words. And for the most part, I even acted indignant when appropriate. But first and foremost, I was after the Samantha Berg story for personal glory and professional advancement. And that didn't sit well with me.

Of course it explained why the case lost much of its appeal after I backed away from it professionally—why I wasn't as thrilled as I thought I should be when I learned that the cops were continuing to follow up on leads. I guess, deep down, I figured that if it wasn't going to make me shine, it didn't hold much luster. Ugh!

We reached the end of town, about five blocks from the 'V,' looped around, and started our way back. The wind whistled across my face and sent a shiver down my neck, the sound of it escaping my lips. "Brrr."

"You cold?" Deputy Ryden asked. "Should we pick up our pace?"

"No," I replied too quickly, leading to an immediate attempt at damage control. "I mean, I'm fine. No need to hurry."

While I wasn't keen on sharing anything more about myself, I didn't want our time together to end either. Once we reached the bar, the deputy would probably leave. Then what? Alone again, I'd most likely examine my conscience some more, which wouldn't be good. What if I uncovered other terrible truths? What if I ended up hating myself? I spent way too much time alone to despise my own company.

We strolled on, Randy whistling to the music that carried faintly from the bar. And me? Well, I pretended that every time the deputy's arm brushed against mine, sexual pheromones formed in the air around us. Silly, I know, but it kept me from doing any serious thinking, and that was the whole point, right? Besides, it was far more titillating than thinking that the buzzing around my head was nothing more than a bunch of gnats.

"Sooo," the deputy said, taking a break from whistling "Ring of Fire," "you're really not going to write about Samantha Berg?"

"Nope. I'm only interested in recipes and a profile piece on Margie. Not exactly exciting, but . . ."

He reached for my hand and gave it a squeeze, the warmth of his touch radiating up my arm, across my chest, and to all points south. "I'm glad," he said. "I didn't want to make trouble for you." I cocked my head, and he replied to the gesture with a chuckle before adding, "What can I say? I'm protective of these people."

I stopped. "Does that include Buddy Johnson?"

I have no idea where that question came from. As I may have mentioned, my mind regularly had trouble keeping up with my mouth. And my mouth had terrible timing, as evidenced by Randy Ryden abruptly dropping my hand.

"Why would you ask about him?"

"Well, when I told you I'd been dancing with him, it was plain to see you weren't happy about it. So what's the story there?"

The deputy walked ahead. "I just don't like him. That's all."

I raced to catch up. "Why not?"

He frowned. "It doesn't matter, does it?"

I opened my mouth but closed it right away again. A sliver of an idea was coming to me, and I wanted to make it whole before I spoke. Since it had come out of nowhere, I knew I needed to give it careful consideration. See? I really was trying to be more thoughtful.

"Hey," I said after some time, hoping his continued silence wasn't a sign that he was angry with me but knowing I'd ask my questions just the same. "Your negative feelings about Buddy don't have anything to do with Samantha Berg, do they?"

The deputy practically tripped over his feet. "You're impossible, you know that?"

"I'm not impossible." I fluttered my eyelashes in a playful attempt at easing the tension I felt building between us. "I'm tenacious. It's the Irish in me."

He snorted. "Don't blame an entire nationality for the way you are. It's not fair to the rest of the Irish."

"Very funny." Again, not much of a comeback, but I couldn't help it. He was getting crabby, and I was getting tired. Or maybe I was merely distracted by the pheromones or gnats or whatever they were. At any rate, our conversation stalled, leaving the void to be filled by the buzzing around my head and the murmuring of the people huddled together on the next block, in front of the bar.

"Why does it matter to you what I think of Buddy Johnson? You aren't writing about the case or the people around here anyway. You're only after recipes, remember?" His tone was less than sweet.

"I can still be curious. It's my nature."

He appeared ready to say something snarky in response but must have thought better of it because he kept his mouth shut for quite a while. "I just don't trust him," he uttered only when apparently able to speak without fear of insulting me.

"Why? Do you think he was involved in Samantha Berg's disappearance and death?"

The deputy blew out an exasperated breath. "How'd you come up with an idea like that?"

I shrugged. "Good-looking guy. Slutty woman. Damaged family. Seemed possible.'"

He sighed. "He and his brother weren't even in town when Samantha went missing. They were in St. Paul at the State High School Hockey Tournament. Hallock wasn't in the tournament, but players from here go down every year to watch the action."

"So?"

"So what?"

"So I sense there's more to the story."

He gently placed his hand against my back. "Come on, let's forget about all this and get some coffee at the café." He playfully wiggled his eyebrows, clearly working to lighten the mood. Although I suspected he was working another angle too. "And if we're lucky, there might be some Cookie Salad left."

"Cookie Salad?"

The corner of his mouth curled upward. "Now don't go all hoity-toity on me. Cookie Salad is goldarn tasty." He embraced a thick Scandinavian accent for those last few words.

"Believe me, I'm no food snob, Randy. Far from it. But I know two things for sure. One, real salads aren't made with candy bars and cookies."

He flashed me a look of disbelief. "They are if they're any good."

"And 'B,'" I said, watching in anticipation of his response to what I was about to say, "I'm not letting you off the hook. You will tell me about the Johnson twins."

His mouth fell open. Yep, he had been trying to sidetrack me. Of course it didn't work. But not being one to gloat, I said nothing. And I even helped him out by closing his mouth with a flick of my finger under his chin.

Chapter Thirty

The deputy's radio crackled, and he mumbled a series of numbers into it before turning to me. "I guess I'll have to take a rain check on that coffee."

"Another accident?"

"No, I just need to get back to the office."

We crossed the street, and when we got to the other side, I rested my hand on his forearm. "Before you go, I want the rest of the story."

The deputy sighed again. Yep, that sighing stuff could easily start grating on me.

"Tell you what," I continued, "since you're in a hurry, I'll even accept the abridged version."

He dropped his head back. "There's just not that much to it." He glanced at me. And with one look in my eyes, he must have decided I needed more of a response than that. "Okay. Okay." He stretched his neck this way and that in an apparent attempt to relieve some stress-induced stiffness. "No one at the tournament remembered seeing the twins the night Samantha disappeared. They saw them the day before and the following afternoon but not that night."

"You mean they didn't have an alibi?"

The deputy scratched his head. "Oh, they had an alibi all right. Father Daley vouched for them. He said they were with him the entire evening. At the game. And the hotel afterwards."

"But you aren't so sure?"

"Let's just say I have a bad feeling about it."

That gave me pause. "Randy, I really hope you aren't pinning the success of your investigation on mere 'feelings.' Not that I'm telling you how to do your job. But I've done that a few times today—gone with my feelings instead of gathering all the facts—and it's left me 'feeling' pretty foolish."

He shrugged. "Well, sometimes that's all I've got. And more often than not, my feelings are right on the mark." He picked up his pace.

"Really?" I marched double time to keep up.

"Yeah. I guess I have good instincts. At least that's what I've been told."

"Hmm." Maybe I was right to wonder about Buddy Johnson. Maybe I was onto something without even knowing it. Deputy Ryden had been doing this investigating thing a lot longer than me, and if he thought . . .

"Well, now that you mention it," I began, "I did get some negative vibes shortly after meeting Buddy." I paused to catch my breath. The deputy walked really fast. "So what do you think? He and his brother left the hockey tournament, drove six hours to get back up here, kidnapped and killed Samantha Berg, dumped her body, and returned to the Cities?"

He slowed down and looked my way. In the pale moonlight, I saw his jaw muscles twitch. "When you say it like that, Emerald, it doesn't sound all that plausible. Although it would explain a lot." He pointed his finger at me. "For starters, together they could have subdued her. A lone person would have had a tough time. I may have mentioned that she was husky."

"But if they came back to town just to kill her, the murder would have been premeditated, right? Do you really believe they could have done that? Wouldn't someone have seen them?" Only when I was done did I realize how fast I'd asked those questions.

Randy held up three fingers, one after another. "Yes. Maybe. And not necessarily. Remember, it was the one-year anniversary of their mother's death—a death they, like a lot of folks, blamed on Samantha. They might have gotten restless down at the tournament, considering the date and all, and headed home. Maybe they did some drinking along the way. Probably some other stuff too. And by the time they got back here, they were all jacked up. They confronted her, and things got out of hand. They killed her, dumped the body, and returned to the Cities."

I finished his thought. "And once back there, they went to Father Daley and confessed their sins, and he offered absolution along with an alibi."

"Something like that."

The deputy motioned me toward his squad car, a brown Ford SUV. It was parked along the highway, in front of the bar. As we closed in, the group that had been loitering nearby dispersed, leaving behind the pungent smell of marijuana. He raised his eyes to the sky in an unmistakable sign of futility.

"You really believe a priest would do such a thing?" I asked the question after a brief examination of some basic beliefs.

Deputy Ryden knitted his brow. "You've never heard of members of the clergy acting improperly?"

He'd missed my point. "I meant would this particular priest do such a thing? It would make him an accessory to murder."

The deputy held his hands out, palms up. "Father Daley loved Lena Johnson. I'm not saying inappropriately, but he loved her. And Samantha put an end to that relationship as well as his friendship with Ole. What's more, he's always been protective of Rosa and the twins. Given all that, I don't think he would have had a hard time forgiving the twins for doing away with Samantha, especially if her death was an accident of some sort."

I was uncomfortable with the notion that a priest would willingly break the law, not to mention one of the major Commandments. Sure, I was aware of abusive clergy, but I didn't know any personally. I'd actually met Father Daley. He had even sung to me.

I shook my head in an effort to clear my mind. "I suppose that in addition to interrogating the twins, you examined their car?"

"Yep, and some of Samantha's DNA was found inside."

"Huh?"

He held up his hand. "Don't read too much into that. Half the cars up here would test positive for her DNA."

"Mmm."

"Nope, there was no damning evidence against the twins. Just my hunch. And they had Father Daley as their alibi. So case closed as far as they were concerned."

"Did they take a lie-detector test?" Now that I'd gotten interested in the investigation again, I wasn't quite ready to let it drop. Not that I'd do anything with the information. I just found it fascinating. "Father Daley told me that Vern took one to prove his innocence."

"Well, the twins never did. Of course they said they wanted to, but their lawyer advised against it. He argued that lie-detector tests weren't reliable. He wouldn't let Rosa submit to one either."

"They lawyered up?"

He grinned as he leaned against the squad car, crossing his feet at his ankles, his arms over his chest. "Lawyered up?" His face was haloed by a streetlight. And like Margie, he appeared amused by me.

"I probably watch too many cop shows."

The wind picked up, and I rubbed my arms briskly against the cool breeze. "Brrr."

"I'd offer you my jacket. But I've got to go. It's dirty anyhow." He thumbed toward the back seat of his car. "I don't know why, but I brought it into the café earlier. And when I grabbed it from the coatroom on my way out, someone accidently dumped a plate of glorified rice all over it."

He stood up straight, and we gazed at each other, both apparently clueless as what to say or do next. I could have asked more about the case, but while staring into his eyes, it had lost all of its appeal again. Go figure.

So, instead, I squared my shoulders, tilted my head to the side, and attempted an expectant look to signal he could kiss me goodbye if he were so inclined. But I must have messed up because he merely scratched his stomach.

"All righty then," I said, and at the same time, he said, "Well, then," and together we chuckled before lapsing into another uncomfortable moment.

"You go first," I urged after a while.

"Well, I just wanted to say again how much I enjoyed meeting you."

"Me too." That's not right. "I mean I really enjoyed meeting you too."

Another awkward moment while he frisked himself. And believe it or not, as nervous as I was, I found myself wishing for a turn at that. Yeah, I know, pitiful. Just keep in mind: A work in progress and in desperate need of a date.

He located what he was searching for—his keys—and said, "Well, I suppose I better go."

I restlessly shuffled my feet, glanced at him, and just as quickly looked away. And that's when it happened. He clasped my shoulders and lightly kissed my cheek. Not exactly the passionate embrace I'd imagined but better than a handshake.

"Margie said you're leaving in the morning." He spoke softly, his eyes mirroring his tone. "I get down to the Cities every once in a while. Sometimes for work. Sometimes to see my folks and my brother. Can I call you? Maybe we could grab some dinner or a drink."

"I'd like that."

He let go of me. "Good. And in the meantime, stay away from Buddy and Buford. They're trouble. And since you aren't writing about the case, quit asking so damn many questions. Don't forget, we still have killers on the loose."

"Killers? Plural? As in the twins?"

He heaved another heavy sigh.

As suspected, those sighs were beginning to bug me.

"This isn't a game, Emerald. It's an unsolved murder. You need to keep out of it. It could be dangerous."

I wasn't sure how he could go from intoxicating to exasperating so effortlessly, but he managed. "I can take care of myself. I've done it most of my life." I showed him my best tough-girl face.

He didn't seem all that impressed. "Tell you what. Leave the investigation to the police, and as soon as the case is resolved, I'll give you a heads-up. Then you can get a jump on the story, if that's what you really want to do."

I sighed. Now he had me doing it! "I already told you I'm not professionally interested in the case."

He studied my face. "I'd like to believe that, but I have the distinct impression you aren't going to let it be. Somehow, you're going to end up mixed up in it."

"Well, maybe your instincts aren't as good as you think they are." I then added under my breath, "After all, you didn't solve the murder now did you?"

"What was that?"

"Nothing. I was just clearing my throat."

He shifted his feet. "Emerald, I like you. And I don't want to see you get hurt. I'd hate for that to happen."

"Me too. Getting hurt is one of my least favorite things."

The deputy closed his eyes, yet his lips kept moving. I think he was silently counting to ten. He opened one eye—just barely—and peeked out at me. "You need to back off, okay? Don't forget, movement doesn't always mean progress."

Who did this guy think he was? Well, he certainly wasn't the boss of me. And what in the hell did he mean, "Movement doesn't always mean progress"? That didn't even make sense.

Here I'd been having a good time, but now I was ticked off all over again, and it was all his fault. I had absolutely no intention of writing about the murder, but I decided right then and there that if he believed otherwise, that was his problem. And if the thought of me asking more questions bothered him, so much the better. Let him stew.

Still, I couldn't help but question why he seemed more concerned about my welfare now than he had earlier in the day. Had he come to care about me? Or was he was simply nervous about my renewed interest in the case.

I suppose it didn't really matter. After this night, I'd be back in the Cities, and he'd be up here in Kennedy. I'd be writing introductions to recipe features, and he'd be doing his police thing. And someday, he'd solve Samantha Burg's murder, or he never would.

Sure, he might call. Perhaps we'd even go out a time or two. But nothing more would come of it. The distance between us would see to that.

I gazed at his lips. He had great-looking lips. It would be a shame to miss out on those lips. To go through life wondering . . . *Oh, what the hell!*

I took to my tip-toes and kissed him squarely on the mouth. "Mmm," I hummed in response to his stunned expression, "you taste good." I then slid my business card, complete with phone number and e-mail address, into his shirt pocket and walked away, having absolutely no idea what had gotten into me.

Chapter Thirty-One

THE MUFFLED SOUND OF MUSIC accompanied me as I strolled to the garden. I rounded the tool shed and literally ran into Barbie. "Ouch!" I grabbed my nose.

She scrambled to regain her footing. "They told me what you lacked in experience and skill you more than made up for in persistence. Boy, they were right about that."

I frowned. "You were eavesdropping?"

She waved away my annoyance. "You would have done the same. We're reporters. That's what we do."

I maintained the frown. "That conversation had nothing to do with news."

"Yes, it did. It confirmed that I was right to invite you to come and work for me at the newspaper. That is, if you ever need a change of scenery. And from what I saw, I think you like the scenery up here just fine."

I rolled my eyes. "Barbie, you're too much."

"No, I'm just right." She flung her ample hips from side to side.

Certain there was no point in arguing, I settled for seeking her opinion. "Since you were listening and most likely heard everything we said, give me your take on Randy's theory that the Johnson twins were responsible for Samantha's death." So I still might have been somewhat intrigued by the case. So what?

She linked her fingers, stretched her arms out in front of her, and cracked her knuckles. "They had an alibi." She shook her hands out. "The way I see it, Randy's focus on them was misplaced. Most likely because of their sister, Rosa."

I wrinkled my forehead so tightly I saw my eyebrows.

"See, Deputy Ryden and Rosa began dating shortly after he moved here. Even when she went off to college, she'd come home every weekend just to be with him. Everyone assumed they'd end up married. They were really happy."

Another pang of jealousy, but I tried to brush it off. "What happened? Why'd they break up?" I kept brushing. My jealousy, it seemed, was stuck to me like cat hair.

"I guess the strain of her mom's death proved too much for the relationship. Well, that and the fact that Randy didn't intercede on her behalf after Samantha was murdered."

We made our way to a garden bench and sat down. "When Rosa and her brothers were repeatedly questioned by law enforcement, the relationship fell apart," Barbie said. "Or, more precisely, Rosa dumped him."

I was developing a strong dislike for Rosa Johnson and was proud that it wasn't entirely based on her incredible looks and sultry voice. "He was only doing his job. Couldn't she see that?"

"He allowed his girlfriend and her brothers to be grilled over and over by FBI agents. That doesn't make for a good romance."

"Why? Did she have something to hide?"

Barbie meowed loudly and clawed at the air.

Okay, maybe I was being a little catty. Big deal.

"Rosa didn't have anything to hide," Barbie stated. "She just didn't like that he refused to stand up for her and the twins. Margie didn't like it either. After a while, Margie got over it, which was quite surprising actually. Rosa never did."

She paused. "The breakup was really hard on Randy. He only recently started dating again. But he's still awfully leery about any relationship that might have serious potential."

"What about Rosa?"

The truth is I wanted to follow up on the whole "he's leery of any relationship with serious potential" thing but refrained from doing so because I didn't want to come across as desperate. Of course some might argue that train had already left the station, given the kiss I laid on him.

"Rosa became somewhat of a recluse," Barbie went on to say. "If she's not at school or in the garden, she's at home. Tonight's the first time I've seen her out in ages."

"I meant what about her on the night of Samantha's disappearance? Where was she? Did she have an alibi?"

Barbie stretched her arms across the back of the bench. "You're itching for a fight, aren't you?"

"Oh, shut up. I'm asking legitimate questions."

She grinned as she took a deep breath. "Well, let's see. For part of that night, Rosa was in the café. She knew Ole was filling in for Margie. She also knew that since it was the one-year anniversary of Lena's death, he'd be having a tough go of it." She clasped her hands behind her head and extended her legs out in front of her. "If I remember correctly, she got to the café around eight-thirty and parked in the alley, which the locals routinely do. She spotted Vern as he was leaving Samantha's house, and they entered the café together." Barbie spoke in a modulated tone, as if reading from a police report, something I suspected she'd done several times during the formal investigation. "They stayed until ten before going their separate ways."

The music stopped inside the bar, and Barbie got to her feet. I remained seated. "The band's taking a break," she said. "I'm going in to spend some time with my honey. You coming?"

I shook my head. "I wouldn't want to intrude."

"You wouldn't be. I'd really like you to meet him, especially since you'll probably be working for me someday." Again, that confident smile.

I let that go too. Even though I was just getting to know Barbie, I already understood it was pointless to correct her or try to change her. "No, you go on ahead. I'll be along shortly."

"Okay. I guess I'll see you later then." And with that, she was gone.

* * *

ALONE, I LEANED AGAINST the bench and reached back into my mind, fully intending to retrieve the questions I had regarding Deputy Ryden's interest in keeping me safe or, in the alternative, keeping me from digging any deeper into the murder case. But somehow I instead latched onto those pertaining to his apparent desire to play the field.

Did I come across as easy? Was that why he asked me out? An "easy" date with no "serious potential"? I checked my blouse. Not too many buttons undone. Not much cleavage showing. No matter how badly I wanted it, not much cleavage would ever be showing.

I reviewed our conversations. Okay, I flirted a little, and I may have said a few embarrassing things. But easy? Well, there was the kiss. But that was at the end, when he was about to leave. And he kissed me first. And I had to kiss him. No woman with a pulse could have resisted. He had some great-looking lips. And it'd been a very long time.

With the band on break, people spilled out of the bar, making the garden less than ideal for reflection. So giving up another sigh, I packed my thoughts away, stood up, and started down the path, not at all sure where I was headed.

I angled behind the shed, stepping around the other side just in time to see Father Daley and Rosa. They'd entered the garden from the main sidewalk, their heads bowed. I watched them for two or three seconds. Then, not wanting them to notice me for some inexplicable reason, I ducked inside.

"Wait a minute." My eyes made a sweep of the dark, cramped space. "What in the hell am I doing in here? What on earth possessed me to jump into the garden shed?"

I held the door latch and listened to the people milling about outside. What would I say if they discovered me? How would I explain hiding in the shed? I waited for an answer.

I expected the little voices in my head to speak up—to tell me what to do—but none of them uttered a word. Figures. The one time I was willing and even eager to listen to their advice, and they were out to lunch. Nope, I didn't hear a thing. Absolutely nothing except for the talking and laughing outside and Deputy Ryden's bumper-sticker wisdom, which echoed through the recesses of my mind. *Movement doesn't always mean progress, Emerald. Movement doesn't always mean progress.*

“No shit,” I muttered. And then my stomach growled. Yes, despite my predicament—or perhaps because of it—my stomach wanted to remind me of its need for food. It always needed food in stressful situations. It growled again, this time making it clear it wouldn’t settle for just any food either. From the images that flooded my mind—images of rich, melt-in-your-mouth chocolate—I knew exactly what it was after—the Traditional Brownies I’d seen at the community dinner. Nothing else would do.

Chapter Thirty-Two

I HELD THE DOOR LATCH with one hand while bracing the other against the adjoining wall. At the same time, I promised my stomach I'd give it whatever it desired when we got back to the café if it would simply agree to pipe down now. It didn't respond, which I took as acquiesence.

The shed was dark, pretty much black on black, although I did spot the gray form of a small table in front of me. It was topped with empty flower pots and bags of dirt. And above it, a window tilted open just a smidge.

Again I reminded my stomach to remain still, at least until the priest and the musician had passed. But it didn't happen. My stomach was quiet, yet even after several minutes went by, the pair never did.

I pushed onto my toes and leaned across the table to get a better view. I didn't see them. Not to my right. Or to my left. No sign of them at all. Not until I glanced at the bench below me. The one outside, just beneath the window. There they were, settling in.

I lurched back and collected myself before creeping forward again. I craned over the potting table, the dense smell of moist soil filling my nose. I peered through the window and spotted the top of Father Daley's graying head angled toward Rosa. She was seated right next to him.

I prayed that my sweaty fingers wouldn't slip from the door latch and that the two of them wouldn't stay long. But only part one of that prayer got answered. I suppose I couldn't expect more, given my spotty church record.

I glanced in both directions. Surely other people would happen by, causing the pair to move on, right?

Wrong. No one came near. The bar patrons had cleared the area, migrating to the sidewalk that ran alongside the highway. I guess the presence of a priest will do that. So here in the garden, Father Daley and Rosa were now all alone—except for yours truly. And here in the garden, all was quiet except for the sound of their voices.

"Rosa," the priest said, "you may get angry with me for saying this, but I'm going to say it anyway. You need some professional help."

Rosa didn't respond, and the priest continued, his words tough but his tone loving. "I believe you're hanging on to the anger you have over your parents' deaths because it somehow helps you feel closer to them. I suspect you don't want to offer forgiveness because, to you, that would be tantamount to abandoning them, maybe even betraying them. But Rosa, dear, that's not a healthy way to live."

"So you think it's okay that my parents were, in effect, murdered, and the person responsible didn't pay for her crime?"

I pushed higher on my toes, not wanting to miss a word.

Through the streaked window, I saw the priest sway. "I never said that. But Samantha Berg is dead. Isn't that punishment enough?"

I watched as a pensive expression found Rosa's face. "She never took responsibility. Not under the law.

"Rosa," the priest continued, "are you telling me that because Samantha never was charged with a crime, you're going to spend the rest of your life in your own private hell? That doesn't make sense. You have to come to terms with everything that happened to your family. Believe me, I know." He paused thoughtfully. "You need to do it for the good of your soul, of course. But you also have to do it for your future. You can't move on if you hold on to all that hatred. It takes too much energy. You'll be too drained to do anything else. On top of that, it'll eat away at you." He paused again. "It might be doing that already. Every time I see you, I see less of the old Rosa, the one I know and love."

"Father, if Samantha had killed my parents with a gun or a knife, she would have gone to jail. But since she only killed their spirits and shattered their hearts, she didn't have to pay for her actions. And that's not right. People have to take responsibility for their wrongdoing, whatever form it takes. It's that simple."

I shook my head, momentarily questioning if I was listening to Rosa or a recording of myself. I'd voiced many of those sentiments about my own parents' passing. I'd uttered some of the same words. And while I didn't care to be in lock-step with Rosa on any subject, we appeared to be in sync on this one.

"Samantha Berg is dead," Father Daley repeated, shuffling in his seat.

"And here I took you for a family friend." Rosa's words were uttered on a wave of emotion.

"I am a family friend. I loved both your parents very much. But—"

She cut him off. "But they're gone. So get on with it, right?" She leaned back, defiantly raised her chin, and spoke in a caustic tone. "No big deal. Just forget about them and move on."

He lowered his voice. "I didn't mean that, and you know it."

I got goose bumps. Their conversation sounded very much like one of my therapy sessions, where I routinely railed against the state for leading my parents to their watery graves. In this current production, however, I didn't much care for Rosa's portrayal of me. She was whiny, and I never was. Or was I?

"I'm sorry, Father. I didn't mean what I said. I'm just stressed out." She absently deadheaded several shriveled blooms from the plant next to the bench.

"All the more reason you should talk to someone."

"I'm talking to you, Father. That's enough, isn't it?"

"Well, probably not. I'm not very objective when it comes to you and your family. I'm too close."

She sniffed with laughter. "You had no trouble whatsoever telling me to see a shrink."

He chuckled while pulling her into a one-arm hug. "That's true. And I want you to think about it." He took a two-beat rest. "In the meantime, I suppose you can talk to me if that will help." Another beat. "Come to think of it, I'd like to know what got you so riled up this afternoon. Yelling at the garden girls? Rosa, that's not your style."

She visibly stiffened. "I'm out of sorts. That's all. I don't like that reporter snooping around here."

I sucked in my breath and strained toward the window, determined to listen more closely.

"Oh, you don't need to be concerned about her. I have it on good authority that she's heading back to the Cities in the morning."

"I still don't like that she's here."

The priest shifted, and the bench squeaked. "Why, Rosa? Why does it bother you?"

My question exactly. She didn't even know me.

"Are you keeping something from me, dear?"

The priest and I were thinking along the same lines.

"Oh, Rosa, you're crying. Here. Take my hanky. Wipe those tears and blow your nose."

She did. She blew hard. So hard he'd never ask for his hanky back.

"There now." He patted her shoulder. "Tell me what's wrong."

I tilted my head and saw Rosa's face illuminated by the light cutting across the garden. "I just don't want her asking a lot of questions. It could cause all sorts of problems."

"What kind of problems?"

We both waited—the priest and me—but again, Rosa said nothing.

"Rosa, did you hear that she was asking about Samantha's death? Is that what's troubling you? Do you know something about the murder? Is that what you're saying?"

Her mouth opened, forming an "O," yet she continued to play mute.

The priest lifted her chin with his finger until her eyes met his. "If you know anything at all, my child, you need to tell me."

I held my breath. I didn't want to miss her response. Yes, I was well aware I was eavesdropping on what amounted to a confession, and that was wrong on so many levels, yet I couldn't help myself.

"Father, I didn't kill her, if that's what you're asking."

I slowly exhaled, more than a little disappointed in her answer and in me for feeling that way. But, then again, I was getting used to being disappointed in myself. Disappointment had often kept me company and certainly had been my companion much of this day.

"I do know her death was an accident, Father," Rosa said in a whisper. "There was no real malice. Not like when she killed my parents. And no, it's not enough that she's dead." The whisper was gone, replaced by huskier-sounding resentment. "I wish it were. Maybe then I'd be able to sleep at night. But it's not. She should have paid for what she did. Under the law. In public. Subject to everyone's scorn."

"Rosa!"

Cymbals crashed inside the bar, and Rosa edged forward. Again the cymbals sounded, and she cast her eyes toward the building. "Father, I've got to go. That's my cue."

"No," he replied, dipping his head close to hers. "You need to stay here and tell me what you know about Samantha Berg's murder."

"I can't. I have to get back inside for the next set."

She abruptly stood, and I stepped away from the window, arching back as far as I could. As I said, a street lamp showered soft light on the garden, and I didn't want to get caught up in it.

"Rosa—"

"Father." She spoke with exasperation. "Maybe later. Maybe I'll tell you more later."

"When?" The man was insistent.

"Tomorrow," she answered far too quickly, most likely saying only what she thought he wanted to hear. "I'll come by the rectory tomorrow."

From the corner of the window, I watched as Father Daley got up and braced Rosa's shoulders with his thick paws. "I'm holding you to that."

"Father, please don't push." Her voice warbled. She was on the verge of crying. "I'm trying. But I have to do this my way. And in my own time."

He wrapped her in a bear hug. "Okay, we'll drop it for tonight. But tomorrow . . ."

She bobbed her head. "Tomorrow, Father."

And with that, they ambled down the garden path, the priest's arm casually draped over Rosa's shoulders. He spoke as they walked, and I could tell from his tone he was attempting to lighten her emotional load. At one point, he even let loose with a belly laugh, but she remained mum. A short time later, though, he made a remark about Green Bean Casserole that actually led her to chuckle, albeit half-heartedly.

Chapter Thirty-Three

Once Father Daley and Rosa were out of sight, I counted to a hundred before opening the door. Since I couldn't explain my presence in the garden shed, I didn't want to take a chance on being seen.

Peeking outside, I sucked in a sharp breath. Rosa was still there. Not right outside the door, like before, but just beyond the garden, on the other side of the alley. She must have circled back after parting company with the priest.

I gently pulled on the door, leaving it open only enough to watch as she stealthily moved toward her pickup truck. It was parked in the alley, between Samantha's bungalow and the Anderson sisters' house.

Reaching the vehicle, she surveyed her surroundings, evidently checking to see if anyone was on to her. Seemingly satisfied that no one was, she removed something from the truck bed. In the dark, I couldn't tell exactly what it was, but it appeared to be a tool of some kind. She tucked it under her arm, eased beyond the truck, and jogged across the Andersons' front yard.

I slipped from the shed to follow her. But first I too grabbed a quick look around. A few people lingered on the front sidewalk, next to the highway, but most had returned to the bar. I had every intention of doing the same. Although that was before Rosa lied to Father Daley about needing to hurry inside. Now I was curious. Now I wanted to find out what she was up to.

I moved toward the pickup, careful to tread lightly on the gravel. I peered into the truck bed. Nothing there but garden tools.

So after another look around, I crept along the side of the truck until I reached the driver's window. Peeking in, I saw only a pair of dirty garden gloves. As if on autopilot, I then edged toward the left front bumper, crouched down, and angled forward.

Rosa was climbing the crooked steps of her great aunts' house. She crossed the porch, illuminated by a single overhead light. She knocked on the door. It screeched opened. She stepped inside. And I darted across the lawn.

I hadn't planned on doing any spying. Common sense had dictated otherwise. But as I may have noted, common sense and I didn't always walk in step. I tended to jump ahead. Although in this case, I slithered.

That's right. I slithered along the exterior of the old ladies' house, my back scratching against the blistering paint. I worked my way from the front porch to the bay window on the home's south side. I assumed, like in most old homes, the dining room was located there. The lights were on. The shades had just been drawn. And shadows lurked behind them.

I inched ahead, squeezing between the house and the thorny rose bushes that bordered it. I glanced at my goal. The side pane in the bay window was open from the top, the sash lowered about a half foot. I pressed against the house. I was partially hidden behind a thick rose bush. No one could see me—at least not much of me—even if they knew where to look. But from my vantage point, I couldn't hear much either. I had to get closer. I had to climb higher. And I had to hurry. Rosa would soon head back to the bar. She was part of the band. And the band was playing. My heart, beating with excitement or panic or a potent mixture of the two, was keeping time to the music.

I checked for something to stand on. Of course there's never a ladder around when you need one, though I did spy an outdoor water spigot about fifteen inches off the ground. If I balanced my left foot on the spigot and held tightly to the window frame with my right hand, I could lean close enough to the opening to hear what was going on inside.

I tested the faucet. It seemed strong enough to support me, so I placed my foot on top and heaved myself up, grabbing the window frame. I grunted, and the voices in the house fell silent. I held my breath and anxiously waited for them to make the next move, which they did. Thankfully, though, it was only to resume their conversation.

Filled with relief, I peered through the gap between the frame and the shade. There, at a round oak table, sat Henrietta, Hester, and their grand-niece, Rosa. Harriet was nowhere in sight. Considering her earlier hysterics, I suspected she was in bed, sedated, and fast asleep.

An eighteen-inch-long dandelion digger lay on the table. I knew what it was because my dad had regularly used one in our yard when I was a kid. It must have been what Rosa had retrieved from the back of her truck.

"I'm taking this with me," Rosa said, fiddling with the rusty, fork-like tool. "It's too dangerous to leave lying around. Two of the garden girls were playing with it this afternoon, as if it were a toy."

The old ladies grumbled, but Rosa remained firm. "No argument. Now I've got to go." She scraped her chair across the bare wood floor and stood, the other two doing the same. All three women then left the room, switching off lights as they went.

I jumped to the ground, utterly disappointed. Here I'd been lurking around the Anderson house, where someone could easily catch me, and for what? Nothing but a lesson on garden-tool safety.

Totally frustrated, I stepped from behind the rose bush and readied myself to run to the back of the house before Rosa exited the front. To avoid suspicion, I planned to walk along the nearby street and down the alley, returning to the bar like anyone else who'd gone for a stroll. Once inside, I'd drink another beer or two, collect my recipe cards, and call it a night. I was tired. And I was done spying. It had led to nothing anyway.

I glanced at the old ladies' porch. Still no Rosa. Breathing easier, I bent forward, swearing I could taste the beer that awaited me. I licked my dry lips and was about to take off when I detected something out of the corner of my eye. I stopped, one foot mid-air.

Two men loomed in the distance. They looked to be standing in the alley, visiting. I stared. No, that wasn't right. They weren't standing. Not anymore. They were walking. And they appeared intent on getting wherever they were going. I stared some more. And I gulped down a large heaping of fear when I realized they were headed my way.

I pulled back behind the bush and dropped to my knees, scraping my nose on a rose thorn in the process. The scratch stung, even worse when I rubbed it with my dirty fingers. I parted some branches to get a better view and pricked two fingers along with a thumb. I wanted to yell but settled for cursing under my breath. I swore because of my fingers and because of the men. My fingers ached. The men lumbered across the lawn. And my heart almost leaped from my chest when I recognized them as the Johnson twins.

Immediately I recalled Deputy Ryden's warning: Stay away from Buddy and Buford. They're trouble. Oh, how I wanted to heed that advice.

I pulled in my shoulders and crouched lower. My mind was spinning with thoughts, much like a hamster on a wheel. How did they know where I was? And how did they know I was on to them? Deputy Ryden wouldn't have told them. He didn't like them. He wouldn't have sicced them on me. The idea was absurd. Around and around went the wheel.

But if not him? No one else knew about my suspicions. No one, that is, except Barbie. She was listening to us. But that didn't mean anything. She wouldn't have betrayed me. We were becoming friends, weren't we? Or was she merely keeping an eye on me?

Questions continued to crowd one another in my brain, making it tough to focus on any one of them. But since the twins were closing in, it didn't seem like a great time for "Q and A" anyway. I had to move. And I had to move soon.

Yet, I remained motionless, stilled by the one thought that had worked its way through the quagmire in my head. If the twins were after me, that meant I was right about them. I might have been wrong about Ole and Vern and some others in between, but I was right about the twins. Well, maybe not "right" exactly. But I knew something was up with Buddy. That much I knew for sure.

Yep, you got it. Killers were coming for me. Yet my fear was usurped by exhilaration and pride. But only for a second. After that, I was a hundred-percent scared shitless again. The Johnson brothers were closing in. I had to run. I had to escape.

I wanted to rise, but my legs wouldn't support me. The muscles were too stiff, and my feet were numb. I must have been paralyzed by self-doubt and fear. Not particularly good timing. But there it was.

If I didn't get away, though, I'd get beaten up—or worse. The "worse" made me shudder. If they murdered Samantha Berg, they wouldn't have any qualms about killing me too, would they?

Buford and Buddy were almost on top of me. I had few options. My body was too frightened to listen to my brain, so my only hope was to use my mouth. I'd often employed my mouth without the aid of my brain, so I knew I could do it. And maybe—just maybe—this time things would work out for me.

I slowly lifted my arm to make my presence known. I had no idea what I'd say, but I had to say something. I opened my mouth.

And Buddy hollered, "Hey, Rosa, Wally sent us to find you. Your songs are coming up."

The twins veered toward the porch. The screen door creaked open. Rosa muttered something. The door slammed shut. Rosa bounded down the rickety steps. And I fell on my butt. Thankfully, no one saw me. At least no one looked my way. Instead, Rosa linked her arms through those of her brothers, and together, they started toward the bar.

For a full minute or more, I remained on my rear, my head flat against the cement-block foundation. It was cool and, hopefully, would stimulate my brain. Obviously, I wasn't thinking straight. One minute the twins were out to get me. The next, they weren't. First, Buddy and Buford were crazed killers. Then they were nothing more than their sister's escorts.

I wearily pushed myself up, using the wall for leverage. I needed to go to bed. I needed sleep. I'd been operating on little more than sugar and alcohol for most of the day, and it was wearing me down, impairing my judgment. I'd understand everything better in the morning. It would make much more sense then.

Still hunched over and stiff, I tip-toed beyond the bay window and around the corner to the back of the house. I moved past the rear stoop, confident no one inside was aware of my presence. The stars softly lit the sky, but no lights burned in the house. At least none that I could see. And I heard nothing but the whispering of the treetops and the indistinct voices of people in the distance.

I jogged along the sidewalk till it ended near the detached garage. I stepped into the grass, the dew licking my feet and ankles. I was almost to the street, a public thoroughfare open to everyone. And from there, I'd walk to the end of the block, turn down the alley, and head back to the bar, where I'd once and for all put an end to my nosing around.

I moved in the direction of the road—quickly but carefully—until I was stopped by the voices. The ones down the road—not those in my head. They were louder now. Much louder, prompting me to dodge behind another bush and peek between some more branches to get a bead on what was happening this time around.

Against the night sky, I saw six silhouetted figures. They were headed my way. And they were talking about . . . that couldn't be right. I listened more closely. Were they truly talking about Oriental Hot Dish?

I pinched my arm. *Ouch!* Okay, I wasn't dreaming. Although the entire day seemed like a dream or, more accurately, a nightmare now that I was frightened all over again. My palms were damp. My throat was like sandpaper. And goose bumps were running a relay race up and down my arms.

I was desperate that the people on the road not see me. If they did, they might ask what I was doing in the Anderson sisters' back yard. And I didn't have an answer. What could I say? And what would they do? Alert the ladies? Call the police? I wrung my hands. I had to hide. Just for a minute. Until they passed.

With no further thought, I put action to those words, whirling on my heels and rushing to the narrow door that led into the

Andersons' garage. I turned the knob, thanked the Lord it was unlocked, and slipped inside.

Like the garden shed, the garage was dark, the only light coming from the moon, a beam or two slanting through its sole dirty window.

I waited for my eyes to adjust. But even then I couldn't see much beyond the outline of a large, older-model sedan. It claimed most of the floor, forcing me to creep sideways to avoid smacking my legs on the oversized bumper or brushing against the fiberglass insulation stuffed between the wall studs.

Reaching the window, I peered outside. The walkers had almost gone by, their retreating forms washed in the light of a street lamp. I scanned the road in both directions. No one else was around. I'd be able to leave in a minute or two and head back to the café. And after I got there, I'd go right up to bed. No nightcap. And no more snooping. Ever!

Feeling safer, though slightly embarrassed, I pivoted away from the window. I inhaled and exhaled slowly and deliberately. I'd overreacted. But that was okay. No one would ever find out about my foray into the Andersons' garage or, for that matter, my close encounter with the Johnson twins and their sister. And if by chance they did, I was ready with an excuse. Hell, I had lots of them. I'd been up for more than eighteen hours. I'd driven 400 miles. I'd met a dozen people and had written down three times that many recipes. And I had done it all on a diet of mostly sugar, with a splash of alcohol thrown in for good measure.

I maneuvered away from the window and toward the door. I was convinced I had nothing to worry about. My actions weren't really out of the ordinary. Okay, they were. But, again, no one would be the wiser.

As stepped forward, however, something prickled my senses. I listened closely but only heard the chirping of the crickets outside. Chalking up my worry to overwrought nerves, I lifted my chin, squared my shoulders, and edged ahead. I was done being scared. I was strong. I could take care of myself. Nevertheless, I felt the need for caution. *But caution's okay*, I told myself. Caution wasn't fear. Caution could be a good thing.

Shuffling between the car and the wall, some insulation must have brushed against my arm because I shivered. I tucked my arms against my sides and reminded myself that caution wasn't fear. Caution could be a good thing. I tentatively moved, one foot in front of the other. I was almost there. Almost to the door. I swallowed, the sound of it terribly loud in my ears. Then I gasped as the door—the same one I had used—creaked open.

The overhead light flickered on, and I froze in place. The light illuminated the silver Buick, pink insulation, and Harriet Anderson. She stared at me, her eyes frenzied, her expression agitated. And I knew at once I was in big trouble. Very big trouble.

Part Four
Heat and Serve

Chapter Thirty-Four

Harriet stepped into the garage and closed the door. "Ya just won't go away, will ya?" She looked haggard. Her features sagged, and her short hair darted every which way, as if she'd just gotten out of bed.

"Pardon me?"

"Ya won't leave us alone." As I'd done only minutes earlier, she slunk sideways along the wall, her hands clasped behind her back.

"I didn't mean to intrude, Harriet. I saw some people outside, and they scared me, so I hid in here. I know that doesn't make sense, but I've had a really long day, and frankly, nothing's making much sense. You won't believe what I thought they were talking about. Hot dish. That's right. Hot dish. How crazy is that? See, I'm just not thinking straight."

"Quiet!" She edged closer. "I'm sick of ya and your nonsense. I've told ya time and time again to stay away. But ya just won't listen."

My pulse quickened. She shouldn't have shaken me so. She was an old lady. But she frightened me just the same. I think it was her eyes. They were fully dilated and reminded me of black, treacherous pools of water. As for the feebleness I'd spotted in her earlier? Well, that was nowhere to be seen. Now she only looked strong and full of stormy resolve.

"I thought for sure I'd gotten rid of ya" She pinched her lips together. "But ya just won't stay dead, will ya?"

I backed up, determined to extricate myself from the scene. I walked in reverse, pressing past the car, but then came to an unexpected halt when I bumped into something. I shoved against it.

It wouldn't budge. So I glimpsed over my shoulder. Shit! There stood a huge snow blower, almost three feet across and four feet tall. I was stuck, absolutely nowhere to go. The wall was to my left. The car was to my right. The monster snow blower was behind me. And crazy Harriet loomed about six feet in front of me.

My heart pounded hard against my chest. "Harriet, you're making a mistake."

"Shush! I told ya to be quiet. You've never been nothin' but a trollop. Ya got yourself pregnant so Carl would hafta marry ya. And he hated ya for it. I know. He told me. He wanted to be with me. But ya made sure that didn't happen."

My jaw dropped as the meaning of her words sank in. Harriet had me confused with Elsa, the woman who'd run off with her fiancée, Carl, almost seventy years ago. "But, Harriet, I'm not—"

"I said quiet!" Her eyes then clouded over with what seemed to be an accumulation of years of torment and hatred. She slowly pulled her right hand out from behind her back. And there it was. The dandelion digger. Rosa had apparently left it behind. "I don't care how many times it takes," she hissed, "I'll do it. I'll kill ya."

I was shocked and scared. Yet, I uttered, "So much for garden-tool safety."

I know. I know. I crack wise when my life's being threatened. Okay, I crack wise all the time. And I'm sure there's some deep-seeded reason for it that my therapist would be more than happy to probe at length. But believe me, it was a discussion for another day. At present, I had to act.

Of course I had no desire to hurt Harriet. She was old and not in her right mind much of the time. Although she did have a weapon. And as she lifted it above her head, she appeared quite capable of doing some serious damage with it, especially if it connected with any of my vital organs.

I glanced around the room. I wanted a weapon of my own. Not to hurt her. Just to scare her away. I scanned the wall next to me, then the one on the opposite side. No weapons. No tools of any kind. I was in a frickin' garage and not a single tool in sight!

Oh, come on, Emme, one of my little voices said, *you don't need a weapon. She can't be very strong. Just go ahead and jump her.*

I didn't want to. I didn't want to hurt her. And there was always the off chance that something could go wrong, and she could end up stabbing me. No, I just wanted to escape. Then I'd run for help. And after that, we'd straighten out this entire mess. It was just some kind of terrible misunderstanding. I was sure of that.

Oh, Emme, it's sweet that you want to work things out, but I don't think she's feeling the love. See that dandelion digger? It's big! It's sharp! And it's pointed at you!

I didn't care. I'd escape. Then I'd get help.

Help? Who's going to help you, Emme? The Johnson twins? Barbie? Can you trust anyone around here?

Answers to those questions were irrelevant. First, I had to find a way out of the garage.

I glanced at the car beside me. It was a four-door sedan with push-button locks. They appeared to be up, which, after a moment or two of consideration, led to a whisper of a plan. And with Harriet schlepping nearer, I figured, it very well could be the only plan I'd get to "test drive" so to speak. Yeah, I know. A wiseass till the bitter end. I only hoped that the "end" wouldn't be anytime soon.

That thought caused beads of sweat to form on my upper lip, while perspiration trickled down my sides. The garage was closed up tight. So stuffy my lungs could barely function, although my stomach was faring far worse. Dread was at war with determination, and currently, dread had the edge, actually pushing a little vomit up into my mouth. I swallowed it back down.

Shuddering from the bitter taste and the situation I found myself in, I reviewed my plan, visualizing it several times over. And when it worked well in my head, I went with it before I could find its flaws or chicken out for some other reason.

I mimicked everything as I saw it played out in my mind's eye. I jerked the driver's door open, jumped in behind the wheel and, in one fluid motion, bounced around, locking all four doors. I then laid on the horn.

I used my free hand to check for a garage-door opener. My objective was simple. I'd back the car out and drive myself to safety. Just one problem. No opener. Not on the visor. Or in the glove box. But that didn't really matter because there weren't any keys in the ignition either. I slouched against the back of the seat, not at all surprised. It had been that kind of day.

As I shook my head in resignation, my eyes fell on Harriet. She was propped against the wall, framed in pink insulation. The car door must have struck her when I yanked it open. I guess I missed it. I was too busy saving myself. But now I wondered if she was hurt. And for a split second, I thought about helping her. However, as she righted herself and charged at me, screaming like a banshee, I dismissed that idea.

I honked some more.

Where was everyone? Why didn't they hear me? Were they all back in the bar? Was the band drowning out my SOS?

Another possibility nudged me like a tap on the shoulder. Oh, my God, were they purposely ignoring me? Was I no different from Samantha Berg? Just another outsider making waves? Just someone else who needed to go away?

As Harriet struck the driver's window with the dandelion digger, I dismissed those questions, choosing instead to concentrate on my honking rhythm. Two long blasts followed by a series of short beeps. Did a minute go by? An hour? I wasn't sure. Harriet pounded on the glass, and I honked my desperate tune. Another minute? Another hour?

Then there was something. Something else. Something other than the honking. I eased off the horn. It was more of a rumbling. Harriet stepped away from the car. Still more rumbling. But this time it wasn't from inside of me. It wasn't fear. Although fear was undoubtedly present. No, this was a mechanical rumbling. The rumbling of . . . the garage door. Yes, the garage door. It was rising. The garage door was rising.

I glanced in the rear-view mirror, eager for deliverance and a peek at my savior. Briefly, I imagined it to be Deputy Ryden. In my mind, he rescued me, carried me off for our date, and we lived happily ever after.

In reality, though, the image of Deputy Ryden morphed into one I couldn't recognize at first. I blinked and checked the mirror again. The picture was getting clearer. Or was it?

I swiveled to see for myself, unable to accept the reflection in the mirror. But there was no mistake. It wasn't an illusion. My actual rescuers were there. And they were none other than Henrietta and Hester. The air in my lungs escaped by way of a long-suffering sigh.

Of course they weren't my saviors of choice. But what choice did I have? And I suppose it made sense. They were in the house. They heard the honking before anyone else. And they came to investigate. Now they only had to talk some sense into their sister. But could they? Would they? Or would they . . . help her?

Remember, Emme, blood is thicker than water.

I ordered the little voice in my head to shut the hell up.

Then I checked the glove box again. Still no garage-door opener. Still no weapon. So I bent over and searched beneath the seat. I only needed a screw driver. Or a hammer. Just a little something to even the score if necessary. But I found nothing except a useless plastic window scraper. I threw it back on the floor. I guess I was on my own, with nothing but a mind full of smart-ass comments and a lifetime's worth of emotional baggage.

"Now, tell me," Henrietta barked, "what in the Sam Hill is goin' on out here? Ya interrupted our snack. Me and Hester here were havin' ourselves some Corn Flake Hot Dish."

Chapter Thirty-Five

THE TWO OLD LADIES SEPARATED, Henrietta slowly looping around my side of the car, where Harriet was standing, and Hester circling from the opposite direction.

"Harriet," Henrietta asked, "what's goin' on here? What's all the hoopla?"

Harriet stood firm. "I gotta kill her again. It didn't take last time."

Henrietta glanced at me. She must have noticed that I'd rolled down the window about an inch and could hear everything being said. "Now, Harriet, quiet down," she warned. "Ya don't know what you're talkin' about."

"Oh, yah, I do. I thought I killed her that night she came to the house. Remember? It was the night ya cooked that Broccoli and Stuffing Casserole, and I told ya not to make it ever again 'cause it caused me to bloat somethin' awful."

"Harriet, you shush now."

Despite my curiosity about what Harriet had just said regarding killing someone, a part of me actually wanted her to listen to her older sister and stop talking. I had no desire to hear about her bloating. None whatsoever. But I guess it didn't matter either way, because I don't think she even heard Henrietta. Rather, she appeared to have slipped into another world.

"Yah," she said, "Elsa thought she was really somethin'. Tellin' me to stop peepin' out the window. Stop watchin' her. Warnin' me to mind my own business. But Carl was my business."

Henrietta glimpsed at me, nervous tension clearly humming through her. "Harriet, shut your mouth. Don't say any more. If ya do, ya could end up in trouble."

Harriet was oblivious to us. She spoke in a soft monotone, the dandelion digger poised in front of her, ready to strike. "She laughed at me, ya know. After all she done, cavortin' with Carl right next door, day after day, all those years, that tramp had the nerve to laugh at me." She cackled like a witch. "Called me crazy and such. Well, I showed her crazy." She cackled again. "Yah, I showed her crazy right in the heart. With this." She shook the dandelion digger.

And I slumped against the seat. There it was. The missing piece of the jigsaw puzzle—the puzzle that had gone unfinished for years. With the final jagged piece now snapped into place, I could see the picture in its entirety. And what a picture it was. Not only had Harriet mistaken me for Elsa, she'd mistaken Samantha Berg for her too.

"Shut up, Harriet!" Henrietta shouted. "Shut up right this minute!"

Something flickered in the depths of Harriet's eyes. She might have been shocked by Henrietta's words, but more likely, she sensed that Hester had edged up behind her.

The smallest sister heaved her shoulders and stretched her arms high into the air in an effort to snatch the dandelion digger away. But Harriet wasn't about to give it up. With a dog-like growl, she elbowed little Hester in the mid-section, sending her across the floor and to her knees. And after that, she pivoted, licking her moustache and slashing the dandelion digger like it was the sword of an old pirate—a pirate insane from being too long at sea.

Henrietta was waiting, and she too fought to wrench the dandelion digger away. Harriet still refused to surrender it. She yanked on the rusty tool and pulled it away, slicing Henrietta in the shoulder in the process. The mother hen let out a blood-curdling scream and crumbled to the floor.

I shoved the car door open just as Harriet lifted the dandelion digger again, its sharp end stained with her sister's blood. Scared as I was, I bent to check on Henrietta. She was sobbing, her brittle hands pressed against her wound. The cut looked messy but not life threatening. Then again, what did I know?

Emboldened by the anger that grew from looking into Henrietta's terrified eyes, I yelled at Harriet. "See what you've done! Now give me that thing!"

I was almost as furious with myself as I was with Harriet. I should have moved faster. I shouldn't have allowed Henrietta and Hester to get hurt. But I was tired. And it had happened so fast. And none of it had seemed real. Yet, it was real. And now Harriet stood nearby, the dandelion digger at the ready.

"Harriet, you've hurt your sisters! You better give me that thing before you cause any more harm."

The old lady backhanded drool from her lips. "I didn't hurt 'em. I'd never hurt 'em. I'm good to 'em, and they're good to me. The last time I killed ya they even helped me do away with your body."

"What?" She continued to surprise me.

"Please, Harriet," Henrietta whimpered, "don't say anything else."

Harriet didn't bother to look at either of us. She just stared ahead, her eyes vacant. "When they came into the entry and saw ya dead on the floor, they wrapped ya in that big rug of ours. The one that used to be under the dinner table. Then we drug ya in here and put ya in the trunk of the car. You were way fatter then." She flashed a demented grin. "We could barely lift ya."

I remained silent. I didn't want to interrupt. I wanted her to keep talking. To tell me everything. That's right. Once again my curiosity overtook my fear and probably my common sense. Again, what can I say?

"You 'member?" Harriet's accent was thicker, her words more ragged. She was getting tired. "We buried ya in that field, under da snow. And we hid the digger in Rosa's garden." Her grin drooped into a frown. "But those kids found it today. And ya wouldn't stay buried." She swayed from side to side, her rant taking its toll.

I carefully moved toward her, planning to grab the digger before she could react. But she saw what I was up to and tightened her grip, her knobby knuckles turning white. "Now I gotta kill ya all over again. Not only for what ya did to me and Carl, but for Rosa too."

"Rosa?" Another surprise. "What about Rosa?"

"Well, we didn't know that field was goin' to get built on. Canola? Why would a canola plant get built here? When we found out, we had to ask Rosa. She'd know what to do."

She gulped air. "We ended up movin' ya to da snow bank. Behind da beet plant. Along da river." She went in search of another breath, but this one was much harder to find. "Bad floodin' was 'spected. Rosa reckoned ya'd float into Canada, bein' the Red flows north. But ya didn't. Ya came back here. Now I gotta—"

"Rosa helped you?"

Harriet wobbled, her eyes blinking uncontrollably. "She didn't wanna. She had no choice. It's tormented her somethin' awful. And it's your fault."

"My fault?"

She waved the digger in the air like a magic wand that would help me understand the world according to Harriet. "If ya would of stayed away from Carl, none of this . . . But, no . . ." Her head rocked.

Another minute or two and she'd be unable to put up much of a fight. "Harriet, I still don't understand. I thought you hated Carl for what he did."

"Hated him?" Tears welled up in her eyes. "I loved him. I've loved him my whole life. Henrietta and Hester just wanted him to pay for what he done, gettin' Elsa pregnant and all. And I agreed he should get taught a lesson. But I never hated him."

A tear trailed down her cheek. I watched for my opportunity. She lifted her free hand to wipe it away. And that's when I jumped her.

I clasped both my hands around the dandelion digger and shook it with everything I had. But she wouldn't let go. She held on tight, staying with me, toe to toe, the two of us circling in a strange and furious dance. Around and around we went, her stale breath hot on my face, her arms hugging my shoulders. I led her. Then she led me.

When I backed her against the car. I thought I had her. But using the bumper for leverage, she propelled herself forward, thrashing with all her might, striving to shove the digger into my chest.

I'm sure my eyes relayed terror. But hers expressed nothing. And even though I was battling for my life, one tract of my mind veered off to something one of my professors had often said: "Don't be fooled. Eyes aren't the windows to the soul everyone thinks they are."

Staring into hers, I wasn't so sure. Maybe my professor had never been up close and personal with a mad woman. As I imagined Harriet's soul to be, her eyes were dark and barren. And they scared the hell out of me.

I pushed against her. But the dandelion digger inched closer to my chest. My grip was slipping. Blood was pulsing through my ears. And fear and Harriet were kicking me in the gut.

Was this the end? Was I going to be done in by an eighty-something granny-type with a crazy disposition and a rusty dandelion digger?

I was about to feel sorry for myself for all the things I'd never get to do—drive in a demolition derby or visit Ireland or eat all the pie I wanted or have a baby or even a pet—when one of the little voices from inside my head spoke up.

Hey, Emme, get a grip! Take care of business, or you'll be known as the woman who got taken down by a geriatric nut job. And if that happens, if you aren't dead already, you'll wish you were.

I didn't think that was true. Nor did I want to follow the advice of my little voices. I still was ticked off at them for not helping me when I was trapped in the garden shed. But this didn't seem like the best time to be holding a grudge. So I drew in a long breath and, on the exhale, shoved against Harriet as hard as I could.

Her body slammed against the car, and she let out a strange noise. A woosh of some kind. She might have gotten the wind knocked out of her. I didn't stop to check. Instead, I bent her backwards over the hood, pinning her there, my faced pressed against her cheek, my tears and sweat mixing with hers.

I had no idea where my strength was coming from. I didn't feel like myself. I was certain I was hovering above the action, while someone who only looked like me fought it out with the hairy old lady. But it was me. Me and my repressed anger. Anger from years of pain and heartache. Anger over this truly sucky day.

I wacked Harriet's gnarly hand against the hood over and over again, until she cried out in pain. She unclenched her fist, and I seized the dandelion digger. It was the weapon she'd used to kill Samantha Berg, and I wasn't about to leave it behind while I ran for help.

With the digger secure, I checked on Henrietta. She remained in a ball on the floor, mewling like a battered cat. For her part, Hester was crouched in the far corner, doing some whimpering of her own. And Harriet? Well, she was still slouched over the hood of the car, rubbing her shoulder and sobbing.

The scene was surreal, and for a moment, I stood there, dazed. How did this happen? I only came to Kennedy for hot dish and Jell-O recipes. Nothing more. Definitely not this.

Henrietta pulled me back into the moment with a noise that was part gurgle, part sob. I stared at her, studying the emotions fighting over her face: fear, mistrust, but mostly desperate need.

You have to go, I told myself. *You have to get help.*

I didn't think Harriet would take off, but I wasn't positive. I didn't think she'd further harm her sisters, although I wasn't certain about that either. The only thing I knew for sure was that Henrietta and Hester needed medical attention. And since I'd left my phone in the bedroom above the café, not imagining I'd have any use for it, I had no choice but to run for help.

As I turned, wondering where I should go and who I could trust, my legs wobbled beneath me. I inhaled and urged my legs to try again. Another step. More wobbling.

I glanced at my destination—the driveway and, beyond that, the alley. If I took my time, I could do it. I could reach the bar. I could get help. I could . . .

I blinked several times, unwilling to believe what I saw. It was Buddy and Buford. They were standing at the entrance to the garage. And no mistake about it, this time they saw me. And this time they headed right for me.

I struggled to speak, but my words got strangled in my throat. I fought to set them free, yet I only managed strange and desperate noises.

"Emerald," Buddy said, palms up, "what's going on here?"

I backed against the snow blower. "I don't know." I forced the words out on a breath filled with fear. "Just stay away!"

Ignoring me, they edged around the car. Closer and closer. Until they spotted Henrietta.

"Holy shit!" Buford shouted. "Did you stab her?"

His face was ripe with confusion. Or was it anger or rage? I couldn't tell. And his question didn't register. It made no sense. Stab her? How could I stab her?

The dandelion digger. I saw it then. It was in my hand. And my hand was poised above my head. "Oh, no . . ." I lowered my arm as new tears stung my eyes. "No, she . . . um . . . tried . . ." My entire body trembled. "She tried . . ."

I blinked back the tears. I couldn't cry. I had to watch them. I couldn't trust the twins. I had to track their every move. At any moment, they could jump me. Two against one. Then what would I do?

I gripped the dandelion digger tighter. I blinked some more. Yes, I saw them. There they were. On the other side of my tears. But no. They weren't alone. Now Barbie was with them. Right next to them. And someone else too.

"This can't be real," I mumbled. It had to be a dream. Why else would Deputy Ryden be here?

I wanted to ask him. I had to find out. But before I could, my world went black.

Chapter Thirty-Six

I DON'T REMEMBER WHAT HAPPENED next. I guess I fainted. When I came to, I smelled fried rice. And when I opened my eyes, I found myself lying on the garage floor, a jacket draped over me. Barbie was seated on the cement beside me.

"Don't move," she said. "You've got quite a bump on your noggin."

My head hurt, but I lifted it anyway. I wanted to shake the cobwebs from my brain. Of course that only made my head hurt worse. But I didn't lie down again. I couldn't. I had to make sense out of what had happened.

I turned on my side and leaned up on my elbow. I spotted Margie at the far end of the garage, tending to Henrietta and Hester. Deputy Ryden and a guy I didn't recognize were huddled outside, in the dark, visiting with the Johnson twins and Harriet.

"I need to talk to someone," I said, my voice froggy.

"Shush. You passed out and hit your head on the snow blower." Barbie nodded at the monster machine. "You were unconscious for a while. You've been in and out some too. So just rest until the doctor gets here."

"But I need to tell someone . . ."

"Hey, Randy," she hollered.

The sound reverberated in my ears. "No, not him. I can't trust him."

"What?" She pursed her lips, her expression suggesting I was daffy. And I probably was. I'd been attacked by a giant snow blower. And I'd been duped by a town full of dangerous nuts.

"Well, if it isn't Sleeping Beauty," Deputy Ryden said as he ambled over.

And to both of us, he added, "The doctor's on his way."

"She definitely needs one," Barbie replied. "She's not making any sense."

Randy glanced at the back of the garage. "Why don't you give Margie a hand? I'll take over here."

"Are you sure?" Barbie looked at me, her face lined with worry.

What was that about? Was she afraid I'd say something to the deputy? Hardly. He was as mixed up in all of this as she was.

Barbie hesitated and only moved on after the deputy again urged her to go. He then took her spot on the floor.

"You gave us quite a scare." He crossed his legs and gently patted my arm, his eyes filled with what appeared to be real concern. But that couldn't be. He was one of them.

I raised my hand to my head, determined to sit up and then get to my feet. "I'm fine. I don't need any medical attention." My fingers brushed against a golf-ball-sized bump, and I winced.

Randy chuckled. "Well, maybe you do, maybe you don't. Why not let the doctor decide?"

I squinted. For a moment, there were two of him. "No doctor. But I do want to talk to someone. I want to tell them what—"

"There's plenty of time for that later." He took my hand. And even though I didn't want to like it, I did. It was big and warm and comforting. And I desperately wanted to be comforted. I was alone and confused and awfully sore. "Besides," he added. "Hester and Henrietta are sharing quite a bit with us. And Harriet's been a wealth of information in her own right. Although with her, we have to parse fantasy from reality."

What did he mean by that?

"Yeah, between all of them, we've developed a pretty clear picture of what happened."

What? Was he suggesting I had something to do with this mess?

I pulled my hand free of his. "I didn't hurt Henrietta. It was . . . her." I nodded at Harriet.

"We know. We know." Again he wrapped his fingers around my hand, caressing the back of it with his calloused thumb.

I leaned a little higher on my elbow. "You know?"

He nodded, his eyes expressing kindness and perhaps a bit of sympathy.

"You know she killed Samantha?"

"We do now. We've heard the whole sordid story. We even have the dandelion digger." He bobbed his head toward the Buick. The dandelion digger was in a plastic bag on the roof. "I'm just sorry you got mixed up in it."

I felt my shoulders relax as I processed what he said and what it meant. Given my cloudy thinking, it was slow going. But after I finally finished, I couldn't help but smile. Deputy Rydan, it turned out, was a good guy. An honest-to-goodness good guy.

Still, I hesitated, not at all sure how my next statement would be met. Even so, I felt compelled to go with it. "So . . . um . . . did they tell you . . . about . . . Rosa?"

The deputy barely moved his head in response. And I immediately regretted asking the question. Then I wondered why I had. I didn't care for any of the possible explanations, jealously being the worst and most likely, with insecurity running a close second.

"She's being questioned in the café." His eyes looked terribly sad.

"I'm sorry," I whispered. And I truly was. Sorry for what he was going through. And sorry for being the jerk who had thrown it in his face.

He shrugged. "You have nothing to be sorry about."

"Yes, I do. Believe me."

He raised his hand and repeated more emphatically, "You have absolutely nothing to be sorry about. You didn't cause any of this."

Maybe not. But I felt bad for him just the same. And, believe it or not, for Rosa too. I guess that while I didn't want her involved with the deputy, I didn't really want her mixed up in muder either.

So maybe there was hope for me after all. "She was only trying to help her great aunts, you know."

I took in a quick breath. While those words had apparently been spoken by me, they felt foreign just the same. Remember, I was Ms. Law and Order. My motto: "You Do the Crime, You Do the Time." I'd never before considered things like "mitigating circumstances." Yet, I went on to say, "She didn't set out to do anything terrible, you know."

The deputy squirmed. "Yeah, well, I guess we'll have to sort all that out."

Yes, we will, I confirmed to myself. And while we were at it, I'd also find out what role Barbie played in all of this. And Margie too. As for Harriet . . .

She was sitting on a stool just outside the garage. There was an older man with her, the guy who'd been talking with Randy when I came to. I suspected he was a cop. Even dressed in jeans and a tee-shirt, he looked the part. He also looked to be questioning Harriet, who appeared more than happy to provide him with answers.

"What will happen to Harriet?" I asked the question of myself, but absently spoke out loud.

The deputy answered, "I'm not sure."

"She's sick you know."

Harriet started to cry. I couldn't hear her, but I saw her dab her eyes with a tissue, as several others, all wadded up, blew around on the ground.

"She didn't know what she was doing." Again I was caught off guard by the turn my thoughts had taken. "The entire time she was here in the garage her eyes were blank."

The deputy heaved a sigh and shifted his legs. "Emerald, she tried to kill you."

My gaze held steady on the old lady. She looked vulnerable again, as she did earlier in the day, not at all like when she was trying to . . . I shooed those images away.

"No, that's not right, Randy. She didn't try to kill me. She wanted to kill Elsa Erickson."

The deputy dropped my hand and ran his own through his hair, unmistakably exasperated. "Elsa Erickson's been dead for decades."

"So?"

"So what exactly are you suggesting, Emerald?" He stared at me, his expression a blend of intense emotions. "What are you suggesting?" He repeated. "Because Harriet gets mixed up sometimes, we should send her to bed without any supper and leave it at that?"

"Not necessarily, but . . ." I let my voice trail off because I wasn't sure what I meant. This was unchartered territory for me. And while I wanted to believe I was growing up and becoming more compassionate, I couldn't help but wonder if my benevolence was, in large part, simply the result of getting konked on the head. And tomorrow I'd wake up just as ego-centric as I'd been earlier in the day.

The deputy cupped my chin with his hand and turned my head so my face was only inches from his own. "Harriet's a murderer." His voice had turned firm and certain. "And those other two are accomplishes." He nodded toward Henrietta and little Hester. "Not to mention that one in . . ." He lowered his hand, unable to say any more. Maybe he wasn't so sure of himself after all.

"Anyhow"—He started over after clearing his throat—"I'm glad we got here when we did."

I thought about that for a second or two. "How did you know to come?"

He leaned his head to the side. "Barbie called me."

"What?" That didn't sound right.

"Barbie called," he repeated. "She heard some commotion over here and sent Buddy and Buford to investigate but thought I'd better stop by too."

I shifted my elbow. "Barbie?" It still didn't make sense.

"Yeah, she's been really concerned about you, watching over you while you were unconscious and everything."

"You mean she wasn't involved with Buford and Buddy?"

"What?" He wrinkled his brow in apparent concern. "You'd better shush, now. And lie still."

I tried to sit up, but my head was a brick. "No, I need to know. I deserve to know what happened." I sounded much gruffer than I intended.

Randy took hold of my shoulders and, in a resigned tone, said, "Okay. Okay. Don't get all riled up. Lie down, and I'll tell you."

I smiled. "Good."

Before I put my head down, I glanced behind me to see what was serving as my pillow. "Is that your jacket?"

"Yeah, and it's still dirty. Sorry."

I sniffed the air. "I thought you said someone spilled glorified rice on it?"

He nodded.

"But it smells like fried rice."

He shrugged. "Glorified rice. Fried rice. Whatever."

Concussion aside, that statement made absolutely no sense. Yet I let it slide. My brain was in no shape to take on very much, and I wanted to concentrate on what had occurred earlier. So I said, "Okay, just tell me about Buford and Buddy."

As I rested my head on the dirty jacket, the deputy covered me with another one—a clean one—wrapping it around my arms and tucking it under my chin. "Well, once upon a time . . ."

"Very funny." Yep, even injured, I was ready with the snappy comebacks. Or not.

Randy cast his eyes downward. "Well, um . . . I guess it's possible that Buddy and Buford had nothing to do with Samantha's death." He voice was low, practically inaudible.

I couldn't help but smile, although, in truth, I didn't try very hard to stop myself. "So your instincts were wrong?"

Randy teasingly glowered. "You're supposed to be quiet."

"Yeah, yeah." I really wanted to give him a hard time, but my head was throbbing. I'd have to wait for another day.

"Besides," he proceeded to say, "if I'm not mistaken, you reported 'bad vibes' from Buddy too. What's more, my instincts weren't totally off. The twins were hiding something."

He once more squirmed on the cement. "You see, to get through the first anniversary of their mother's death, they evidently barricaded themselves in a hotel room down in the Cities and drank themselves unconscious. And while they won't admit it, I think there were some other chemicals involved too. You know, anything to numb the pain."

I turned my head to catch a glimpse of Buddy and Buford. They were standing outside, behind Harriet. And they weren't moving a muscle. From the look of it, they were intimidated by the cop. Understandable since even in street clothes, the guy resembled an army drill sergeant.

"Anyhow," Deputy Ryden said, "from what we've learned, Father Daley found them or found out what they were doing and agreed to cover for them. Not because of Samantha. It had nothing to do with her. He just didn't want the twins in trouble for underage drinking. Or, more likely, illegal drugs."

"So that's why no one saw them? That's why they refused to take a lie-detector test?"

"Exactly."

"And Father Daley told you all this?"

"No, he won't say a word. At least not yet. Priest confidentiality and all. But the boys confessed parts of the story." He paused. "We may not be members of the clergy, but we have our ways." He raised an eyebrow.

"On top of that," he continued, "I received some information late today, before coming back to the bar, that corroborated my suspicions about Buford and Buddy and their illegal drug use. I just can't go into it right now."

"Fair enough. But it makes me sad."

"What do you mean?" He stopped for a beat. "Are you telling me you feel sorry for Buddy?" Another beat. "Hey, you didn't fall for him after just a couple of dances, did you?"

I attempted to laugh, but my chest ached too much. Most likely I had some bruised ribs to go with my bruised noggin. "No, nothing like that," I uttered after a shallow breath. "But the information you received explains why you seemed more concerned about me tonight than earlier in the day."

"And?"

"And here I thought you were showing more interest tonight because, at some point after our dinner together, you discovered you really liked me." Yep, head injuries and all, yet I could still flirt. It was downright shameful.

"I do like you."

My face grew warm. At least I had the decency to be embarrassed. "Well, um . . . ," I stammered. "Tell me . . . um . . . tell me the whole story about Samantha Berg's death." When flustered, change the subject. Words to live by. "I want all the details."

Randy squirmed some more. He really shouldn't have been sitting on the cold, hard, concrete floor, but I was glad he was. "We've only been here a while, so we don't know everything. But it appears that when Vern went to Samantha's house that last night, he ripped her a new one for destroying Ole and Lena's family. With it being the one-year anniversary of Lena's death, we didn't find that too surprising." He took my hand in his and played with my fingers. A simple gesture that felt pleasantly intimate.

"Back then, Vern also told us that Samantha became furious with him. Again, not surprising. But now, tonight, we learned from the Anderson sisters that after Vern left Samantha's house, Samantha noticed that Harriet had been watching them and decided to take her left-over rage out on her. So she headed next door."

He glanced at Harriet before proceeding with his story. I did the same. She was once again wiping away tears.

"Anyhow, Samantha wasn't aware of Harriet's fragile state of mind. If she had been, she probably would have stayed home or gone to the bar, like she'd promised Jim.

"She supposedly taunted Harriet, which sounds about right. Samantha loved to badger people. But most weren't unstable. It drove Harriet over the edge." He shook his head.

"She apparently grabbed the dandelion digger from her gardening box, which also serves as a bench in the entry. We're checking it out right now." He nodded in the direction of the old ladies' house. "She stabbed Samantha, thinking she was killing Elsa Erickson, the woman who stole her boyfriend some seven decades earlier."

The deputy raised his eyes to the elderly man standing over him. "Oh, Doc, I didn't see you there." He unwrapped his legs and rose to his feet. "This is Emerald Malloy."

"Hi, Emerald, I'm Doc Watson."

The old man bent down next to me. His face reminded me of driftwood, and he had more hair growing over his eyes and in his ears than on top of his head.

He flashed a pen light in my eyes and felt around my head and neck. "Since you were out cold for a while, I'll need to run some tests. And I'll want you to stay with me at the hospital tonight." He glanced at his wrist watch. "Or what's left of it."

I fidgeted. "I really don't think I need—"

"Exactly. I really don't think I need you second-guessing me. I'm the doctor. You're the patient."

"Doctor, I didn't mean—"

He interrupted again, "And you never know. You might like it. Some women actually enjoy spending the night with me." He winked, and the deputy chuckled. "So let's get you into my car. You've been waiting here too long as it is."

He looked to Randy. "She doesn't appear to weigh much. Think you can carry her?"

"No," I lifted my arms in protest. "No one needs to carry me."

"Well," the doctor said as he stood, kneading what appeared to be a sore back, "I don't have a gurney here, and you, young lady, aren't going to walk. So . . ."

Before I could object further, Randy threw aside the jacket that covered me and scooped me into his arms. "I promise I won't drop you." And without another word, he trailed the doctor out the garage and down the driveway.

Not knowing what to do with my arms, I clasped them in front of me. But that left me feeling as if I might fall, so I ended up draping them loosely around the deputy's neck. And only because my head hurt an awful lot, I rested it on his shoulder.

He moved slowly across the alley, where small groups of gawkers gathered, watching and waiting for who knows what. And after a glimpse at them, I again burrowed my head between his neck and his shoulder.

Reaching the car, the doctor opened the front passenger door, and Randy carefully slid me onto the seat. "I have to stay here a while," he said, settling me in. "But later, after Doc gives you a clean bill of health, call me, and I'll come get you. You'll need a ride because your car's at the café, and that's where it'll stay until Doc says you can drive." He slipped a business card into my shirt pocket. "My personal cell number is on the back." He winked, and my face grew warm. He was teasing me for shoving my business card into his pocket after kissing him earlier.

"In the meantime," he added, his forehead again falling into thoughtful lines, "just remember, you're safe."

"Huh? What do you mean?"

He leaned closer. He smelled like fresh air and pine trees. "Your brain's putting up a good fight right now, Emerald. But at some point, it's going to give in, and you'll fully realize what happened here tonight. That may frighten you. But that's okay. Just let Doc know. He'll help you through it."

"Randy, until you brought it up, I'd managed to avoid thinking about pretty much everything that occurred tonight." I felt myself blush, yet added, "At least the bad stuff."

He smiled, his face within kissing distance of mine. "Yeah, well, you won't be able to pick and choose for long," he replied. "But Doc will talk to you more about that at the hospital."

He pulled back, then must have decided, what the hell, because he dipped forward and lightly brushed my lips with a kiss. I quivered, and he chuckled. "Now, I'm not bragging, Emerald, but those shivers have absolutely nothing to do with your concussion. My kisses have that effect on all the women."

With a smirk on his face, he yanked his head from the car and hollered, "Hey, Doc, she's cold. Must be the shock. You got a blanket in the trunk?"

He gently closed the door, and I laid back and shut my eyes. My head was pounding, but I couldn't get rid of the stupid grin on my face. I could feel it as I pictured him kissing me. Sure, he was goofy and, at times, infuriating, but I liked him just the same.

As for the stuff he'd said about me being unable to keep my mind off bad things? Well, he didn't know me all that well. I was quite accomplished at keeping the boogeymen at bay. I'd done it for years. Sure, sometimes my emotions got the better of me. But that's why I saw a therapist, although I did my best to avoid thinking about anything that might upset me. To date, it had proven to be a fairly effective strategy, even if my therapist—and now Deputy Ryden—didn't seem to endorse it.

I shifted in my seat. Where was the doctor? I was chilly and wanted that blanket. I was tempted to open my eyes and check for him, but the gawkers were still out there. I could feel them staring. So I kept my eyes shut and took my mind off my goose bumps by focusing on the music softly playing on the car radio.

It was a favorite Kristofferson song of mine—from my parent's era. It carried me back to evenings when I was young, and the three of us would dance in our living room. And now, tonight, after the song was over, the last few lines replayed through my mind, a family reverie I apparently wasn't ready to let go. "*'Cause the moral doesn't matter. Broken rules are all the same. To the broken or the breaker. Who's to bless, and who's to blame?*"

That's what I thought. Just a warm memory to comfort me during a tough time. But then one of my little voices broke in and said, *Hey, Emme, do you really know? "Who's to bless, and who's to blame?"* And after that, images flashed through my head. Images of Ole and Lena, Samantha Berg, Vern and Vivian, the Johnson twins, Rosa, Father Daley, and the Anderson sisters. "*Who's to bless, and who's to blame?*" More images. My parents crashing through a guardrail. Me accepting a check written in blood. Samantha taunting Rosa. And Harriet stabbing Samantha.

I yanked my eyes open. My lips were quivering. And my hands were shaking. "*'Cause the moral doesn't matter. Broken rules are all the same. To the broken or the breaker. Who's to bless, and who's to blame?*" My breath caught in my throat. And tears began to fall uncontrollably down my face.

"Damn!" I didn't want to give into my feelings. The last time I did, on the anniversary of the death of my parents, I think I cried for six or seven hours. And it changed absolutely nothing. It only led me to think about things. Hard things. Painful things.

Beyond that, it merely made me hungry. No, not hungry. Ravenous. And here I was on my way to a hospital. An institution not known for fine cuisine. Not even particularly good comfort food. So tell me. How was I supposed to make it through the night?

Recipes from Hot Dish Heaven

One-Arm Hot Dish

1 lb. lean ground beef
1 can stewed tomatoes (chopped)
1 can tomato soup
1 c. macaroni
Salt and pepper to taste

Brown the ground beef. While the meat is browning, cook the macaroni according to the directions on the box. When the meat is brown, rinse it with water to remove the excess fat. (I tell my customers that by doing this, my hot dishes are "low fat.") Then add the stewed tomatoes and the tomato sauce. Finally, drain the water from the noodles and add the noodles and seasonings to the meat mixture, gently mixing them. Simmer over medium-low heat for ten minutes, stirring on occasion. This dish is good with a green salad. (Note, all of my recipes are for "normal" portions. I double or triple them for café or when I'm doing a church luncheon.)

Chocolate Frosted Mint Bars

1 c. white, all-purpose flour, sifted
1 c. white Crystal sugar
1 can Hershey's chocolate syrup
4 eggs

2 c. powdered sugar
½ c. margarine (don't use butter)
½ tsp. mint extract
3 drops green food coloring

6 tsp. margarine (don't use butter)
1 c. chocolate chips

Preheated to 350°. Mix together the flour, Crystal sugar, eggs, and chocolate syrup and bake that mixture in a 10-x-13-inch greased, brownie pan for about 20 minutes. The bars are done when a toothpick is stuck into them and comes out clean. Don't bake them too long. Cool the bars at room temperature or in the refrigerator. (Note, during the baking process, you may have to use a toothpick to poke air bubbles that form in the mixture.)

With a mixer, beat together the margarine, powdered sugar, mint extract, and food coloring from the right-hand column until it's thick and creamy. Spread the mixture over cooled bars. Then chill until the topping is set.

Mix the margarine and chocolate chips from the bottom, left-hand column in a small saucepan over low heat until the mixture is melted. Stir regularly. Pour the mixture over the mint-topped bars, spreading it carefully. Place the bars in the refrigerator until cool and set. Cut the bars into squares before the chocolate topping becomes too hard. If you wait too long, the frosting will crack when you cut it.

ꕥ Carrot Bars ꕥ

2 c. white Crystal sugar
4 jumbo eggs
3 small jars of baby-food carrots
2 tsp. baking soda
1 tsp. salt
1½ tsp. cinnamon
1 c. chopped walnuts

Preheat over to 350°. Mix together the Crystal sugar, eggs, and baby carrots. Add the soda, salt and cinnamon. Stir well. Pour mixture into a greased and floured 12-x-18-oz. pan. Bake for 25 to 30 minutes. Use the toothpick test to determine when the bars are done. After the bars are cool, frost them with the cream cheese frosting described on the pumpkin bar recipe card.

ꕥ Uncle Ben's Hot Dish ꕥ

1 box Uncle Ben's Original Recipe Long Grain and Wild Rice
1 c. fresh or frozen vegetables (e.g., corn and/or beans; slightly cooked if frozen)
1 lb. lean ground turkey
¼ c. chopped onions
½ c. chopped celery
Salt and pepper to taste

Cook the rice and accompanying seasonings according to the directions on the box. In the meantime, brown the turkey. When the meat and rice are done, combine and add the vegetables, onions, celery, and salt and pepper. Bake for 30 minutes at 350° and serve with hot biscuits. It's kind of like a one-pan Thanksgiving dinner.

Note: I like to use real wild rice instead of the Uncle Ben's variety. I get it from a guy who still goes ricing the old Indian way on the Mississippi River. For every pound of hamburger, I add two cups of cooked rice. I also add a bit of beef broth for moisture and extra flavor.

ꕥ Tater-Tot Hot Dish ꕥ

2 lb. lean ground beef
2 cans cream of mushroom soup
Tater-tots
1 can whole kernel corn, drained, or 1 c. fresh blanched corn
1 can green beans, drained, or 1 c. fresh blanched beans
Salt and pepper

Preheat over to 350°. Brown the beef. When done, rinse it with water to remove the excess grease. Add the cream of mushroom soup, corn, and beans. Stir. Add seasonings to taste and stir. Place the mixture in a 9-x-12-inch, greased, casserole dish. Arrange a single layer of uncooked tater-tots on top of the mixture. If you're artistic, you can even make a design. My sister, Vivian, makes pinwheels and a real nice houndstooth pattern. Bake for about 40 minutes, until the tater-tots are cooked through. Serve with baked bread.

ꕥ Lena's Chili Hot Dish ꕥ

1 lb. lean ground beef
1 pkg. chili seasoning mix
1 can stewed tomatoes (chopped)
1 can tomato soup
1 can dark kidney beans, drained
1 c. macaroni
Grated American or cheddar cheese

Brown the ground beef. While the meat is browning, cook the macaroni according to the directions on the box. When the meat is brown, drain the fat, add the seasoning mix, stewed tomatoes, soup, beans, and stir. When the macaroni is done, drain the water and add the noodles to the meat mixture and gently stir. Sprinkle as much cheese on top as you want and let it simmer, covered, over medium-low heat, for ten to fifteen minutes. This dish is good with crackers or corn bread.

Tuna Noodle Hot Dish

½ package wide egg noodles
1 can cream of mushroom soup
1 c. frozen peas, slightly cooked
1 can tuna, drained and flaked
Salt and pepper to taste

Preheat over to 350°. Boil noodles according to directions on the package. Drain and pour noodles into a buttered casserole dish. Stir in the soup, the tuna, and the cooked peas. Add salt and pepper to taste. Bake 30 minutes and serve with raw vegetables. Note, for something a bit different, after the hot dish has baked for 20 minutes, sprinkle the top with shredded cheddar cheese and return it to the oven for the final 10 minutes.

Blondies

½ c. butter-flavored shortening
1½ c. firmly packed light brown sugar
2 jumbo eggs, slightly beaten
1 T. hot water
2 tsp. vanilla
1½ c. all-purpose flour, sifted
¾ tsp. baking soda
¼ tsp. baking powder
¾ tsp. salt
1 c. Semi-sweet chocolate chips

Preheat oven to 350°. Cream shortening. Add the sugar. Beat. Add the eggs. Beat. Add the vanilla and water. Beat some more. Add the flour, soda, baking powder, and salt. Stir only until mixed together. Don't overstir, and don't use a beater. Fold in half the chocolate chips. Spread the mixture into a greased 10-x-13-inch pan and sprinkle the remaining chocolate chips on top. Bake for 20 to 30 minutes. Use a toothpick to test for doneness. Don't overbake. These bars are especially good if you put one of those grates in your pan, so every bar is a "corner."

Pumpkin Bars

4 jumbo eggs
1 c. vegetable oil
2 c. white Crystal sugar
1 15-oz. can of pumpkin

2 c. all-purpose flour, sifted
½ tsp. salt
½ tsp. cloves
2 tsp. baking powder
2¼ tsp. cinnamon
¼ tsp. nutmeg
1 tsp. soda
¾ tsp. ginger

3 T. margarine
1 8-oz. package cream cheese
1 tsp. vanilla
3½ c. powdered sugar

Preheat over to 350°. In a large bowl, mix the ingredients listed in the first column. In a second bowl, sift together the ingredients from the second column. Add the dry, second-column mixture to the first-column pumpkin mixture. Stir well. Pour into a greased and floured 12-x-18-inch pan. Bake 25 to 30 minutes. Use the toothpick test for doneness.

In a separate bowl, cream the margarine and cream cheese. Mix in the vanilla. Stir in the powdered sugar and beat with an electric mixer until creamy. Frost bars when they're cool. You may want to use this frosting for the carrot bars too.

Cheeseburger Hot Dish

1 pkg. Kraft Macaroni and Cheese
1 lb. lean ground beef

1 T. minced onions
Salt and pepper

Prepare the macaroni and cheese according to the directions on the box. Brown the ground beef. When it's done, rinse it with water to remove the fat. (Those with heart trouble will appreciate that.) Add the meat to the macaroni and cheese. Stir. Add the onions and gently stir a little more. Finally, salt and pepper to taste. This hot dish is good with buns and pickles.

ഇ Jell-O Delight ഋ

3-oz. pkg. strawberry Jell-O
16 oz. cottage cheese
9-oz. container of Cool Whip
1 small can fruit cocktail, drained

Mix dry Jell-O into cottage cheese. Fold in Cool Whip and fruit cocktail. Refrigerate for several hours before serving. Nothing beats a little Jell-O Delight!

ഇ "Regular" Jell-O Salad ഋ

3-oz. package of orange Jell-O
1 small can of mandarin oranges, drained
Miniature marshmallows

Cook the Jell-O as directed on the package. When partially cool, stir in the oranges and add a single layer of marshmallows on top. Then refrigerate until set completely. You may want to try strawberry Jell-O with fresh, sliced strawberries and marshmallows. Or, try cherry Jell-O with bananas. And, of course, you can't go wrong with the all-time favorite of lime Jell-O mixed with shredded carrots. This is especially popular among the seniors. And for you health nuts, I think it does count as a vegetable.

ഇ Pizza Hot Dish ഋ

1 lb. lean ground beef
¼ tsp. oregano (other Italian seasonings too, if desired)
1 can tomato soup
1 standard can of pizza sauce (about 16 ounces)
Salt and perpper to taste
8 to 10 oz. wide egg noodles
3 to 4 oz. Parmesan cheese
2 c. mozzarella cheese

Preheat oven to 350°. Brown the ground beef. Drain the grease. Rinse the meat with water. Add the soup, pizza sauce, oregano, and other seasonings. Meanwhile, cook the noodles according to the package instructions. When noodles are done, drain and gently stir into the meat mixture. Place half of the mixture in a greased casserole dish. Sprinkle half of the cheeses over it. Top with the remaining meat mixture. Sprinkle with the rest of the cheese. Bake for 30 to 45 minutes. Serve with garlic bread and a green salad. It's so good folks will think they're at one of those fancy Italian restaurants.

ꟷ Halfway Bars ꟷ

1 c. butter-flavored shortening
½ c. light brown Crystal sugar
½ c. white Crystal sugar
2 egg yolks
1 T. cold water
½ tsp. baking soda
2 c. all-purpose flour, sifted

6-oz. pkg semi-sweet chocolate chips
2 egg whites
1 c. light brown Crystal sugar

Preheat oven to 350°. Mix together ingredients from the first column and pat into an 8-x-13-inch cake pan. Sprinkle with chocolate chips. Then beat the egg whites until stiff. (Cold beaters—left in the freezer for a while—will help to stiffen the egg whites.) Add the brown sugar to the egg whites. Stir gently before spreading the eggs mixture over the dry mixture in the pan. Do not let the egg mixture touch the sides of the pan. Bake for about 35 minutes or until golden brown. The toothpick test will not work.

Special-K Bars

1 T. water
1 c. white Crystal sugar
1 c. light corn syrup

1 c. peanut butter
6 c. Special-K cereal
9 oz. semi-sweet chocolate chips
9 oz. of butterscotch chips

In a sauce pan, mix ingredients from the first column. Bring the mixture to a rolling boil. Remove pan from the heat immediately after it starts to boil. Stir in the peanut butter until completed mixed. Pour the mixture over the cereal and stir gently. Spread the mixture—minus whatever you've eaten—into a greased 9-x-13-inch pan and pack lightly. Melt the chocolate and butterscotch chips together and spread them over the cereal mixture. Let set before serving.

☙ Hester's Favorite Jell-O ❧

1 can cherry pie filling
¼ c. sugar
1½ c. hot water

1 large box of cherry Jell-O
1 can coca cola

Dump the ingredients in the left-hand column into a kettle and bring it to a boil. Add cherry Jell-O. Stir and let cool. Add the can of regular coca cola and stir until the bubbles disappear. Chill until firm. Cover with Cool Whip. I know this sounds like a weird Jell-O recipe, with soda pop and all, but it's actually very good.

☙ Lemon Bars ❧

½ c. butter
1 c. flour
¼ c. powdered sugar

1 c. sugar
2 T. flour
½ tsp. baking powder
2 eggs, beaten
5 T. lemon juice

Preheat oven to 350°. Mix the flour and sugar from the first column. Melt the butter and add it to the flour-sugar mixture. Stir. Pat the mixture into a 9-x-9-inch greased pan and bake for 15 minutes. Meanwhile, mix the sugar and eggs from the second column. Add to that mixture the flour and baking powder. Stir. Mix in the lemon juice. Spread that mixture over the baked layer. Bake for another 25 minutes. Dust with powdered sugar.

≈ Three-Bean Hot Dish ≈

1 lb. ground beef
1-lb. can of pork and beans
1-lb. can butter beans, drained
1-lb. can kidney beans, drained
1 T. brown sugar
1 T. yellow mustard
3 T. catsup
Salt and pepper

Brown the ground beef. Drain the fat from it and rinse it with water if desired. Add in all the ingredients listed in the second column and stir. Then gently mix in kidney beans and butter beans. Finally, add the pork and beans, stirring very gently so as to avoid making mush. No, you certainly don't want mush. Simmer for about 15 minutes and serve.

≈ Snicker Salad ≈

4 green apples, sliced and chunked (leave the peelings on for extra flavor)
4 Snickers candy bars (regular size), cut into quarter-inch slices
1 regular-size container of Cool Whip

Mix the ingredients together. Chill for 30 minutes. Serve. Makes eight to ten servings of salad. And if you add a couple more cut-up candy bars, you can call it dessert!

≈ Chocolate Caramel Bars ≈

German chocolate cake mix
1 14-oz. bag caramels, unwrapped
1 can sweetened cond. milk
1½ sticks of margarine
1 c. chopped walnuts
1 12-oz. bag semi-sweet chocolate chips

Preheat oven to 350°. Pour dry cake mix into a bowl. Set aside. In double boiler, melt caramels in one-half can of sweetened condensed milk. Set aside. In a second pan, melt margarine. Add remaining sweetened condensed milk. Pour into dry cake mix. Stir until mixed. Add nuts. Press one-half of mixture into a greased and floured 9-x-13-inch pan. Bake for six minutes. Remove from the oven. Immediately sprinkle with the chocolate chips. Top with the caramel-milk mixture. Crumble or drop the remaining cake mixture over the bars. Bake 15 to 18 more minutes. Refrigerate at least one-half hour before cutting. Tastes incredible with milk—or wine.

ঌ Chocolate Cherry Brownies ও

1 pkg. Pillsbury-Plus Devil's Food Cake Mix
1 can (21 oz.) cherry pie filling
1 tsp. almond extract
2 eggs beaten

1 c. sugar
1/3 cup milk
5 T. margarine
1 pkg. (6 oz. or 1 cup) semi-sweet chocolate chips

Preheat oven to 350°. Grease and flour a 10-x-15-inch pan. In a large bowl, mix all of the ingredients from the first group. Stir until well blended. Spread batter in the pan. Bake for 20 to 25 minutes. Use the toothpick test to determine doneness. Do not let the brownies cool.

For the frosting, combine the sugar, milk, and margarine in a small saucepan. Bring the mixture to a boil. Boil one minute, stirring constantly. Remove pan from heat. Stir in the chocolate chips until smooth. Spread over warm brownies. Cool completely before eating, although you don't need to wait to lick the frosting pan.

ঌ Pistachio Salad ও

1 box Jell-O instant pistachio pudding
9 oz. Cool Whip
20-oz. can crushed pineapple
2 c. mini-marshmallows
¼ c. chopped walnuts

Fold the dry pudding mix into the Cool Whip. Add the pineapple, marshmallows, and walnuts. Stir gently. Refrigerate for several hours before serving.

➳ Irish Baked Hot Dish ☙

2 lbs. lean ground beef
1 can green beans, drained
1 can tomato soup
Salt and pepper
6 medium-sized potatoes
2/3 cups warm milk
1 egg, beaten
Paprika

Preheat oven to 350°. Peel potatoes. Boil until soft. Drain and set aside. Brown ground beef. When done, drain grease and rinse with water. Add the beans and soup to meat. Stir. Season with salt and pepper to taste. Spread into a 9- x 13-inch greased casserole dish. Add milk and egg to the boiled potatoes. Whip until smooth. Add salt and pepper to taste. Spread potato mixture over meat mixture. Bake for one hour. Serve with hard rolls.

➳ Chicken Wild Rice Hot Dish ☙

1 c. wild rice (uncooked)
1 chicken, deboned and cut into small chunks
1 can cream of mushroom soup
1 can cream of celery soup
1 c. milk
1 pack dry onion soup mix

Preheat oven to 350°. Place the rice in a standard casserole dish. Spread chicken chunks on top of the rice. In a bowl, mix together mushroom and celery soups, along with the milk. Pour over the rice and chicken. Sprinkle the dry onion soup mix on top. Cover and bake for two hours.

꧁ Nut Goodie Bars ꧂

1 12-oz. bag butterscotch chips
1 12-oz. bag semi-sweet chocolate chips
1 18-oz. jar creamy peanut butter

1 c. butter
3 oz. regular vanilla pudding
2/3 c. evaporated milk
2 lb. powdered sugar
2 tsp. maple flavoring

16 oz. Spanish peanuts

Bottom layer: In a medium saucepan, melt butterscotch and chocolate chips, along with peanut butter, over low heat, stirring occasionally. Spread half of mixture in buttered 10-by-15 jellyroll pan. Refrigerate until firm.

Middle layer: In medium saucepan, melt butter over low heat. Stir in the pudding powder and evaporated milk. Cook until thickened. Do not boil. Add powdered sugar and maple flavoring. Stir until completely combined. Spread over the chocolate layer. Refrigerate for 30 minutes.

Top layer: Stir peanuts into the remaining chocolate mixture. Reheat over low heat if necessary. Spread the peanut-chocolate mixture over the nougat layer. Refrigerate until firm. Cut into squares. Transfer leftovers to a container with a tight-fitting lid. (You probably won't have any leftovers.) Store them in the refrigerator.

ᘓ Seven Layer Bars ᘐ

½ c. (1 stick) margarine
1½ c. graham cracker crumbs
1 14 oz.-can sweetened cond. milk
1 c. (6 oz.) butterscotch chips
1 c. (6 oz.) semi-sweet chocolate chips
1-1/3 c. flaked coconut
1 c. chopped walnuts

Preheat oven to 350°. In 9-x-13 cake pan, melt the butter in oven. Evenly disperse the butter across the pan. Sprinkle cracker crumbs over the melted butter. Pour condensed milk evenly over the crumbs. Top with ingredients in the second column, in order, from top to bottom. Press the bars down firmly. Bake for 25 minutes or until bars are light brown. Let cool before eating.

ᘓ Egg-Bake Hot Dish ᘐ

1 standard bag of frozen shredded hash-brown potatoes
1 c. diced ham (cooked)
½ c. bacon (cooked and broken)
¾ lb. ground Italian sausage (cooked and drained)
1 c. shredded sharp cheddar cheese
1 c. shredded mild cheddar cheese
½ c. onion (diced)
½ c. green peppers (diced)
½ c. red peppers (diced)
10 eggs (combined with ¾ c. milk and lightly beaten in a bowl with a whisk)

Preheat oven to 350°. In a buttered casserole dish (approximately 10-x-13 inches), spread frozen potatoes. Sprinkle cooked meats over potatoes. Add cheese. Layer on onion and peppers. In separate bowl, beat eggs. Wisk in milk. Pour egg-milk mixture on top of everything. Bake for 60 minutes. Let cool for five minutes before cutting and serving.

℘ Apple Square Bars ℘

10 cups sliced apples (try several different kinds for a mix of flavor)
2/3 c. sugar
¼ c. flour
1½ tsp. cinnamon
1 tsp. vanilla

Mix all of the above ingredients and set aside.

4 c. flour
1 tsp. baking powder
1 tsp. salt
1¾ c. Crisco
1 egg, beaten
½ c. water
1 tsp. vinegar

Combine dry ingredients from the second group. Cut dry mixture into Crisco. Add in the beaten egg, water, and vinegar, one at a time. Stir until dough forms. Divide into six parts. Wrap parts separately in freezer paper and freeze for several hours. Do not use it right away. Before using dough, allow it to thaw for several hours, until it is at room temperature. Then roll it out.

Preheat oven to 400°. On a lightly greased cookie sheet, roll out thawed pie dough for the bottom crust (form into a rectangle). Pour apple mixture on top of the dough. Roll out dough for top crust. Lay it over the apple mixture. Slit top crust so it is well vented. Bake 40 to 60 minutes or until crust is light golden brown and filling is bubbling through the venting.

In sauce pan, stir together 1 c. powdered sugar, 1 tsp. vanilla, and 1 tsp. water. Add more water and vanilla as needed until mixture is smooth and to your taste. Drizzle over warm bars—do not let the bars cool first.

ꕥ Cookie Salad ꕥ

2 3.4-oz. pkg. of instant vanilla pudding mix
2 c. buttermilk
12 oz. of Cool Whip
1 20-oz. can of pineapple chunks, drained
2 11-oz. cans of mandarin oranges, drained
½ pkg. (11.5 ounces) of fudge striped cookies

In a large bowl, mix together pudding mix powder and buttermilk. Fold in the Cool Whip. Mix in the pineapple chunks and the oranges. Chill until ready to serve. Crush the cookies and mix in just before serving.

ꕥ Glorified Rice Salad ꕥ

2 c. cooked white rice (cold)
1 14-oz can crushed pineapple, drained
¼ c. sugar
1 c. miniature marshmallows
1 c. whipping cream
1 T. sugar
1 tsp. vanilla
1 c. maraschino cherries, sliced

Mix rice, pineapple, first sugar, and marshmallows in a bowl. In a second bowl, whip the cream stiff (works best if you put the beaters in the freezer for 15 minutes ahead of time). Add the vanilla and the second sugar. Fold cream mixture into rice mixture. Chill. Decorate with sliced maraschino cherries before serving. Serves 6 to 8.

℘ Traditional Brownies ℘

½ c. butter
2 squares unsweetened chocolate
1 c. sugar
1 tsp. vanilla
¼ tsp. salt
2 eggs
½ c. flour

Preheat oven to 350°. Melt butter and chocolate separately in microwave. Stir together until smooth. Beat in sugar, vanilla, and salt. Beat in the eggs, one at a time. Slowly stir in the flour (don't use a beater). Pour batter into greased 8-inch-square pan. Bake for 25 to 30 minutes. Use a toothpick to test for doneness. Do not over bake.

℘ Green Bean Casserole ℘

1/3 stick butter
½ c. diced onions
½ c. fresh mushrooms, sliced
2 c. fresh green beans, sliced
3 c. chicken broth
1 10¾ can cream of mushroom soup
1 2.8-oz can French-fried onion rings
1 c. grated cheddar cheese
Salt and pepper to taste

Preheat oven to 350°. Melt butter in a large skillet. Sautee onions and mushrooms in the butter. In separate kettle, boil the green beans in the chicken broth for 10 minutes. Drain. Add the beans, mushroom soup, onion rings, and salt and pepper to the onion-mushroom mixture. Stir well. Pour into a greased 1½-quart baking dish. Bake 20 minutes. Top the casserole with the cheese and bake for another 10 minutes or until the casserole is hot, and the cheese is melted.

Oriental Hot Dish

2 onions, chopped
1 c. celery, chopped
3 T. butter
1 lb. ground beef
½ c. white rice, uncooked
1 can cream of mushroom soup
1 can cream of chicken soup
1 c. water
¼ tsp. pepper
1 T. soy sauce
1 can water chestnuts, drained and sliced
5 oz. chow mein noodles

Preheat oven to 350°. Brown onions and celery in butter. Remove from pan. Brown ground beef and rice. Add in the cooked onions and celery. Add the soups and water. Stir. Mix in the pepper, soy sauce, and water chestnuts. Pour into one-quart, greased, casserole dish. Cover. Bake for 20 minutes. Uncover and bake another 20 minutes or until hot all the way through. Sprinkle chow mein noodles on top and serve.

Corn Flake Hot Dish

2 lbs. frozen cubed hash browns
½ c. melted butter
1 tsp. salt
½ tsp. pepper

2 T. minced dry onions
1 can of cream of chicken soup
8 to 12 oz. sour cream
3 c. shredded cheddar cheese

¼ c. melted butter
4 c. Corn Flakes

Preheat oven to 350°. Mix together ingredients in the first two columns. Place in buttered 9x13-inch cake pan. In a bowl, mix butter and corn flakes. Scatter over the potato mixture. Cover with tin foil. Bake for 45 to 60 minutes, uncovering for the last 15 minutes of baking. Let stand for 10 minutes before serving. This dish tastes great with ham and brown beans.

Broccoli and Stuffing Casserole

2 lb. fresh broccoli florets
2 eggs, beaten
1 onion, chopped
1 10¾ can cream of mushroom soup
½ c. mayonnaise
10 oz. dry stuffing mix
½ c. butter, melted
1 c. shredded cheddar cheese

Preheat oven to 350°. Cook the broccoli in a large pot of salted boiling water until slightly tender. Drain. Meanwhile, in large bowl, combine eggs, onion, soup, and mayonnaise. Place a layer of broccoli in a lightly greased 9-x-13-inch baking pan. Pour the sauce mixture over it. Spread stuffing mix—directly from the box—over the sauce. Drizzle butter over the stuffing. Sprinkle the cheese on top. Back for 30 minutes.

Chicken Fried Rice Hot Dish

1 pkg. Rice-a-Roni Fried Rice*
2 T. margarine
1½ c. water
*Rice seasoning mix from Rice-a-Roni box
1 lb. uncooked, boneless, skinless, chicken breasts, cut into one-inch pieces
1 c. frozen peas
2 eggs, beaten

In a large skillet, cook rice mix and margarine over medium heat, stirring frequently, until rice is golden brown. Slowly stir in the water, the seasoning from the rice mix, and the chicken. Bring to a boil. Cover, reduce heat to low. Simmer 15 minutes. Add the peas. Simmer 5 more minutes or until the water is absorbed. Increase the heat to medium. Add eggs. Cook and stir until the eggs are set—about 2 minutes.

Watch for the next installment in this series
by Jeanne Cooney:

Hot Dish Heaven:

A Second Helping of Murder and Recipes

Coming 2014

Turn for a sneak peak!

Chapter One

I swerved to miss the sugar beets that littered the road. It was late October, and I was back in the northern Red River Valley, only thirty miles south of Canada. The air was cold, and the wind was strong, howling at me through my car windows. I drove east along Highway 11. I was just outside of Drayton, on the Minnesota side of the river, headed for Kennedy, the sun riding low on my shoulders. The half-dozen beets I was attempting to avoid must have fallen off the semi-trucks used to haul them from the fields to the pilers.

Don't let me fool you with words like "pilers" or even "sugar beets" for that matter. I really don't know much about either. I'm not a farmer. My name is Emerald Malloy, Emme to my friends. I'm a twenty-six-year-old reporter for the Minneapolis paper. I write for the Food section, although the word "write" may likewise give you the wrong impression. I mostly compose lead-ins for articles that highlight recipes. But a few months ago, on my first trip to Kennedy, Minnesota, I not only acquired recipes for a feature on "church cuisine," I solved a murder.

It was a front-page story. I got a piece of the by-line and everything, which should have thrilled me since I thought I had wanted to be an investigative reporter. But in the end, I actually ached for the people involved and felt more than a little guilty for what I'd done to uncover the crime, regardless that my actions were anything but deliberate. And when my editor explained that the article had earned me a full-time position on the crime beat if I wanted, I told him I'd have to think about it.

So that's what I'd been doing for the last couple months. Thinking. And since I can multi-task, I had also volunteered to return to Kennedy for more recipes from Margie Johnson, the owner of Hot Dish Heaven, the local café. It turned out our readers loved seeing their favorite hot dish, Jell-O, and bar recipes in print. So we were planning another full-page spread.

When I called Margie to ask if I could visit again, she said, "Oh, ya betcha. Just be careful once ya get off I-29 there. The state highways and county roads are scattered with beets. Yah, even though most everybody's done haulin' for the year, the roads are still a mess."

The beets were much larger than had I expected, although, in truth, I wasn't sure what to expect. I knew sugar beets were used to make the alternative to cane sugar. I also knew they were big business up here. And while I was pretty sure they didn't grow in cube form or in those tiny packets found on restaurant tables, I didn't think they'd look like potatoes on steroids either. Yet they did.

I turned onto County Road 1 and, from there, County 7, as Willie Nelson sang, "On the road again. I can't wait to get on the road again." I bounced over a few more beets and the large clumps of dirt that accompanied them, pretty sure Willie would have changed his tune if he'd actually been in the car with me.

Up ahead, I spotted what I assumed was a piler. It was nothing more than a mountain of sugar beets in a wide-open field, the mountain surrounded by heavy equipment, including a conveyor belt of some kind. A couple semis, fully loaded, idled in a line nearby, while a few people rushed around outside a small, guard shack-like building.

Aside from that activity, all was quiet. The roads were empty, and now with harvest over, the flat, treeless fields that stretched to the horizon were black and barren. They made for a bleak picture, one that reminded me of something Margie had once said: "This may not be the end of the world, but we sure as heck can see it from here."

By the time I entered Kennedy, the sky had fallen gray. Red and gold leaves blanketed the ground, as if already preparing for the cold winter ahead. And a dirty white pickup passed, moving in the opposite direction, the driver acknowledging me by briefly lifting his index finger from the steering wheel. I nodded in return before crossing the railroad tracks and taking a right onto Highway 75. Up the road, I pulled in across from Hot Dish Heaven.

Only two pickups were parked along the highway, but the makeshift parking lot next to the grain elevator was crowded with vehicles and men, about five or six of each, constituting quite a gathering in a town of 193 people. I didn't recognize anyone, but that didn't surprise me. While after just one visit, I knew more people here than I did in Minneapolis, where I lived a monastic life, I couldn't expect to be familiar with everyone. Not yet anyway.

I exited the car and leaned forward, touching my toes. Following a six-hour drive, stretching was necessary since I'd stopped only once for the bathroom and refills of gasoline, Diet Coke, and M&Ms. Righting myself, I adjusted my sweater and jeans and, with a shiver, wrapped my corduroy jacket tightly around me, wishing at the same time I'd worn my winter coat. I then hurried across the road with the wind, smelling of dirt and damp leaves, pushing me the entire way.

A cute, short-haired, white dog sat near the door to the café, but as I approached, he edged away. "Don't be afraid," I said to the little guy in my friendliest voice. Nevertheless, he scampered down the sidewalk.

I opened the heavy door to the café and shuffled inside. The place was deserted. I didn't see anyone. Not even Margie. Though I did *hear* her. She was in the kitchen, singing along to the jukebox. It was playing Maura O'Connell's version of "Livin' in These Troubled Times."

I knew the song because my parents were big music fans, particularly folk and country-rock, and I'd continued the tradition. "Brings you down to buy a paper if you read between the lines that no one seems to have the answer to livin' in these troubled times."

I listened for another second or two while glancing around the room. Nothing had changed. Hot Dish Heaven was small and dark, the walls covered in plaster and wainscoting, along with yellowing advertisements, both professional and handmade. As for the booths, they were upholstered in black vinyl, marked by the occasional piece of duct tape, while the tables inthe middle of the floor and the counter up front were framed in chrome and topped with stained Formica.

"Hey, anybody home?"

"Oh, my goodness!" Margie scurried from the kitchen, drying her hands on a towel that ended up flung over her shoulder. "If you aren't a sight for sore eyes." She enveloped me in a warm embrace before stepping away. "Now let me getta good look at ya." She scanned me up and down. "Uff-da, you're still so skinny I bet ya have to run around in the shower just to get wet." She grinned. "Otherwise, ya look great. I love that hair, ya know." She yanked one of my long, orange curls. "Remember, we have very few redheads around here."

That may have been an exaggeration. I'd never spotted any redheads in the area. The northern Red River Valley, you see, was home to Scandinavian-Lutheran farmers, most of whom were tall, with solid builds, blonde hair, and blue eyes, much like Margie herself, even if Margie, admittedly in her early sixties, was now more gray than blonde. I, on the other hand, was an oddity in these parts. I'm Irish-Catholic. And at five-foot-five, slim—not "skinny"—with long, curly, carrot-red hair and emerald-green eyes. I stood out like a bagpiper at a lutefisk dinner, as Margie once said.

"It's good to see you, Margie." My smile stretched wide. I really liked Margie Johnson. During my previous visit, you see, I had ended up incapacitated for a few days, and Margie took care of me. In spite of repeatedly telling her it wasn't necessary, I loved every minute of it. Having lost my mom at a tender age, I guess I craved motherly attention. And since Margie had never married or had children of her own, she must have enjoyed providing it. Throughout those three days, we spent hours visiting and became good friends, regardless of our age difference. And while I'd often spoken with her on the phone between then and now, it wasn't the same as seeing her in person. "You look wonderful" I added.

She patted the sides of her head, clearly trying to tame the hair that had escaped the ponytail that hung loosely at the nape of her neck. Next, she tugged on her tee-shirt, which, along with her jeans and sneakers, comprised her usual work uniform. "Your eyes must be goin'," she replied with a moderate Scandinavian accent. "Kind of strange for someone so young."

Somehow, my smile managed to stretch a little wider. "Tell me, do you have time to sit and catch up, or are you too busy preparing for the big feast?"

Margie was cooking for the beet banquet her nephews, Buddy and Buford, were hosting that evening in the "middle room"—the room that bridged the café and the VFW. The meal was to show their appreciation to the people who'd worked for them during harvest. Margie said it was something most of the farmers did every year.

"Well, I gotta keep cookin', so why don't ya come on back to the kitchen, and we'll talk some there. And don't worry none, I won't make ya do much." She snickered as she put her arm around my shoulders and led me to the kitchen after first pulling the plug on the juke box. "I still can't get over ya bein' a food reporter, given what a terrible cook ya are."

I squinted, feigning indignation. "But I can copy down recipes with the best of them, can't I?"

She gave me a squeeze. "That's for darn sure, kiddo. Business has been boomin' since that newspaper of yours published the piece about me and my food. I've had folks in from as far away as Crookston and Thief River Falls. And like I told ya on the phone, I even got a nice review from that famous food critic over at the *Grand Forks Herald* there."

I pulled my purse from my shoulder, set it on the metal worktable, and took a seat on a nearby stool. Margie wiped her hands down the front of her tee-shirt across the words, "Let me spend eternity in Hot Dish Heaven." She always wore the same shirt, just a different color. Today's was royal blue.

"If ya care to, Emme, ya can stack some dinner plates on the counter while we gab." She made the passive request—the only type uttered by these humble Scandinavians—while checking the oven and stovetop. Both were teeming with various hot dishes, the scent of onions and peppers permeating the air. "We'll be feedin' about a hundred, countin' the workers and their families. The counter will serve as our buffet table, just like the last time ya were here."

I nodded and headed for the large, painted cupboard at the back of the kitchen. I knew my way around. During my prior stay, the café and the adjacent VFW had co-sponsored a benefit dinner and dance, and I'd helped out some.

"I'm glad ya got here when ya did," Margie went on. "The temperature's droppin'. The weather's supposed to get real ugly. Ya wouldn't wanna be on the road then." She paused. "There's a storm front in Canada, and it's headed our way. There's a good chance we'll get a bunch of snow dumped on us. And the way the wind blows around here, snow always means a potential blizzard." She grimaced. "Another Halloween blizzard. Good thing everyone around here makes their kids' costumes big enough to fit over their snowsuits."

She paused once more, a guilty expression on her face. "I probably should of called and told ya about the forecast. I didn't want ya to cancel your trip. Besides, those weather folks never know what they're talkin' about. That storm might miss us altogether."

She pivoted toward the stove to stir the contents of a large frying pan. "Just to be on the safe side, though, plan on pluggin' in your car." She glanced in my direction, her eyes twinkling. "Ya do have a head-bolt heater, don't ya?"

I shook my head. "No need. My townhouse came with a garage."

She chuckled, waving her spoon. "I was just kiddin' anyways. It's too early in the season to plug in your car." She set the spoon down. “And I have jumper cables if ya can’t start it in the mornin’.” She laughed some more as she checked the other pans.

When she was done, she turned my way. “But like I said, I’m sorry. I really should of given ya a ‘heads up.’”

I dismissed her apology with a wave of my hand. “Margie, it’s not your job to keep tabs on the weather for me. I could have listened to the radio, but instead, I played CDs the whole way here. And since I had no intention of delaying my trip, I didn’t listen to any weather reports this week, either.”

As I spoke, I couldn’t help but contemplate the prospect of being stranded in Kennedy for a few days. It actually made me a bit giddy.

And apparently I didn’t hide my feelings very well because a smile lit Margie’s eyes and curved the corners of her mouth as she said, “I bet the look on your face is tied to thoughts of being snowbound for a few days with Deputy Ryden. Am I right?”

At the mere mention of his name, my cheeks grew warm, and I was sure they were turning as red as my hair.

Randy Ryden was a Kittson County deputy sheriff. I had met him the last time I was in town. We hit it off—well, not at first, but eventually—and since then, we’d talked twice on the phone. And had also exchanged four or five emails. We even went out to dinner when he was in the Twin Cities two weeks ago, visiting his folks. For our date, I shaved my legs and the whole works, hoping we’d end up back at my place, taking our relationship to the next level—the horizontal one.

I know that sounds sleazy on my part, but believe me, it had been a while—if a while means longer than I can rememberk. Besides, it didn’t matter because he got called away before anything happened. Though not before inviting me to stay with him while in town this time around. And I planned to do just that as soon as he returned from western North Dakota.

He was helping in the oil fields. Not working with oil but doing law enforcement stuff. The oil boom had caught the police out there off-guard, so cops from around the region were lending a hand. Until he got back, which he expected would be the following afternoon, I'd stay in one of two rooms above the café. Margie rented them out to short-term guests. They were the closest Kennedy had to a hotel.

"Margie, I'll admit I like the guy, but that's all I'm going to say on the subject." In truth, that was all I could say without getting hot and tongue-tied. Randy Ryden, you see, was tall, dark, and handsome, with a build that reminded me of rugged mountains—rugged mountains I wanted to climb all over. And more importantly—well, at least *as* importantly—he was genuinely nice, not something I was used to. "As I've told you many times, my track record with guys isn't great. So I'd rather not jinx myself by talking about what's going on between Randy and me."

Margie's smile remained while she poured two cups of coffee and handed me one.

"Now, put away that goofy grin of yours," I scolded with no conviction whatsoever. "There's not much to tell." I couldn't help but add, "At least not yet."

Margie chuckled and continued to tease. "Well, if ya don't wanna share your secrets with me, that's your business, I reckon. But it seems kind of cruel since I nursed ya back from the brink of death."

I rolled my eyes. "Don't be so dramatic. I had a concussion, nothing more. I was hardly at death's door."

I did my best to sound nonchalant, but my muscles tightened as I spoke. I guess I still was "working through the psychological aftermath" of nearly being killed during my last visit. At least that was how my therapist had explained my ongoing battle with anxiety.

That's right. I see a therapist and have for some time. Even so, I remain pretty messed up. Makes me wonder about people who've never sought counseling. They must be batshit crazy and not even realize it. Yet they walk around unsupervised. Kind of scary, huh?

"Well, if ya won't spill your guts," Margie playfully whined as she retrieved an oblong Tupperware container from the refrigerator, "how about a little somethin' to fill 'em up?" She tugged on the plastic lid. "I know ya hate sweets, but—"

Before she finished speaking, I grabbed a bar from the tub and took a bite, savoring every morsel and ignoring the likelihood that she was using sweets to weasel information out of me. It was a risk I had to take since I loved sweets. Especially Margie's sweets.

Margie was not only a great cook, she was an award-winning baker. She had won lots of county fair ribbons over the years and, at my insistence, had finally entered a dozen different baked goods in last year's Minnesota State Fair. She walked away with three firsts, five seconds, and four thirds. That's right. Twelve for twelve her first time out. Despite that, she cast off her success by saying, "Well, I sure as heck didn't deserve that many ribbons."

In turn, I had argued that she was the best baker around, and with my penchant for sweets, I considered myself an expert on the subject. I also begged her to quit being so modest. To that, she'd replied thoughtfully, "Well, maybe you're right. I'm getting' arthritis, and I don't deserve that either, so, yah, maybe it all evens out." I had to bite my tongue to keep from laughing.

"Margie," I said, returning my attention to the present, "how did . . ." My voice trailed off. I wanted to find out how these incredible frosted banana bars had fared in the state ribbon competition but got distracted by an unexpected feeling—a feeling that something was terribly wrong.

I'm not suggesting I'm psychic. Hell, I don't even know if I believe in that sort of thing. I'm simply saying that one moment I was chatting with Margie, and the next I was overtaken by a sense of danger. Or was it tragedy? I couldn't tell. But it hovered in the air, thick and dark, much like the sky, now that a storm was brewing. And despite being in Margie's warm kitchen, I shivered.

∞ Frosted Banana Bars ∞

½ c. butter or margarine, softened
2 c. white sugar
3 eggs
1½ c. mashed ripe bananas (about 3)
1 tsp. vanilla extract
2 c. all-purpose flour
1 tsp. baking soda
Pinch of salt.

Preheat oven to 350 degrees. In a mixing bowl, cream the butter and sugar, using an electric beater. Then beat in the eggs, bananas, and vanilla. In a separate bowl, combine the flour, baking soda, and salt. Add it to the creamed mixture and stir it together with a wooden spoon. Pour the batter into a greased, 15 in. x 10 in. x 1 in. pan. Bake for 25 minutes or until done per the toothpick test. Cool.

½ cup butter or margarine, softened
1 8-oz. pkg. cream cheese, softened
4 c. powdered sugar
2 tsps. vanilla extract

For the frosting, cream the butter and cream cheese in a mixing bowl, using an electric beater. Gradually add the powdered sugar, beating the mixture with an electric beater. Add the vanilla and beat some more. Then spread over the cooled bars.